♡

For Kathryn

Christine
Castigliano

the

TWINS

of

TESSAR

a novel by
CHRISTINE CASTIGLIANO

STELLA MIA PRESS

for my grandma, Goldie Mae Thorpe

ACKNOWLEDGEMENTS:
This book wouldn't exist without many blessings: the creative and
practical gifts of my parents; the love of my family; the generous arms
and listening skills of close friends; a richly entwined community that
feeds me daily. I am lucky to have studied the craft with several fine
writers, particularly Ursula K. Le Guin, Bruce Coville, Octavia E. Butler
and Jane Yolen. Many thanks to the instructors and fellow writers of
Clarion West Workshop '99, and to writer friends who showed me that
it could be done: Deborah Davis, who read and commented on the first
and many subsequent drafts; Glenn Savan, whose life as a novelist was
so appealing; and Barbara Berger, who pointed the way with a gentle
hand. This book owes much of its current shape to the editorial insights
of Barbara Nichols, Y. Sue Thorpe, and the Hedgebrook writers group:
Judy Bentley, Janine Brodine, Terri Miller, Susan Starbuck, Kate
Willette and Mary Wright. I offer thanks and respect to Lao-Tsu, Carl
Jung, Frank Baum, Orson Scott Card's *Alvin Maker*, Neil Gaiman, Alice
Walker, and the creators of the Marvel X-Men.

ISBN 978-0-9822499-0-1   1.4

Cover and book design: Christine Castigliano
Royalty-free stock photography: photos.com
www.twinsoftessar.com

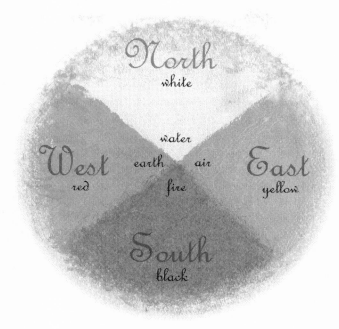

North
white

water

West   earth   air   East
red   fire   yellow

South
black

prologue

*O*nce upon a time, in the nothingness before time began, there
was only Spirit and Matter. Spirit and Matter were so
attracted to each other, so entranced by the other's differences,
that they drew close together and joined as one. The result of this union
was a magical child, a world.

Like a cell dividing, the young world expanded into four
quadrants, North, South, East and West, born of the four elements of
Air, Earth, Fire, and Water. The grandchildren of the union became
the four primal races of mankind: the Black, White, Yellow, and Red.

This ancient world lives on, preserved at the center of creation and
reflected in our dreams and myths. The spirits, beasts, people and gods
that walk this world call it Tessar.

Four gods and goddesses are entrusted with keeping the sacred *knowledge ~ and the Balance ~ of the four lands of Tessar. Ching, god of the East, is responsible for the force of Change. Star Mother, goddess of the West, holds the spirit of Love. Logos, god of the North, embodies Logic. Shanga, goddess of the South, is devoted to Strength.*

Once every hundred years, each of the deities feels a stirring in the deepest, most primitive place in their soul. Each knows it is again time to seed the next generation. At midnight, when their longing is strongest, the deities find their way to one of many gateways that lead to our world.

In an unknown year of the 20th century, the god of the East slipped through a cold spring to the electric city where his village had once stood, to seek his mate in a crowded high-rise.

The goddess of the West climbed a river bank to a high, deserted plain, searched the horizon and found a highway sign that pointed to the man she would meet that night.

Stepping from the lake, the god of the North knew that a woman who loved to dance was in a town not far away.

The goddess of the South rose up from the ocean and ran alongside the cliff's edge to find the man she had seen in her dreams.

At dawn, when the sun's light kissed the Earth, each of the four gods regretfully stole away from the arms of their mates. Each of them made their way back to Tessar, passing through the ancient gateways hidden in the spring, the river, the lake and the ocean.

The goddesses prayed that the human seed within their bellies would grow in strength, beauty and wisdom, and become children who would one day return to their Earthly home. And the gods also prayed that their unborn children would grow in strength and beauty inside their human mothers, and one day become wise enough to make the journey home, to Tessar.

1

*G*et back home and feed the chickens like I told you!

Yolanda ignored the voice in her head, climbed over the broken-down fence and ran across the fields out toward the sycamore at the edge of MacGroder's farm. She longed to climb into the arms of the old tree like she used to, to get away from Mama, to dream, to hide in a book. Yolanda wished she could just go on like that, as if everything was fine and she hadn't seen that face staring back at her in the mirror this morning. But she ran on past the sycamore tree and up toward George's Mountain.

This time, she had to tell somebody.

The George's was the biggest of the lumpy hills that stood like a wall around the Huskaloosa Valley. All Yolanda knew was that Miz Becca, the old midwife, lived somewhere near the top. As she trampled up the deer tracks at the foot of the mountain, she worried about what she'd say when she found the midwife. It wasn't going to be easy to tell her.

She could still picture his face, especially his sparkling green eyes that looked exactly like hers, only brighter, more alive somehow.

don't you go up there, talking crazy

I'm going, Mama, and you can't stop me.

Yolanda climbed harder, remembering. It had still been dark when she woke from a nightmare and went to the bathroom for some water. Usually she avoided looking in the mirror with its long crack that broke her reflection into two pieces that didn't quite match up. Plus she hated how she looked: green eyes, fat lips, big square jawbone, and feisty red curls that broke combs and bent brush bristles. But this time Yolanda glanced in the mirror, and her reflection began to change.

All by itself.

Her face melted into a swirling pool of eyes, nose and mouth, and when it stopped her cheeks looked a lot thinner, one eyebrow arched up higher than the other, and her hair was chopped off, as short as a boy's. Matter of fact, it was a boy, staring back at her through the crack in the mirror. And he was fine to look at, even with the same stubborn jaw, the same thick mouth and the same green eyes as hers.

you didn't see nothing

Did, too!

Yolanda hiked on through a long stretch of briars, her jeans catching on the thick undergrowth. She climbed higher through muddy creek beds until she came to a pine needle trail through a wide hall of trees. She could walk easier there, but she couldn't stop thinking about that face in the mirror.

At first she'd reckoned it was only a dream or that she'd been sleepwalking, but when she pinched herself, it hurt. Yolanda flicked on the TV and sprawled on the sofa with Jimson, the orange and gray kitten she'd found in a ditch a few weeks back. Nothing was on but a boring farm report. Hog belly futures. So she scooped up Jimson and went to turn off the TV. A wave flickered across the glass, her reflection started to swirl again, and her hair shot up, short and wild. She frowned, but the reflection smiled. It was him.

"Cripes! How in the world?" Yolanda keeled backwards into the coffee table, and Jimson scampered under the couch.

Nervous, Yolanda went to make some toast. She found a piece of day old bread, checked it for mold and had dropped it in the toaster when she noticed a big smear of grease on the side.

we may be poor, but we don't have to be dirty

That was one of Mama's favorite sayings. Yolanda grabbed a rag and rubbed the metal until it shone. But then she saw her reflection on the side and it started swirling, again, just like on the mirror and the TV, and when it stopped swirling she had short hair, thinner cheeks and one eyebrow arched higher than the other. He smiled at her, again.

Yolanda's heart flip-flopped faster than a fish in a five-gallon bucket, but she didn't look away. She blinked. He was still there, smiling, his eyes blazing like green fire. She could have stared at those eyes forever.

Then he opened his mouth and said her name, real slow, as if it was a magic word to open a secret door. "Yo-lan-daaa..."

Did his voice fill the room, or just her head? Wasn't there something sad in it?

In that moment she knew who he was, and why he was there. It was her twin, the one she'd never known, the one Mama wouldn't talk about. And he needed her, bad.

Yolanda reached out to touch him, as if there wasn't a toaster and God-knew-what-else standing between them. He lifted his hand too, but when their fingers came together, the metal was hard, and hot enough to burn.

"Mew," Jimson wove himself around her ankles, hungry.

Yolanda glanced down and the spell broke. She looked in the toaster again, longing to climb back into his eyes, but she only saw herself leaning over the plywood counter with a smelly old rag in her hand.

it's high time you stopped staring at that toaster and fed the chickens!

Dang it, Mama! I don't need you telling me what to do!

But she knew it was time to tell somebody. Only who? She'd never told a soul about the things she could see, nobody except Mama. And Mama hadn't taken to it at all. Told her she was crazy, and a fool, too.

The neighbor lady Mrs. MacGroder was nice, but there was no way in heaven she would understand. And even though she hadn't made a fuss about Yolanda living on her own so far, if Yolanda told her what she saw in the mirror she'd definitely call in some folks from town. Somebody from church or school or the police would start asking questions. Sooner or later they'd come after her with a piece of paper that said she'd have to go live with a foster family or somewhere even worse.

No, it had to be somebody who would keep it quiet, and somebody who knew the truth. It had to be Miz Becca, although Yolanda hadn't seen her in years and didn't even know if she was still alive, up on George's Mountain.

What if she laughs? What if she thinks I'm crazy?

Yolanda decided to go ahead and look for the midwife anyway. She changed into jeans and a flannel shirt, put on one boot and cursed the other one gone missing until she found it tangled in Mama's gold crocheted afghan. She tidied up, fed Jimson some corned beef hash leftovers, banged out the crooked screen door, watered the baby pea plants out in the garden, fed the chickens and took off running for George's Mountain.

Now she was only halfway up and it was past noon already, judging by the sun sitting high among the branches. Yolanda's stomach groaned and her mouth was as dry as dirt.

Should have brought some food and water. Dang, I even left my toast behind.

Yolanda hiked on, climbing over fallen logs, busting through brambles and skirting around narrow ledges until she came to the gravel road that led to the top. It felt good to be out of the woods, on a road that led somewhere. Still, the late afternoon light was dimming fast. Wicked March winds cut right through her jean jacket. Her legs wobbled like Jell-o, her head felt woozy from hunger, and her hands got clammy with the dread of what she was about to do. Yolanda clenched her jaw and determined herself to keep going, to find Miz Becca, and when she did, she'd go ahead and ask her about her twin.

lord almighty, don't go blabbing it all over!

"Shut up, Mama! You're supposed to be dead! Why won't you leave me alone!" It felt good to yell like that. And it was safe out here in the middle of the woods, where nobody could hear her talking out loud to a ghost that was only in her head.

Yolanda kept her nose down until she spotted an opening in the pine trees where a faded green trailer squatted in the center of the clearing. Could that be Miz Becca's place? She stuck her sweaty hands in her pockets and slowed down, getting closer, her boots crunching on the gravel.

A cloud of black birds screeched out from the trees. Then she saw Miz Becca standing out in front, as if she was waiting for something. Or somebody.

2

*M*ing stopped long enough for Jade to catch up, long enough to take in a deep breath and stare at the Palace of the Ten Thousand Things. It stood so tall and bright on the eastern horizon, gold and red in the fading sun, and with so many curved pagoda rooftops. The palace was much bigger and more intimidating than she'd imagined, even from a long distance across fields of millet. On the outside it appeared to be worthy of the journey, but would she find what she hoped for on the inside?

Jade wobbled up the hill and stood beside Ming. Her yellow tunic was as wrinkled as her face under a wide straw hat, and she was covered with fine brown dust, but her eyes crinkled with joy. "Finally, the Palace! I thought I would die before we saw it."

"It must have over a hundred rooms," Ming said.

"Tch, tch. It's well over a thousand, perhaps even ten thousand." Jade laughed, her mouth full of crooked teeth.

Jade could always make Ming smile, no matter how serious she felt. "Ah yes, one room for each of the Ten Thousand Things. Thank goodness I have you here with me to explain everything...!" she said. "Let's go, it's not far now,"

She quickened the pace a bit in spite of the dull ache in her feet and shins that never went away after so many days of walking. From the mountains at the western border they had traveled many rough roads and dusty fields to reach this valley in the central plains. Although the spring air was chilly enough to see her breath, her palms felt hot. Soon she would finally meet him, the great Ching, god-king of the East. What would he look like? She pictured broad cheeks and fierce, dark eyes. But would there be kindness in them?

Ming imagined bending forward toward him, honoring him with the most humble, graceful bow that had ever been made.

She would then perform the double happiness combination she had practiced many times for the occasion. But what would happen after that? Would he speak first? What would she say? How would she begin to mention the delicate matter of their relationship, of her own birth? Her jaw clenched and unclenched and she walked even faster.

"He-ya, Ming, slow down, please!" Jade said. "I'm too old to be thumping across the countryside like a rabbit. Ching will still be there if we walk to the Palace, like respectable people."

"So sorry. A thousand apologies." Ming waited for her, made a short bow, and then decided to take more care to match her steps to her older companion's.

The closer they came to the Palace, the more she worried.

"Jade, how should I – how can I ask him?"

Jade's eyes twinkled under her hat. "So, even the young warrior, master of many disciplines, is not always so sure. Hmm. Tell me. What instructions did your teachers give you when we left the valley of the wind?"

How could she forget? Ting and Tan had said it so many times in her years of training: Breathe. Just breathe.

Ming stopped walking and drew in a long, slow breath. As the air flowed into her lungs she felt the chi, her life force, gather in the center of her body and flow out to her limbs. Her muscles softened, her forehead smoothed and her feet felt more solid, connected to the ground. She smiled inwardly.

I will know. I will know what to do, and what to say, when the time comes.

3

*M*iz Becca's face was the color of strong, milky tea, and her long dark braids were streaked with gray. She wore black stretch pants and a black western shirt with small pink flowers, buttoned up to the neck of her skinny body. She also had on the tiniest pair of black cowboy boots that Yolanda had ever seen.

"Well, if it isn't Mae Crick's girl. Yolanda, am I right?" Miz Becca walked closer, her face open and friendly. "Such a pretty name."

Yolanda couldn't tell if Miz Becca was in her forties or her eighties. She sounded much younger than she looked, and her voice was as sweet as maple candy.

"Now I wonder, what brings you all the way up the George's on this fine day?"

don't tell   don't tell

"I – uh –" Yolanda kicked a pinecone under the trailer, then decided to just get it over with. "Miz Becca, did I ever have a twin brother? You gotta know, since you birthed me and all."

"My, my. Now that's a good reason to come all the way up here." Miz Becca nodded toward the trailer. "Come on in and we'll have ourselves a chat. Looks like you could use a drink of water."

Yolanda shrugged and followed her up the aluminum steps. With its dark wood paneling and green carpet, the inside of the trailer felt like the deep woods and smelled like moss and topsoil. There was only a small wooden table against the kitchen window, two folding chairs and a nest of blankets in the corner.

Miz Becca filled a coffee cup with water from a milk jug and put it on the table along with a half-empty bag of sunflower seeds. Yolanda sat down, guzzled three cups of water and grabbed a handful of seeds, salty and good.

Miz Becca scooted in her chair and leaned over her elbows. "I hope you don't mind me asking about your ma. She's passed on, what's it been now, about three months?"

Yolanda could tell she wouldn't get an answer without some small talk first. "Yes, Miz Becca."

"Please, call me Becca. I've been wondering if you'd pay me a visit. You've been taking care of your ma for years. Now she's gone and you've got nobody. A girl needs a body to talk to, even if she is darned good at looking after herself."

Yolanda turned away, spit her sunflower shells into her empty cup, and grabbed some more.

"What was it she died of again?" Miz Becca asked.

"We never did find out the scientific reason," Yolanda said between mouthfuls. "Mama wouldn't go to the hospital."

"Didn't like hospitals," Miz Becca smiled. "Stubborn."

"You got that right. She said, 'I was born in this house and there ain't no reason why I can't die in it, too.'"

"Uh-huh," Miz Becca said, "that sounds like Mae."

"She got pretty weak 'round Christmas, though. Wouldn't eat or drink a thing. She was just a bag of bones..." Yolanda's voice cracked a little. She hadn't said this much to anyone in a long time.

"Uhmm. Did you have any help, taking care of her?"

"Our neighbors, the MacGroders, called in a doctor. She was young and pretty. Said it was probably cancer, and left some pills for the pain. After that Mama got real quiet and didn't move much, until she —"

Yolanda closed her eyes and remembered that day when Mama passed. It was during a soap opera. She didn't feel much of anything that day, even when they carried her out. Not sad, not relieved, just empty.

"Watching your mama go like that, that's a hard thing for a girl your age. Let me see, you'd be 'bout 13 by now, am I right?"

Yolanda nodded.

"I'll bet you miss her."

"Well, in a way," Yolanda said, frowning. "But she wasn't much good to talk to. Ever since she got sick."

"Hmmm?"

"She could be pretty mean at times. Plus, she'd never tell me anything. Seems like everybody in Huskaloosa knows more about my family than me."

"How's that?" Miz Becca asked.

"Well, the town kids used to pester me with this old rhyme on the way to school."

"What was it?"

Yolanda hated that verse, yet she knew it by heart. She chanted in a singsong taunting voice, just like the town kids did:

"Where's your daddy, girl, don't you know?
You were so ugly that he had to go.
Where's your mama, girl, can't you say?
She's too mean to see the light of day.
Where's the other baby that was born that night?
Devil took the child, it was such a fright."

"My, my, my." Miz Becca's forehead creased into rows of furrows, deep enough to plant potatoes. "What did you do?"

"I ran home to ask Mama. I asked her about my Daddy and where he was; I asked her if there was another baby, if I had a brother or sister, but she refused to say it; she just yelled at me to change the channel. I asked her again and again, but I never did find out." Yolanda kicked the table leg, hard, and the whole trailer shook.

"Mama never said a thing to me but 'don't let the dishes set, Yolanda,' or 'the broom ain't going to sweep the house itself, Yolanda.' 'Starving chickens can't lay no eggs, Yolanda.' It went on like that all day long. And just when I was about to sit she'd think of something else."

don't you sass me to her, going on and on like a stanley steamer! now get on home like i told you

Miz Becca cocked her head and frowned as if she'd heard Mama's voice. But she couldn't have, could she?

Yolanda figured it was time to get down to business. "So, did I ever have a twin brother? You gotta know."

Miz Becca sighed. "I guess there's no harm in telling you. There was a little baby boy. Came about an hour before you."

Yolanda took a breath. So that old rhyme about a twin was true. But she knew that already.

"What ever happened to him?"

"Well, your mama didn't expect twins; if only she'd come to me sooner. Anyway, she couldn't nurse him with you still coming on, so I wrapped him and set him in a basket by the woodstove to keep him warm. He was such a scrawny little thing. With twins, sometimes one or the other doesn't get enough of what they need. And you were having a heck of a time making your way into this world, feet first, what they call a breech. Finally out you came, just a little bit blue, and I put you on your mama's chest. She sang an old lullaby, I recall – "

"Two Babes in the Woods." Yolanda remembered that sad old tune about the pair of little babies who got left out in the woods all alone. It used to make her tear up, back when she could cry. "So what happened, to the other baby?"

"Nobody knows, nobody knows. When I went to fetch him to your mama, that little baby boy was gone, basket and all." Miz Becca looked down at her hands and frowned again.

"Didn't anybody look for him?"

"Good heavens, child, we looked everywhere! The men got their guns and dogs and combed the whole county, but nobody'd seen or heard a trace. Poor Mae was never the same after that. I suspect that's why she took sick. Just couldn't bear it, poor woman, especially without a man by her side."

An old familiar ache crept up again, the yearning for a real family: a real daddy, a mama that wasn't so mean, a sister or a brother. Now it looked like Yolanda might get part of her wish. A brother! After so long alone, it would be awful good to have somebody she could count on.

"It was him, in the toaster," she said, half to herself.

"What's that?" Miz Becca perked up.

don't tell   don't tell!

"Nothing, I, –" Yolanda stammered.

Miz Becca smiled. "It's all right."

Yolanda's cheeks burned hot and her heart beat down under her jacket. She felt like running all the way back down the George's, but knew it was time to tell. "I-I saw him. I saw my twin brother in – in a reflection."

Miz Becca didn't laugh, she didn't frown, and didn't look at Yolanda as if she was spooky, crazy, or both. She just nodded, waiting for more.

"First, I saw him in the bathroom mirror. The reflection swirled for a second, and I saw a boy, looked just like me. Then I saw him again, on the TV, and again, on the toaster."

it was only your eyes, playing tricks

"What was that?" Miz Becca asked.

"I said, it was him –"

"No, after that. Something about 'your eyes playing tricks'?"

don't tell   don't tell!

"I – I don't know!" Yolanda looked out the window at the darkening sky. How in the world could Miz Becca hear Mama's voice? This whole thing is getting too crazy. I got no business up here, telling things I shouldn't even be thinking to a woman I hardly know.

"It's all right, you can tell me. Might feel better if you did." Miz Becca smiled, and the pair of crows' feet deepened around her eyes. She sounded so nice, and smelled good, too, like lavender and pine.

Still, Yolanda didn't feel like telling any more. "I gotta go now," she said, scooting back from the table.

"Yolanda." Miz Becca's deep brown eyes were like cups of hot chocolate, warm and sweet and full of comfort. "Let's get a few things straight. Now, you may not have liked your Mama much, especially after she got sick, but you loved her, right?"

Yolanda nodded, just a little.

"And now, after she's gone, she's still trying to look out for you. She still talks to you. But you don't want to hear it."

Yolanda nodded again.

"And today, you saw your twin brother, in a mirror."

"And the toaster," Yolanda said, biting her lip.

Miz Becca's smile lit up the room like Christmas. She put her arm around Yolanda's shoulder, gave her a squeeze and said, "By the Four, she's got the gift."

a gift? ha! now that's what i call crazy!

Yolanda looked down at Miz Becca's crooked hand on her shoulder, pulled away and stood up.

"I'm sorry, child. I only thought you might be needing somebody to hold on to," Miz Becca said. "And it's *not* crazy."

"Thanks – for everything. But you can stop calling me 'child.' I don't need anybody." Yolanda stumbled out the trailer door into the twilight, and hugged her jacket against the chill.

"Come back anytime…" Miz Becca called out from the doorway. "If you want to know more about your talent."

Yolanda wheeled around and hung her thumbs on her jeans. "Talent? All I know is chores and chickens."

"Those things are good to know," Miz Becca said.

"Darn right, if you want to eat," Yolanda said.

"I'll bet you're good at it, too. I'll bet you know what the hens need to lay their best. I'll bet your garden is a real prize winner."

How did Miz Becca know? Yolanda didn't go around bragging about the size of her hens' eggs or all the pounds of beans and potatoes she got from only a ten-foot-square patch. "What does that have to do with anything?" she said.

"You tell me. You're the one who's got the vision."

vision? ha! don't listen to that rubbish, it's all a pack of lies

Deep down Yolanda knew Mama was the one telling lies. Her whole life Yolanda had seen and known things that other people didn't see or know. She'd learned not to shout it out loud when somebody told a whopper, especially if it was the minister or a teacher. She knew better than to make a fuss at the store when somebody took something without paying for it. For years she'd done a great job of ignoring all that, so she wouldn't call attention to herself, and get in trouble with Mama. She was doing fine, keeping it all under her hat. Until he showed up.

"What the heck is 'vision,' anyway?" Yolanda said the word as if it was a disease, or a vegetable she didn't like.

"It means you can see the truth, child. What's really there, if you learn how to look. And I hope you do, 'cause it sounds like there's a whole lot of truth coming to find you."

4

*D*arkness filled the sky when Ming and Jade reached the stone wall surrounding the Palace of The Thousand Things. Their breath sent clouds of fog into the night air as they stood before the iron entry, coiled with metal dragons.

"Isn't it too late for visitors?" Ming said.

"Not for you," Jade said, "honored daughter."

"I don't feel honored, or worthy. Just filthy and tired."

"We have traveled a long way," Jade said. "If Ching is half as great as his reputation, he will understand."

Ming nodded.

"And don't worry so much. I will introduce you." Jade smiled, and beckoned for Ming to lead the way.

The gate was unguarded, and so they opened it and went in. The road was paved with flat stones wide enough for twenty, with ancient willows overhanging both sides. Large gardens lay in shadow beyond the trees. The full moon rose behind the Palace as they came to an inner wall with another entry, a large circle of wood cut by a square door in the center. A row of guards stood stiffly in green tunics and black trousers on both sides of the entry.

Jade approached the tallest and bowed deeply. "We are pilgrims from the Fung Mountains, come to seek an audience with Ching, may he be blessed with a hundred lifetimes."

The guard did not answer, or even nod.

"I beg your pardon, this is most unfortunate. Perhaps you may not have heard." Jade said, louder. "May we go in?"

The leader did not move; the others stood like stones, too.

"Strange," Jade whispered.

Ming saw that the gate stood open a hair, and nudged Jade toward it.

"Thank you for your kind permission." Jade bowed to the silent guards once more as they pushed it open.

A long marble hall led through a forest of tall red columns. They walked slowly down the hall to another massive pair of doors, painted gold, with two stone temple dogs crouching on either side. Ming stepped up to the door and rapped it. The sound echoed in the vast emptiness of the hall. No one came to answer.

"Maybe everyone is in bed for the night," Jade whispered.

"Maybe we should wait here until morning," Ming said.

"Wah! I am too old to sleep on these marble steps! Surely we will find someone awake inside."

Ming felt uneasy as Jade helped her slide the heavy door open. Inside was as cool and black as a tomb, and smelled of ancient dust; a fitting place for a god-king to withdraw from the world. Once Ming's eyes grew accustomed to the dark, they crept forward into a large anteroom with a tall ceiling and at least a dozen doorways that opened to shadowed hallways. Jade pointed to another row of guards standing in the dark against the far wall. Were they real men or only statues, like the stone dogs at the door? They didn't move or even make a sound as Ming and Jade made their way to the center of the room.

Ming bent her knees in warrior pose, waiting. All was still, except for a rattle in Jade's chest, remnant of a long bout with a cold, and a scurrying sound that could have been a mouse. Ming heard a muffled laugh. She traced the sound to a location deep inside one of the passages. Then she heard a woman's voice, high and strong, coming from the same hallway. A man's voice shouted in anger.

Could it be Ching?

5

ecca watched Yolanda stomp down the road, her hair a blaze of wildfire, every bit as stubborn as her mama Mae. There could be trouble if the girl just goes on like that, not knowing what's inside her. Still, there was considerable danger in letting it come out. It had to be the right time, and in the right way.

Becca stepped down from the trailer and onto the trail where she did her best thinking. She opened herself to the signs that revealed the way. She sensed a hundred smells and small movements in the darkening forest. She heard the horned owl in his favorite haunt, a hollow cedar tree struck by lightning years ago.

"Oooooht," he called down from a burnt branch.

"Evening," Becca nodded. "A girl came to see me today. She's got quite a gift on her. It's the sight this time."

He blinked, twice.

"I could send her over." She tasted the air. "Moon's full, this very night."

Becca heard a young raccoon lumber over a hill of pine needles, clicking his teeth in agreement.

"You're probably right," she sighed. "I've not seen one this strong for – well, it's been way too long. An old fool like me could begin to hope."

The raccoon chattered a quick warning before he scampered off. Becca tightened her sweater and hiked further up the trail. Her heart ached from so many disappointments over the years. So many young ones never made themselves into what they could be. They'd squandered their talents, used them only to get what they wanted.

Would Yolanda be any different?

Becca saw a bit of moonlight caught on the spokes of a web and peered at the spider in the center, munching her dinner, a beetle.

"The girl's got spirit," she said, "but no faith to speak of. Thinks she can do it all alone. Well, she won't get too far that way, will she?"

The spider didn't answer, but the spiraling pattern in her web echoed the path Becca herself had taken, so long ago: the road to Tessar. It had been a hard road, but it was still the best road for such a one as Yolanda.

That's it, then.

The moon shone down from a cloudless sky, newly round and full of possibilities. Becca crouched to the trail and tucked her head against her shoulder. Although it felt right and good to change, her bones cracked as they shrank and bent inward. Her fingers fanned out into the spines of wings; her skin sprouted tufts of blue-black feathers. Both feet clawed the dirt for balance as her entire body compacted into a tight, strong bird shape. Last, her wings unfolded like a dark blossom and lifted her up and off the trail.

The night wind ruffled her feathers as she flew over the pines and under the moon. Her nostrils followed the scent of water, and then her quick, black eyes spotted the stream below. She listened for all the night creatures and insects scurrying among the trees, and then heard Yolanda crashing through the bush.

Becca flew down to her, her heart as calm as the still, deep pool that lay at the top of the mountain.

6

ing motioned to Jade, and they crept down the long marble hall toward the sound of the voices. As they got closer she distinguished three unique voices, becoming louder and more elevated in tone. They rounded a corner and stopped just before an open doorway where light spilled onto the floor. The people inside spoke a different language. It sounded harsh, not flowing like the Eastern tongue, yet Ming understood every word.

"He must go, now," a deeper, man's voice, said.

"But Niko, he's exhausted," the woman said. "Let him stay and rebuild his strength first."

"She's right," a younger man said. "That little trick took more out of me than I expected. That's why I need her now."

"We must stay the course," the deep voice said. "You both agreed to the plan. It's a precisely timed machine –"

"Niko, stop going on about the plan." The woman interrupted the man. "This is only a tiny adjustment. Surely you can abide that."

Ming drew her head closer to the open door, to better grasp the meaning of this argument.

"I'm telling you, it's not the right time. Even if it was, she's of no use to us. She doesn't know anything."

"If you had told me about her sooner –" the young man said.

"She's not important."

"She's important to me," the younger man said.

"The East is done. Let Yakos have this," the woman said.

"Narissa, as usual, you underestimate the realities of the situation. We don't know what the people will do. They will get hungry. They could revolt. They will demand Ching."

Ming's ears perked up at the mention of Ching. She leaned her head forward just a fraction, to try and look into the room without being seen. Jade tugged on her arm, her eyes full of worry. The conversation stopped.

Ming heard a click-clack on the marble floor, coming closer. Her knees bent and lowered, in case of attack.

The woman stepped out into the hall, a full head taller than Ming. Light-skinned, her hair color was a blend of four sacred metals: gold, silver, copper, bronze. A Northerner, here in the Palace? Yet she wore a pink silk robe of the East, embroidered with a delicate web pattern.

"You may be right, Niko," she said in her own tongue.

A tall Northern man appeared behind her, with silver hair and slightly darker skin, wearing a deep blue uniform. "What have we here, a pair of spies?"

"No, we are only pilgrims, come to —" Jade said.

Before she could finish, Jade's head slumped forward. She fell against Ming, who caught her and lowered her body to the floor as she checked for signs of injury. She could see nothing. In the same tenth of a second, Ming calculated the distance to the woman, to the man, and readied for a spring kick just as the younger Northerner stepped into the doorway.

His hair shot up from his forehead, as red as poppies. Though no older than Ming, he carried himself with great purpose and strength.

"What are you doing!" he challenged the older man.

Ming re-positioned her stance to take all three, but then her mind lost all focus. All thoughts of attack were pushed aside by a sweet feeling of peace and contentment that filled her entire body. She knew that everything would be fine. She didn't need to bend in warrior stance any longer. As Ming let every muscle relax, her body fell gently to the floor near Jade. And when her cheek landed on the marble it was not cold and hard, but as soft as a cloud, drifting toward heaven.

7

*Y*olanda could barely see her way in the deep woods. It was crazy to walk down the mountain at this hour; still, not as crazy as Miz Becca's talk about a 'gift,' or Mama's voice cranking in her ear, or her twin brother's face that never seemed to go away. Moonlight caught on the dewy pine boughs, glistening green, reminded her of his eyes. The trail ahead was the same golden color as his skin. Even the wind seemed to whisper "Yo-laan-daaaa" with his voice.

That's it. I'm going nuts. Seeing things, hearing things that can't be real. She hiked faster down the mountain path. Maybe I should go live with the people from church after all. Maybe God will have mercy on my soul. Maybe He'll make this all go away.

A big black bird swooped over her head, and then a twig snapped somewhere behind her. Somebody was out there!

double dog! this is no place for a young girl after dark

Yolanda spun around and saw Miz Becca stepping out from the shadows. "What are you doing, sneaking up on me like that!" she said.

"Full moon's rising, child. Come with me," Miz Becca said.

"Where to? The loony bin? I don't believe any of that stuff about 'vision,' and a reflection being real. I just want to know what's wrong with me!" Yolanda hadn't meant to sound like such a whiner.

Miz Becca took a breath. "There is nothing wrong with you. Your vision is a talent, as I said. A power. But you can't learn to use it properly around here. Now this may sound strange, but there is another world besides this one. It's an old place – the place where dreams and magic come from. They call it Tessar, meaning 'four.' Your brother is there."

ha! she's just an old fool, filling your head with a bunch of garbage

Miz Becca's eyes blazed and her voice changed to thunder. "That's only your fear talking. Don't listen! Come with me, even if you don't believe." She turned back into the woods, hiking uphill toward the top of the George's.

What if she's right? Maybe there is such a thing as vision. What if he really is in that other place? If I don't go now, I may never find out.

Yolanda hurried to catch up. Miz Becca looked back at her and winked, then took off alongside a trickling creek that became a rocky stream. The path ended at a waterfall, with huge slabs of rock on either side that looked too steep to climb. Yolanda grabbed a hold high above her head and tried to clamber up, but her feet slipped against the slick moss.

you'll fall, break your neck!

Yolanda lost her grip and her balance, and landed in the stream on her backside. "Dang it! Dang the day I was born."

Somehow Miz Becca had already made it to the top, and leaned over the edge with her arm out. "It was a fine day. Blue skies and everything. Here's a hand up for you, child."

"I believe I told you to stop calling me that!" Yolanda ignored Miz Becca's outstretched hand and spotted another way up. She clambered up and slid her belly over the ledge, and then stood up. The waterfall flowed from a pool of water that glistened in the moonlight.

"Say, isn't this Hanging Lake?" she said.

Miz Becca wasn't in sight, and didn't answer.

"Hey! Where'd you go?"

Yolanda's voice echoed back across the water. Except for a crow flying over the lake, she was alone.

Crazy old lady. Drags me up here, talking crazy, and then she just leaves. Dang it!

Yolanda tightened her jacket and watched the full moon rising over the trees that circled the lake. What did Miz Becca say? Something about it being full tonight?

As the moon rose higher, Yolanda saw its reflection – a twin – shimmering on the still water. She stared at the spot, hypnotized by the light. The water started swirling. And then the familiar face with green eyes appeared on the surface and smiled, just like the man in the moon.

"Yo-laan-daaa…" A whisper came across the water. There was longing in it, a feeling she recognized.

He needs me.

Yolanda edged toward the lake. Her boots squished in the mud with a soft sucking sound. It was nuts to think about it, but to actually go into a freezing cold lake, at night? She saw his face, glowing and golden, and took a step toward him.

don't be an idiot. you're not going out there!

I can do what I want, Mama! Besides, I'm already wet from falling in that damn stream.

With a snort of a nervous laugh Yolanda kicked off her boots and threw them into the weeds along with her jacket. Icy water crept up her shins, and then she went farther, up to her knees. A couple more steps and she stood chest-deep, gasping from the cold.

flabbergast it! you'll catch your death!

"Yo-lan-daaa…" he whispered.

Yolanda took a breath and kicked out to the deeper water at the center of the lake where she'd seen his reflection under the moon. Her swimming churned up the water so she couldn't see anything on the surface, but a round shape glowed down below, like another ball of light near the bottom. His face shone there, rippling and changing deep under the water.

"Yo-laan-daaaa…" His voice definitely came from below.

cheese and crackers! come to your senses, girl!

Yolanda had swum to the bottom of MacGroder's pond many times. She took a deep breath and dove straight down toward the light. When she came to where the bottom ought to be, the glowing ball of light was still further down. Green and gold currents flowed around her like a whirlpool, bringing her farther and farther down to the light. Yet he was always deeper, always out of reach.

How long had it been since she took a breath? Too long. Panic gripped her throat. Her fingers clawed at the water as if it were a hole she could climb back out of. She fought to hold on to her last scrap of breath, until finally she had to take in a gulp of cold water. She gagged and sputtered, but didn't drown! Once she stopped fighting it got easier, and the water felt like air in her mouth and lungs.

Yolanda dove farther down to the ball of light where her twin's face shone faintly. At the outer edge millions of shimmering golden droplets danced around her like tiny fireflies. She wanted to laugh, it was so beautiful. She swam in farther, but couldn't see his face anymore. The center of the fiery ball was so bright it hurt her eyes. She swam around it again and again, searching for any sign of him, but couldn't see or hear him at all.

Where are you, dang it!

As Yolanda's hope sank, the gentle current that had carried her down to the ball of light became a force of gravity. Instead of floating light and weightless, she sank heavily into a thick, mud-colored mist, moving farther and farther away from the light. She felt trapped in an endless dream, falling through molasses, with a silent scream stuck in her throat.

Help me!

Finally her feet touched bottom, on a spongy sort of ground. Her legs buckled under her and she collapsed. Yolanda stood up slowly, all in one piece, thank heaven, and with no broken bones.

Somehow the lake water had become air; she was completely dry. A strong wind whipped the legs of her jeans and blew her hair across her face. Yolanda turned all the way around, but every direction looked the same: nothing but thick fog, the goldish-green color of a three-day-old bruise.

What is this place, Hell?

Mama always said I'd end up there.

8

𝒯he ground felt solid and flat under Yolanda's feet, but she couldn't see anything. The horizon was just a smudge between heaven and earth. She peered into the fog looking for a sign of her twin. There wasn't even a twinge of that magnetic tug she felt whenever she saw him. Where were those wide-open arms she'd pictured herself running to? Brothers are supposed to watch over you, be there for you, not lead you into some bottomless water hole and leave you there to sink. A ball of hopeless rage rose up from her belly and climbed into her throat. She cupped her hands to her mouth and bellowed as hard as she could. "Hey! Where are you?"

No answer.

"Isn't anybody here? Anybody?"

you just had to go jump in that lake. now look where it's got you

"Dang you!" Yolanda stomped her feet and cursed. She cursed her mama, her long-gone daddy, Miz Becca, everybody in Huskaloosa and the whole of creation. After all the cursing and stomping was done she stood red-faced in the middle of nowhere. She still wanted to find him, but had no idea where to look. Or even how to get back home.

Yolanda staggered against the wind, feeling the ground ahead with her toes to make sure she didn't fall off a cliff or something. Not that it mattered. She'd already gone off the map, although it couldn't be Hell. The ground was too mushy, and there wasn't a lick of fire, or brimstone, whatever that was.

What was the name of that other world Miz Becca had been going on about? Tess-something. Yolanda wished she'd paid more attention. She stumbled on, not caring which direction. She just had to keep moving, to keep her mind off the fact that she was both lost and crazy, and might never get back to the Valley, or to her right mind, again.

In time the wind blew patches of fog away, lifting it like a blanket so she could see some of the ground underneath. It looked like plain old dirt, just the same as back home. As the fog thinned she could make out some lumpy shapes not too far up ahead. She half-walked, half-ran toward it, hoping for a house, but it was only a sunken pit of cracked mud, surrounded by creepy-looking trees. The branches hung so low and spidery they seemed to grow back into the ground like roots.

Banyan trees. That's what they are. Yolanda had never heard of banyan trees, but the word was there in her mind, as plain as if the trees had said it themselves.

talking trees! ha! now you are gone, full crazy

"I didn't say the trees could talk!" she said.

"Aaa-waa-eeeeeee...awh, awh, awh, awh!"

A screech came down from the trees, sounding like a cross between a turkey vulture and a cat in heat. Yolanda practically jumped out of her jeans. She could have sworn she heard something else under the wild screeching. Something like words.

A lean streak of gold fur darted behind the vines, and then a small face with shiny black eyes and a leathery mouth peered down at her. A monkey! Yolanda had only seen them on TV. The monkey swung from vine to vine on a tail as long as her arm, scrawny, and with a dirty white underbelly.

"Aweeeee-ah-ah-ah-ah!"

Yolanda heard the monkey's screech, but she also heard 'Good morning,' in English. It was in her head, the same as she'd heard 'banyan trees.'

talking monkeys. my word!

What kind of a place is this?

The monkey swung so close that his face was right up against her face, so close she could see a little chunk of stuff in the corner of his eyes. He opened his mouth so far she could see an inch of black gums and both rows of yellow teeth. He screamed, "I am a girl-child of the North, and you are an immortal monkey!"

"What the – ?" Yolanda's jaw dropped open like a wide-mouthed bass.

The monkey leapt away, jumping from tree to tree, jabbering about immortal spirits and a bunch of other things that didn't make sense.

"Lord in heaven above us all," she whispered. "Oh Lord, oh Lord, oh Lord."

"Thank you," the monkey smiled.

"U-umm, where am I?" she said, not quite believing she was talking back to him.

"Aieeeah," he said. Home.

"Home?" she frowned. "It's your home, but it's not mine."

"Home is where the harp is."

Funny, she'd just thought of that old line before he said it. Only he got it wrong. "Don't you mean 'heart'? Home is where the *heart* is."

"There's no place like Rome."

"O-kaaay, whatever," she said. "Hey, since you can talk, maybe you can help. I'm looking for somebody. He's about my size. Green eyes. Have you seen him?"

"Your brother. Very important. Big guy." He swung within an inch of her nose and picked up a strand of her hair with his long, thin fingers. "Red. Color of fire. Color of Mount Vesuvius in the morning. Color of –"

"Let go!" Yolanda backed away from him. "Hey! How did you know he's my brother?"

"The way," he said. "The way, the way, the way, the way." He chattered as he leapt to a shaggy branch above her head and scratched himself in a couple of rude places. "Monkey see, monkey do."

Once again, she'd been thinking the exact same thing before he said it. "What are you, a bloody mind reader?"

The monkey twisted around to look down his back then checked his legs and arms, one by one. "Bloody! I'm bleeding!"

"You're not really bloody," she laughed. "I heard it on TV once. I liked the way it sounded."

"The way. The way it sounded. The way the way it sounded." His head went up and down like a bobble-head toy.

"Yeah, the way it sounded!" she said.

"The way it sounded sounded sounded!"

"Just forget the way it sounded, ok? Isn't there anything around here? Any houses, roads, a Quick Stop —"

"What's a quick stop?"

"A place to get stuff, you know, gas, pop, all kinds of junk."

"Junk?" The monkey's head tilted sideways.

"You know, food and junk. Candy, chips, whatever."

"Where do you put the junk?"

Yolanda smiled. "In your mouth! You eat it."

"Do you have any junk to eat?"

"Nope." Then she remembered a half-eaten stick of beef jerky she'd stuck in her pocket a week ago. That stuff never goes bad. She pulled it out of its sticky plastic wad and tossed it over.

The monkey caught it, bounced up and down on his branch and shrieked "thanks." He shoved the whole thing into his mouth and chewed from side to side, his lips pulled up high so the jerky juice squished out. "Ah, delicious! Where do you come from, with such junk?"

"Huskaloosa, USA. The Valley, not the mountains."

The monkey pressed his palms and fingers together, and then bent his head forward like he was praying. "Ah, valley and mountain. Yin and Yang. The complete Tao."

"No, it's Hus-ka-loo-sa, like I said."

"Do flowers still grow in Hus-ka-loo-sa?"

"Yeah, I guess so. Don't flowers grow everywhere?"

"Ah, but none like the flowers of the East. So fragrant, so sweet, they melt the stony heart of old Mount Yao himself. But now, the flowers will not grow." The monkey's face drooped and he folded his arms around himself for comfort.

"What's the matter?" Yolanda asked, and then realized he'd gotten her off track again. "I'm sorry, about the flowers and all, but I've got to get moving. Is there a road around here? Can you show me the way?"

"The way, yes!" The monkey perked up again.

"You keep talking about the way… where is it?"

"If there is a way, it will come to you."

"So what do I do now? Just sit around? Doing nothing? That's stupid!"

"Ooooh," the monkey whistled. "Sit around. Do nothing. Be stupid. That's what is."

Yolanda shook her head. "I've got to find somebody who knows what's going on around here."

The monkey sighed, long and slow. "A king knows many things. He knows he is the last spirit walking. He knows your kind is in the palace. What do you know?"

"Nothing, I guess." Yolanda shrugged. He was no help at all. She looked out past the banyan grove. The fog had burned off and the sun shone bright and clear; she could see a long way into the distance. Wide fields of gold-colored grain spun out in all directions.

Millet. The word came to her mind.

"What is this place?" she said, turning back to the monkey, but she couldn't see or hear him among the trees. He was gone, just as suddenly as Miz Becca. And her twin.

lord almighty. now it's disappearing monkeys!

"Oh, shut up, Mama!" Yolanda kicked the base of the closest tree, almost hard enough to break her little toe. "I've got enough trouble without you talking in my ear!"

She limped out of the grove, half-expecting Mama to pipe up again, but all she heard was a dead quiet as if her nagging voice was really gone. Like her friend the monkey. Though she was no better off than before, at least she could see the way ahead.

"The way!" Yolanda laughed out loud and started walking.

9

$\mathcal{N}$arissa lounged in her favorite chair, the rosewood carved with clouds, sipping jasmine tea. Nikolas worked across the table in his high-backed throne carved with a thousand animals: cranes, snakes, panda bears, and dragonflies. She smiled at the irony of their choices, that she liked the cloud chair and Niko preferred the animal.

She sniffed the air, in the same way that some will sense the weather, and noticed a touch of longing in the atmosphere.

"We have a visitor on the way, Niko," she said, twisting a strand of gold and copper hair around her finger.

Nikolas didn't even look up from the giant stack of scrolls, maps and documents that had cluttered the long table since they'd taken the Palace. He jotted something fast, and then stopped to suck the end of his peacock quill before he rummaged under another stack for another essential bit of paper and read it ferociously, nodding. He'd always agonized over every tiny detail, anticipating and calculating every possible move and countermove.

His obsessively linear skills and logic were useful, but Narissa preferred the power of instinct. She sighed and left the comfort of her cloud chair and walked to the rice paper window. It was impossible to see through the stuff, still, she knew without looking that someone was coming.

"Ming. Open the window," she said, annoyed with the new servant who stood by the door with a slack expression on her lovely round face. Narissa would not open it herself, even though she stood much closer and it would take several minutes for the girl to get there.

Ming shuffled to the window with some difficulty and slid the wood frame to one side. From this height in the Palace tower, Narissa could see far across the golden yellow fields of the East, shimmering in the afternoon heat. She saw a dot on the horizon that appeared to be coming closer.

"I'd better get out the good china," she said.

"What?" Nicholas looked up over his pile of papers, frowning. "What did you say?"

"Oh, for the sake of the heavens, pull your nose out of there and look." Narissa pointed outside with a tapered pink fingernail that perfectly matched her silk robe. "It may be the one we've been waiting for."

Niko stood up and squinted, but clearly couldn't see. "You take care of it; you've got help." He looked over his spectacles at Ming, and the older servant, Jade. "I've got to finish this section. It's absolutely vital." Niko sat down and bent over his papers again.

"Which is it?" Narissa pretended to care. "Total Unification or – ?"

Not surprisingly, Nikolas didn't respond. Narissa turned to Ming. "Prepare the yellow guest quarters and draw a hot bath. Tell the cooks to prepare a feast for an esteemed visitor arriving within the afternoon."

She noted the servant's tiny steps as she made her way slowly toward the door.

10

*Y*ellow hills of dry millet rolled along as far as Yolanda could see. The fog piled up in the distance like cotton candy, in shades of pink and blue and purple, as pretty as a picture book. The wind blew right into Yolanda's face, though, always pushing against her. Strange that there weren't any signs of life: no bugs, birds, or critters of any kind. The whole place seemed way too quiet and empty.

After a long time just walking, and not coming across a road or anything more interesting than an abandoned molehill, she caught a flash of light glinting at the horizon. She squinted. What was it? A building of some kind?

She ran over the fields until she could see it better. It was some kind of castle, with tall towers and a stone wall all the way around, but with strange rooftops, like square boats, on top. The word 'pagoda' popped into her head. She remembered seeing a pagoda in one of her books back home, "Around the World in a Thousand Pictures." Yolanda loved the photographs of folks riding elephants, princesses in bejeweled headdresses, kids crouching in mud huts with nothing on but a couple of twisted rags; she used to pretend she'd go someplace far away like that someday. Now she was farther than she'd ever dreamed – was it China? Yolanda ran even faster toward the golden pagodas.

If it's gold, it's got to be good, right?

Yolanda was totally out of breath when she reached the wall, over eight feet high, built with massive chunks of stone and topped with red clay tiles. She turned left and walked to a rusty iron gate that squeaked open to a wide road, paved with perfectly round stones and lined with rows of dried-out willow trees. The road led to another, shorter wall that surrounded the huge castle with its five tall towers with pagoda roofs. Everything was gold or marble, carved with curlicues and scrolls.

you don't belong in there. you're just a nobody from nowhere

Mama was right. Yolanda looked down at her filthy jeans with the ripped knees. Her shoeless feet were caked with mud and bits of millet. Her hair hadn't been combed in two days, and she didn't smell very fresh. She wasn't even fit for the hardware store back home, but there was nowhere else to go. She walked the deserted road toward the palace.

"Hello," she called out. "Is anybody here?" No answer.

Yolanda noticed some shadowy shapes beyond the trees. She crept into a huge garden with hundreds of gray stone statues. She passed every kind of animal: foxes, lions, lizards, cats; and weird creatures, too: dragons and monsters of every size and shape; human bodies with elephant heads, peacock tails or about a hundred arms and legs. Some of them even looked like sea foam or giant plants from Mars, but all the statues had a look of shock on their faces, like wild things that got cornered.

Yolanda hurried back to the road. She came to a huge wooden gate, a square hole cut out of a large circle of wood. The gate opened to a long hall with slick marble floors, red columns along both sides, and a set of stairs with another huge gold door at the top. A couple of crouching statues guarded the base of the stairs, looking like a cross between a dragon and a lion, with huge popping eyes and fangs. The words 'palace dogs' came into her mind. Those dogs looked mean enough – and real enough – to bite her head off.

don't you do it don't you go in there

Dang it, Mama! There's no place else.

Yolanda could almost feel the dogs' breath as she hurried past them and up the marble stairs. The doors hung from a sliding track, about ten feet tall and four feet wide, decorated with jewels and carved symbols. What do you do at a door like that, knock? Before she got up the nerve, the door slid open, just a crack. Yolanda bit her lip as it inched slowly to the left, as if all by itself.

11

wo ladies stood in the shadows behind the door. One was about Yolanda's age and about the same height, while the other was much older and barely reached to her chin. She supposed they were Japanese or Chinese, judging by the nice points at the ends of their eyes and high eyebrows. The ladies looked as perfect as painted dolls with their shiny black hair done up in big knots and folded ribbons and long yellow robes trailing on the floor. Pretty as they were, their faces had no expression. They didn't say a word. After they'd stared at her awhile they bent over and bowed to her, the same way as some Chinese people she'd seen on TV once.

So this really is China. Hanging Lake must be even deeper than I thought. Ha!

don't trust 'em, they're different

Shoot, Mama, they don't look dangerous.

Yolanda didn't know if she should bow back, or curtsey? She nodded her head a couple of times, but they still didn't do – or say – anything. She'd have to do the talking.

"I – um, I'm looking for somebody. A guy. Red hair and green eyes. Looks like me."

The older woman nodded slowly, then spoke a jumble of twangy words that sounded like "ouchoo-ya-da."

Yolanda knew exactly what she meant: "Come, follow me."

She said it in Chinese, but I heard English, just like how I heard the monkey. But did they understand what I said?

Before she had a chance to ask, the two women turned inside with slow, jerky steps. They slid down the dark hallway like a couple of zombie snails, dragging their yellow robes behind them. Yolanda wiped her sweaty palms on her jeans and stepped through the doorway in her mud-soaked socks. Nothing she could do about that.

Once Yolanda's eyes adjusted to the dark, she noticed that the walls and floor were shiny black marble with gold decorations everywhere: flowers, trees, birds, bugs, animals, people. The Chinese ladies walked so slowly Yolanda had lots of time to see everything. Every so often they passed a hollowed opening in the wall with a tiny figurine sitting inside. Yolanda heard names come into her mind as she passed by: 'Bodhisattva' and 'Buddha,' fat and smiling, sat on cushions; demons and dragons crouched wild-eyed, ready to pounce. Though no bigger than mice, they were as lifelike as the statues out in the garden, with every hair, tooth and claw perfectly carved in wood or stone.

Next they came to a long row of men with gray-yellow skin and stern faces, wearing brass helmets and armor over loose black clothes like pajamas. Were they soldiers or statues? How could they stand so still, without even breathing? Yolanda was tempted to give one a poke to find out for sure, but then the ladies slid open a tall door.

The long yellow room had a huge red rug covered with patterns, painted wall hangings, and fancy carved chests. The girl shuffled to the far wall and slid open a pair of windows that looked like milky paper instead of glass, while the older lady pulled aside some gauzy curtains that surrounded a large bed covered with bright colored pillows.

A wave of weariness came down on her, and she felt as tired as somebody who'd climbed a mountain, swum through the bottom of the world and walked a hundred miles of yellow fields. "I wish I could just sink into those feather cushions for a little nap," she said, half to herself, but the older woman motioned her through another door.

Though it was only a bathroom, it was bigger than her whole house back in the Valley. The walls, the floor, the ceiling and even a tall tub in the corner were all made of black marble with veins of gold. Hot steam rose off the tub of water; the ladies nodded at her to get in.

"Um, do you always keep hot water in there?" she asked. "Or maybe you saw me coming, and filled the tub?"

They didn't answer, in Chinese or any other language. The older one reached out to fumble with the button on Yolanda's jeans, while the young one bent down and lifted her left foot to take off her sock. She wasn't used to having anybody touch her, much less take off her clothes.

rude as hell, that's what it is!

"Hey, is this how you do things around here?"

No answer. When the older one tugged her jeans halfway down, Yolanda grabbed her arms to stop her. "Hold on just a cotton-picking minute! I can take off my own underwear, thank you!"

The women must have understood because they slowly backed out the door, bowing and nodding. Yolanda stripped and perched on the tub's wide marble edge and poked her toe in. Youch! The water was scalding, and so deep she could barely see the bottom against the black marble. She stepped in and found a ledge to sit on, thank Jesus. Her skin turned as pink as a blushing pig, and she sunk to her ears in the sweet-smelling water.

"Yo-lan-da..." A whisper rose up from the water and bounced off the marble walls.

Yolanda sat up. Her reflection started to swirl around and around like a whirlpool, and then the face with the strong jaw, green eyes and red hair floated up and smiled at her. Her heart beat faster than she could think. She'd wanted to see him so bad, but now she felt queasy, as if she'd had too many french fries.

"Yolanda. You've come to me at last," he said, in a voice that matched his face: bold and sure. Not like her, always wondering if she'd made a mistake.

But he was the one who'd made a mistake, ditching her back in Hanging Lake.

"Yeah, I came," she said, looking away at the wall. "But if you expect me to dive into this tub after you, well, you can forget it."

His chin puckered into a pout that reminded her of Mama. "I hoped you'd be glad to see me again," he said.

"I might be, if you hadn't left me at the bottom of that lake. Where did you go, back into a mirror or a toaster or something?"

"Please forgive me, Yolanda. This is not what I wanted for you. But don't worry. Nikolas and Narissa will –"

"Who the heck are they?" she butted in. "I don't even know your name!"

"Oh! I thought you knew. I am Yakos."

"Yakos...what kind of a name is that? You show up in the weirdest places, calling me like you're in some kind of terrible trouble. Then, when I follow you, you leave me alone in a damn fog bank! How do you do it? Appear and disappear in things? What is this place? And how the heck am I gonna get back?"

"You have many questions. And you will have answers..."

"Well, I better get some answers right now –" Yolanda gripped the side of the tub to stand up, but didn't want him to see her naked. She sat back down with a thud. Yakos' face rocked on the water, all broken up in a patchwork of waves.

"Sorry," she said, forcing a smile.

"You are an intelligent young woman," he said.

"I stopped going to school."

She said it to spite him, but Yakos only laughed. His eyes sparkled like green jewels, which made her forget how mad she was, for the moment.

"An ordinary school is not the place for you. Narissa and Nikolas will teach you everything you need to know."

"But when can I see you? For real? If you are real, that is."

"I am most certainly real," he smiled. "And you will see me, when the time is right."

"I know what that means: just shut up and do as you're told. I've heard that before."

He raised one perfectly arched eyebrow. "Hmmm. You are even more like me than I imagined. That's very good. Good night, Yolanda."

Yolanda watched her brother's face swirl away like an oil slick in the rain. "Wait! I still don't –"

But he was gone, again. Yolanda slapped the water with her hand.

12

*M*ing walked back into the black room filled with billowing steam carrying a silk robe over her arm. It wasn't the mist from the young lady's hot bath that filled the corners of her mind with gentle warmth. It was something else, something peaceful and soothing. She knew how to keep that feeling close. All she had to do was the one task whispered by the Master, and then the next.

Get the girl dressed. Take her to the dining hall. Bring the food from the kitchen, and serve it to the girl.

The older woman that Ming called Jade carried a square cloth towel. She held out her hand for the young Northern girl to get out of the water. The girl didn't take it, though. She tried to cover herself while climbing over the steep tub walls, slid on the marble and nearly fell to the floor.

Ming lunged forward to help the girl find her balance, but her own legs felt tight and pinched, as if bound together with barbed wire. She wobbled and almost tripped over, which brought a new feeling of worry that didn't fit so well with the dreamy cushion of comfort that she preferred.

Something was wrong. The feeling passed, though, like a bird flying overhead.

The girl took the towel from Jade and dried herself. Ming draped the silken robe around her shoulders, wrapped it tightly around her body several times before tying the sash at her waist. Jade led her to the dressing table chair, and together they combed her wet hair, twisted it on top of her head, and held it with a silver comb with charms.

The girl looked very familiar with her red hair up, but Ming didn't know why, and didn't care. The feeling of peace blew through her mind again like a warm breeze. Her first task was done.

13

*Y*olanda's headdress tinkled like a bell as the two Chinese ladies led her out the door and into the long hallway. The fancy robe was way too tight around her legs, so she could only take baby steps, but it made her straighten herself up, the way a princess ought to walk.

ha! some princess. you're just a nobody from —

Shut up, Mama. Yolanda tilted her chin higher.

The ladies led her around several turns until they slid open a door to a huge room painted with swirling fog and clouds. It was empty except for a long, low table on the bare wood floor. The ladies slid a panel of the foggy mural to one side, took three pillows from a hidden closet, put them on the floor beside the table and motioned for her to sit on one. Surely they could afford chairs, in such a fine place!

How to get down on that pillow in this tight dress?

Yolanda bent her knees and twisted downward, but the silk pillow slipped out from under her and slid out of reach. Her backside bumped on the floor so loud it almost echoed.

"Well, well. Here she is." A man's voice spoke in English. Not Chinese.

Yolanda jerked her head around to see a tall, silver-haired man with a deep tan walk with long strides toward the table. He wore a dark blue uniform with gold buttons, and looked like a boat captain character on Mama's soap operas.

Yolanda scrambled on all fours to grab her pillow, and shoved it under her bottom about as gracefully as a toad.

"I am Nikolas, master of this Palace."

The man bowed very slowly, though not as low as the Chinese ladies, then stared right into Yolanda's face. His eyes were crinkly around the edges like a kindly old gentleman, but they were as blue and cold as chips of ice from the North Pole. It almost hurt to look into them.

Yolanda glanced down at her hands. Stop shaking! A trickle of sweat ran down her side. What to do, what to say? She couldn't stand up; she'd never get back on that pillow.

well, just don't sit there like a bump on a log

Nikolas clapped his hands sharply. The Chinese ladies shuffled toward him, bowing over and over.

"Does she talk?" he said, like an order. The ladies nodded. "Well, then, why not to me?" Nikolas moved closer. His shadow fell across Yolanda's lap.

"Niko, what are you doing to our guest?" A female voice, husky and smooth, spoke from the doorway.

A tall lady glided across the floor in a long pink Chinese dress with slits on the sides that showed her legs. Though not young, she could have stepped off the cover of a fashion magazine. Her blonde-and-copper hair was pulled up tight, her cheeks stood out from her face, and her cat eyes were the same blue as Nikolas'. She smiled the whole way to the table, as if she was thinking of something funny that no one else knew.

Nikolas straightened up. "Narissa. Late, again."

"So sorry to disappoint you, Niko. Again."

Narissa glided to Yolanda and held out her hand. "Welcome, my dear."

Yolanda did not know what to do with a hand like that, glittering with gold and jeweled rings. Should she shake it up and down, the way Reverend Weaver pumped hands after church, or kiss it? People were always kissing the queen's hand in fairy tales. Her own palms felt slick with sweat.

"Don't be offended by her lack of decorum," Nikolas said. "She doesn't like me, either."

Narissa dropped her hand as easily as a falling leaf, and frowned at Nikolas. "Niko, please. You've embarrassed our guest." She smiled at Yolanda, flashing a set of the whitest teeth she had ever seen. "It is a pleasure to meet you! I pray the servants have shown you to your room, and that you found everything to your satisfaction?" Narissa used a lot of pretty words that rose and fell like a tumbling waterfall. And like a waterfall, she kept on gushing. "Nikolas. Isn't it astonishing how much she resembles our Yakos? The green eyes, the red hair. He tells us your name is Yolanda. A lovely name for an exquisite young woman."

Yolanda's cheeks blushed so hot they could have caught on fire. She knew she was as plain as a post, and had known it all her life. Still, it was nice of Narissa to say that. But what to say back? Nikolas and Narissa's eyes roamed over her like searchlights, probing, asking.

"Y-Yakos told me about you," she finally said.

"I trust he said nothing but kind things." Narissa gave Nikolas a sideways smile.

"All he said was you were going to tell me everything. So where the heck am I? And how did I get here?" Yolanda's hand flew up to cover her mouth. She hadn't meant to blurt it out like that. She bit her finger, to make it hurt.

"My dear, you are an honored guest in the Palace of the Ten Thousand Things, the greatest treasure in all the East."

"The East. Isn't that China?"

"No, dear, this is not China, although there are many similarities," Narissa clapped her hands and nodded toward the wall. The two ladies shuffled to the mural and slid the panels together so the painting was whole again. She swept her hand through the air with a grand style. "Welcome to the Eastern quadrant of Tessar, the golden land of air."

Tessar! So she did get to that place Miz Becca talked about! In the mural, that thick yellow fog hung over the entire countryside, with only a few things poking through: hills dotted with pines; clusters of pointed roofs, and the golden Palace with its five pagodas. At the far left, a small city perched on the edge of a large lake or ocean. Near the top of the mural there were a few mountains with giant clouds piled around the peaks. Were the clouds actually moving?

"Delightfully mysterious, isn't it?" Narissa said.

Yolanda frowned; everything around here was a mystery. "So what is Tessar, anyway? I only went into Hanging Lake and then, and then, well, how did I get here?"

"Through a doorway," Nikolas said, as if that explained everything.

"Sure, I came through the door. They let me in!" Yolanda pointed to the two Chinese ladies.

"No, no, no," he chuckled. It was the kind of laugh that sounded like he didn't mean it. "A door between the worlds, my dear. A gateway."

A gateway. Sure. Yolanda clenched her jaw. Some people act so high and mighty about what they know, as if they know everything about everything and have known it all since the beginning of time.

"Niko, she doesn't understand." Narissa reached out to pat her hand, as if Yolanda were her favorite niece. "Don't mind him, it's just his way. We thought Yakos had told you."

Yolanda's stomach growled out loud. Nikolas glanced at the empty table and snarled at the two servants. "Hasn't she been served yet?" They bowed ten times, opened another hidden panel and rustled with plates and things.

"May we join you?" Nikolas asked.

All Yolanda could do was nod. Thank goodness Nikolas sat across the table; Narissa sank gently, kneeling on the pillow beside Yolanda without a bit of trouble.

The Chinese ladies brought out huge platters loaded with food that looked strange and smelled even more strange. She heard the names of the dishes in her mind: Imperial Quail Eggs. Soup of Nine Wonders. Shrimps Stuffed with Seven

Happinesses. Perfumed Rice. Pork with Peppered Plums. Whole Enchanted Fish. Braised Duck Feet. Duck feet?

The ladies gave her a plate and a pair of skinny black sticks. Chopsticks. Oh lord. Don't they have forks in Tessar?

Yolanda was starving. She crossed the sticks in one hand the way she'd seen on TV, and grabbed a chunk of gooey fish. It jumped out from the chopsticks, slid down the front of her robe and onto the floor.

flyin' fish! now that's how a real princess does it
Hush it, Mama!

Luckily Narissa and Nikolas didn't see, because the ladies were busy pouring tea. Yolanda nudged the fish under the table with her toe, and snuck a piece of pork with her fingers. It tasted much better than she expected, rich and salty and sweet. She reached out for another, and another.

"Our guest seems to be enjoying our little feast," Nikolas said, as she stuffed another hunk into her mouth.

A dribble of plum sauce hung from her lower lip; she licked it clean. Nikolas and Narissa's blue eyes were all over her. That old blush came up again, hotter than July.

"Chopsticks can be so very difficult when you're not used to them. Here's the way." Narissa showed Yolanda how to rest one stick on her middle finger and to use her thumb and forefinger to move the other chopstick against it.

"Thanks." Yolanda picked up a duck foot and waved it in the air.

14

*N*ikolas stared incredulous at the ignorant girl – his own half-sister? – holding her food up like a trophy.

"Bravo," he said dryly, barely containing his impatience and rage that he'd been made to spend this precious time on her, when other matters were so pressing.

"Now that you're here and getting settled, you'll find that Tessar truly is a wonder," Narissa waved her arm in her usual way, highly dramatic. "It's the oldest world, the first world, the very center of creation."

"Isn't the first place supposed to be the Garden of Eden?" Yolanda asked, between open-mouthed bites.

"Oh, yes, it's called that in the Bible, of course. Tessar has been variously named, in the sacred texts, myths and so on, depending on which of the four quadrants the believers came from."

"Tessar actually means 'four,'" Nikolas said, happy to assert some contextual meaning into this ridiculous conversation. "The four lands born of the original union of spirit and matter."

"What?" Yolanda frowned.

"Niko, let me explain," Narissa said. "Tessar is not so very different from your world. In fact, it's the archetype, the first draft, the original. The four quadrants of Tessar – the East, West, North and South – these quadrants mirror the primary continents of Asia, America, Europe and Africa. Each has its own unique race of people with their own customs and languages, their own spirits and gods."

"Spirits and gods..." The girl actually stopped eating for a moment to ponder that.

"Tessar is the place of dreams and myths, the living world of the ancients. That is its power." Narissa settled back into her pillow and took a sip of tea, finally finished.

Nikolas had to correct her on a few key points. "Tessar is an ancient land, but that is NOT its power. It remains primitive only because its people never cared for progress. They have none of the advances of your world, no tools beyond the medieval. But as you discovered this morning, the distance between us is not so very far."

He nodded to Yolanda. Didn't she appreciate his attempt at understanding? She only glanced up from her plate at him.

"Our mission is to bridge the worlds, to bring the modern way to this ancient land." Nikolas folded both arms across his chest and smiled for the first time in a while.

"What does all that have to do with me?" Yolanda asked, her voice shaky.

"Your brother, Yakos, wants you here," Nara said. "And he is our greatest hope for the future of the realm."

"He must be pretty smart," Yolanda said.

"It's beyond mere intelligence, my dear," Narissa said.

Nikolas had to admire her patience. She really did have a way with the young ones.

"Yakos was raised from the cradle for this role," she continued. "Every moment, even in sleep, was spent training. He has developed more power in his thirteen years than most achieve in a hundred."

"Yakos has proven his power in battle, but he is not yet ready to win the war," Nikolas said. He narrowed his eyes at Yolanda, realizing for the first time that it might actually be interesting to know her strengths and weaknesses, if they could be put to use.

"Why are you staring at me?" Yolanda said.

"Because you are one of us," Nikolas said, matter-of-factly. "We are the future gods of this place."

Yolanda's jaw dropped open; she looked like a drowning fish.

"My dear Yolanda," Narissa said. "All your life, you've always known there was a true purpose waiting for you, something far beyond that waste of a valley where you were born. Yakos wants you to join us now, the gods of Tessar."

15

*I*t's all lies, lies and blasphemy

Gods? Another world? This time, Mama's right. This is all a big load of crap.

Yolanda threw down her chopsticks. "I may be a nobody from nowhere, but I'm not as dumb as I look. All your talk about being gods and all, it's a pile of – well, I don't believe it! Yakos was stolen when he was a baby, so how come you know so much about him? You probably took him! Now, he's only a reflection! If you don't tell me what's really going on, I'm gonna –" Yolanda struggled to get up from the pillow.

"You are so tired. You've had such a long journey." Nikolas sounded like a nice old granddad.

Yolanda's eyelids felt heavy, too heavy to hold up anymore. Her head became light and woozy, as if the yellow fog had rolled back in and found a home inside her brain. She dropped back down to the pillow with a dull thud.

"What the? What you –" At first Yolanda tried to resist, but the warm feeling filled her mind so she couldn't think or speak anymore, and didn't want to.

"Niko, what are you doing?" Narissa said.

"Don't worry, Yolanda," Nikolas said. "We know what's best. You need sleep, that's all. A good, long rest."

Yolanda lolled on her pillow like a roly-poly toy. Narissa put her arm around her. Somebody else had done that. Who was it? Miz Becca. She put her arm around me. Yes. It was important to say it, but Yolanda's tongue forgot how to talk. The memory faded, like smoke melting into the air.

"Good, good. Everything is fine now. Just fine." Nikolas' words seeped into her entire body like truth.

Yolanda couldn't hold her head up too well anymore, but everything was fine, just like Nikolas said. It didn't matter that she crumpled over, fell back from the arm that held her, slipped off her pillow and bumped her head on the floor. She felt as light as air, and as peaceful as the clouds rolling over the yellow plains of the East.

16

*Y*olanda, Yo-lan-da..."

Someone called Yolanda's name through the winds of a dream where she swam through the fog looking for something important. Her eyelids fluttered open and she found herself in a huge bed with flimsy draperies drifting gently in the breeze. She'd seen a bed like this before, in a nice yellow room just like this one, but couldn't remember where or when.

"Yolanda, darling. Are you awake?"

A graceful hand with long fingers, jeweled rings and gold bracelets pulled the curtains aside. An older blonde woman leaned in and smiled, showing her bright white teeth. She looked familiar. What was her name? Nara?

"Good morning, my dear. How do you feel? You gave us quite a scare, fainting after dinner like that."

"Where am I?" Yolanda asked.

"In the Palace. Don't worry, you are safe," the woman said.

Yolanda's brain felt as thick as day-old oatmeal. She tried to sit up, to get some sense back into her head, but she could barely lift her shoulders off the pillow. It felt like a giant hand pressed her down to the mattress.

"There now, don't try to do too much." The woman smoothed the silky feather blanket down around her legs.

A man with gray hair and deeply tanned skin drew aside the curtains. "How is she, Narissa?" he said.

Narissa. That's her name. Yolanda had seen him before too, but his name was a blank.

"She's only just waking." Narissa smiled up at the man. She held the smile a little too long, like maybe she didn't mean it.

Yolanda ordered her legs to move, to roll off the bed and stand up, but they just lay there like a couple of crippled dogs. She couldn't even wiggle her toes.

"Something's wrong with me," she said.

"Shh, dear. You're exhausted, that's all. It's nothing that a good long rest won't cure," Narissa said.

"But my legs. They won't move. I can't get up!"

"Don't worry, my precious flower. You aren't going anywhere, are you? Nikolas and I will take care of everything, and give you anything you could ever need."

"I need somebody to help me get up!"

"There, there, dear, just lay back and relax."

Nikolas – that was his name – stared at Yolanda with deep blue eyes. "What are you looking at?" Yolanda said.

"Nikolas is concerned about you." Narissa gave him another strange smile. These people acted nice, but something wasn't right.

Yolanda wondered what to do. Her stomach growled. It felt like an empty, gnawing hole that needed to be filled, soon. "I'm hungry," she said.

"Of course, you must be famished! I'll have the servants bring you something nourishing." Narissa smoothed Yolanda's forehead with cool fingers while Nikolas stood beside the bed, staring at her, nodding slowly.

A warm, cozy feeling seeped into Yolanda's body. Narissa was right; she felt so tired. Maybe her bones were asleep, and that's why they couldn't move. She let out a sigh. The weight on her chest and legs grew heavier, sinking her down into the feather bed, but it wasn't so bad. She knew she should stay alert, to figure things out, but couldn't put two thoughts together anymore. Why not sink into the dream, as soft as a cloud?

17

*M*ing shuffled down the long corridor, balancing a tray heavy with soup, grilled fish, rice and fruit. With each step she felt a dull pain in her feet shoot up into her legs, gripping her shins like the claws of a dragon. Every other corner of her soul was filled with the orders. Nothing mattered but to bring the tray to the girl. As long as she allowed only the orders to enter her mind, the sweet fog kept the pain down.

She entered the yellow room, relieved. Her task was nearly done.

"Food! Thank God, I'm starved," the young mistress said.

Day after day, all she did was lie in her bed and eat the food that Ming brought. But this time Ming noticed something else about her. Red hair. The girl has red hair.

Ming's brain was no better than a stale ball of sticky rice, so thick and dull she didn't often hear the sound of her own thoughts. She ignored her orders and stopped to listen to this new thought, although the pain shot up into her thighs and the tray trembled in her hands. She caught a fleeting memory of another red-haired stranger she'd seen only once, a young man who looked very much like the girl in the bed. But he was not weak like her. He was strong. So young, yet already a master.

The way I was, once.

Ming caught her breath in surprise. To see a glimpse of her true nature was like finding a gold nugget buried under a mountain of stone. She tried to grasp it, to hold on to it, never to lose it again. The pains shot up higher into her thighs and hips, but she held the thought firm.

"Ming!?" The master had come into the room. "What in the Four are you doing?"

The sweet cloud filled her mind again, and all thoughts faded under a single command: Bring the tray. Bring the tray to the girl. Ming lifted one quivering foot and then the other. Tea and soup sloshed out of their bowls as she made her way to the girl's bed.

18

*N*arissa returned from the kitchens, weary of spending her considerable talents on Yolanda and the servants. She hadn't realized how empty she'd become. With Yakos gone and Nikolas playing the mastermind, she needed something to do, something more than feeding the prisoner.

How did I let myself become the queen of maintenance?

She glided toward Nikolas' usual spot at the head of the table and decided to speak directly, an approach that had been occasionally effective through the many years.

"Niko, it's been over a week. We must stop. This was only an experiment, to test her, to see how she would react. But it's gone on too long."

"I am aware of the passage of time," Nikolas did not even look up from his papers.

"Surely we have more important things to do than to baby-sit her. I can't do anything with her. Can't find the gift."

"You shouldn't try," he said. "It's too dangerous."

Narissa paused for a moment to change tactics, to think in Nikolas' terms: cold logic. "Since you are convinced that she knows nothing, then it follows that she can do nothing," she said. "What is the number one rule of power? Don't use a hammer when a feather will do."

"In this case, it is necessary," he said. "Yakos didn't understand the risks of having her here, and neither do you. We do not know what she is capable of."

"Exactly my point, Nikolas. We do not yet have the knowledge to assess her. I propose we let her be this morning, only for an hour or two. Then we'll know exactly what measures are required."

Nikolas glanced up and made eye contact for the first time since the conversation began. Although he would never acknowledge that her point of view was valid, he understood her with a depth that only a twin can share.

He knows I'm serious and won't back down. He knows I don't have to ask him, that I have other ways to get what I want.

Narissa looked into his arctic eyes and wondered how serious he was, how attached to holding the girl. A wave of calm like a warm breeze passed into her body.

No! He wouldn't actually use his gift on me, to get me to shut up? That line hadn't been crossed in many years, a disaster.

"Remember the last time, Niko," she said.

Nikolas scowled and looked back down at his papers. "All right then," he said. "But you are responsible, when your little experiment fails."

19

*Y*olanda, darling. Wake up."

Yolanda tried to lift her head, but it was too heavy. Her eyelids felt heavy, too. Light seeped in under her lashes, too bright. She opened them only halfway.

"It's time to wake up."

A woman leaned over her. Narissa. Her face was in shadow, blocking the light from the window. "How are you feeling?"

"Uhhhmm." Before she could think of something to say, Yolanda's stomach growled, louder than a grizzly. "Hungry."

Narissa snapped her fingers and called to a figure standing by the door. "Jade, go and see what's keeping Ming with Miss Yolanda's breakfast. That girl is slower than a stone turtle." She turned back to Yolanda. "Other than hungry, how do you feel? Can you think clearly?"

Yolanda shrugged her shoulders, as much as she could.

"Can you remember anything? You've had such a hard time with that lately."

Yolanda frowned and stared up at the ceiling, trying to think back. "Umm, I think I remember yesterday."

"Yesterday is good! Very good. What happened yesterday?"

"Hmm. Ming brought me some stuff to eat. Then, I guess I fell back asleep."

"Oh, dear. It's such a pity you've not been well, just when I'm becoming so very fond of you." Narissa smoothed the covers around Yolanda's legs and looked at her as if she were her favorite thing in the whole world. "Now, Yolanda, I'd like to ask your help with something."

"What can I do?"

Narissa pulled the bed curtains aside and pointed to a statue of a monkey that sat cross-legged on a carved table on the opposite wall. "Perhaps you can move that little monkey for me."

The monkey was bigger than a cat, with mangy gray fur and lips pulled back in a wide grin. He looked so real, and familiar, too, but Yolanda couldn't think why.

The door slid open and Ming came in with a tray. The room filled with delicious smells: steaming rice, seafood, jasmine tea. Yolanda's stomach leapt for joy. "Is that my breakfast?"

"Ming, wait there by the door." Narissa walked to the monkey's table and slid a smaller table out from underneath the larger one. "Yolanda, I'd really prefer that the monkey be moved here, to the small table."

"But I'm hungry!" It was more than just a craving; Yolanda's belly begged to be filled. Quick.

"I know how ravenous you must be," Narissa said, "but I've asked you to do just this one thing. Then you may have your breakfast."

Yolanda tried to get up to move the darn monkey, but she couldn't lift her head off the pillow. "I can't. I can't even get out of bed!"

"I don't want to you move it with your hands; I can do that myself. I want you to do it from where you are now."

Yolanda frowned. "That's crazy."

Narissa laughed. "Not so crazy here, in Tessar! If you try, you may find that you can move it another way. Perhaps you can ask the monkey to move. Or you could imagine it. But you must really want it to happen."

The smell of the rice made her mouth water. Yolanda didn't give a dang about moving that monkey or anything else except getting some food, but she stared at the monkey and concentrated hard: go ahead, move! It didn't budge.

"I can't do it," she said.

"Have you tried using your – all your will?" Narissa asked.

"I told you, I can't do it!"

The monkey seemed to be laughing at her. She knew that she'd seen him before, and he'd laughed out loud and jumped around a lot. "What's wrong with that monkey? He used to be alive."

"How do you know this?" Narissa came back and sat on the edge of her bed. "That's a very interesting talent you have."

Yolanda's eyes opened. "Talent? Somebody else said that."

"Well, well. That's very, very good! That sounds like a real memory. Now, who was it who said this to you?"

"I don't know. When you said 'talent,' I just knew that I heard it before."

"Can't you remember anything else?"

Yolanda shook her head.

"This may be important, don't you think? Try hard to remember. Close your eyes."

Yolanda squeezed her eyes shut and saw a thousand tiny lights like stars against a black sky. A picture floated out of the darkness: a woman's tanned, wrinkled face with marbled eyes and a pair of long braids. A sweet voice, talking crazy.

"It was an old lady in the woods, Miz Becca. She said I had a talent. Vision, she called it. That's it."

"That's very good, dear. I'd say your memory was surprisingly good." Narissa's face bloomed into a wide smile. "Now try again. What else do you see?"

Yolanda closed her eyes again. Other pictures came into her head: an old cabin in a lonesome patch of weeds; a sick woman under a crocheted blanket; a boy's face in a cracked mirror; a midnight lake with a round moon.

what the heck are you doing, lazing around in bed all day? it's high time you got up, missy!

Mama! Yolanda forced her head and shoulders up off the pillow and leaned on her elbows. Her head pounded, dizzy. "I want to get up!"

Narissa's eyes opened wide, and she smoothed the feather quilt across Yolanda's chest and around her legs. "Oh, dear. I'm afraid it's simply not wise to over-excite yourself in such a condition."

"What condition? Dammit, I'm sick of lying here all the time! Get me up!"

The heaviness on her chest and legs pressed down even harder, and her belly cramped up like a fist. Yolanda strained to sit up but finally sank back into the soft mattress, spent.

"There, now. That's better. Just relax." Narissa stroked her forehead. "Ming. Bring Miss Yolanda her breakfast."

20

"Scree! Scree!"

Becca followed the hawk's path against the sunsetting sky with an ancient longing in her heart. Though she longed to fly, these days she was bound to the ground, to the creeks, hills and hollows of the Huskaloosa territory. She spent her days poking under rocks and scratching tree bark, reading signs. Did the earthworms squirm like they should? Were the beaver's dams built to last? Did the honeysuckle bloom in time for the bees? Mother Nature didn't usually need a meddling old woman like her, but things hadn't been quite right this spring, not since the last full moon, when Mae's girl went through to Tessar.

Maybe it was unwise to send her off that way, all alone, as if there was nothing more at stake than another lost child trying to find her place in the world. The signs spoke of many things, but they couldn't tell Becca if Yolanda had found her twin brother in Tessar, or if she'd begun to learn to use her talent. The only way to know for sure would be to go back there herself.

Becca scratched among the dead twigs of winter with her walking stick and saw new shoots, both woody and green, sprouting up. Some came in stunted and strange, bent back on themselves, as if they wanted to crawl back into their seedpods. She'd heard frogs singing in the early evening, but they jumped around crazy and never made it into the pond to mate. The wind felt more like March than May, carrying a bite instead of the promise of warmth.

Little things, maybe, but when you added them up together it looked like spring was resisting the change to summer. Something, or somebody, was clogging up the works.

Bah! What does it have to do with the girl?

Becca hiked up and over the last hill and headed back to the Georges when a gray mouse scurried out from a pile of withered leaves. He cocked his head up at her, his eyes shining like a pair of tiny, deep pools, and squeaked. Twice.

"I can't go back to Tessar now, not with all the babies due," she said. The mouse let out another peep before it ran off.

"You're right. There's always more babies coming, always will be." Becca frowned and leaned into her stick, feeling her age for the first time that day. She took notice of the shade of the sky before setting off again. The moon would be full tonight.

21

"Caw! Caw!"

Yolanda heard a wild squawking sound through a thick veil of sleep. A bird just didn't make sense; must be a dream.

"Caw! Caw! Wake up!"

She settled deeper into her pillow and wished that the talking dream bird would fly back to wherever it came from.

"Caw! Caw! Wake up! Listen!"

"Shut up. Leave me alone," she mumbled.

Just as she sank back into sleep, she heard a ripping sound. Cold air blew the bed curtains into a frenzy. A big black bird had flown into the paper window and stuck its head halfway through, flapping like mad to get in the rest of the way. A crow, most likely.

"Ming! Wake up! A dang bird tore the window open."

Ming's round face rose up from her alcove near the door. She slowly stood up, tightened her robe around her waist, and inched across the rug toward the window.

Crimeny, I could get to the moon before Ming'll get to that window.

The bird squawked. It had almost gotten its wings free.

"C'mon, Ming! It's gonna –"

The bird broke through and swooped in toward Yolanda's bed. It darted at the curtains, found the opening and flew in a loopy circle over her body.

Her arms were so heavy and stiff she couldn't lift them off the bed to bat it away. She couldn't even raise her head more than an inch. "Get out-a-here, you dirty stinkin' bird!" she shouted.

The bird landed on her right leg, then hopped onto her left foot. "Ming! It's on me! Hurry up!"

Ming was only halfway across the room.

The bird stared right at Yolanda, its black eyes flashing yellow in the morning light. "Caw! Caw! See! Look!"

Yolanda heard the 'caw', but she also heard the words underneath the sounds: 'look' and 'see.' Look and see what?

The bird pecked at the blankets around her feet and legs. "Caw! See! Look!"

"I see you, pecking at me. Stop it, or I'm gonna –"

Yolanda stared at the crazy bird as it hopped up and down her legs, pecking and then pulling way back, like a tug of war. But there was nothing to tug on, nothing in its beak.

"Caw! See! Look!"

"I can't see a thing, you blasted bird!"

Ming finally made it to the bed. She pulled the curtains aside and reached for the bird, but it darted up into the canopy. She followed it around to the other side. The bird was faster. It hopped up and down Yolanda's legs, cawing and pecking at the covers. "Caw, Look! See!"

What in creation does that dang bird want me to see?

Yolanda's eyes got tired and blurry from staring so hard. She blinked and let them rest for a bit, and that's when she saw something, like a grayish wisp of smoke in the bird's beak.

"What's that stuff in your mouth?"

"Caw! Caw! See truth!"

The black bird grabbed another wispy thread and flew right up to Yolanda's face. Her eyes crossed and everything got more blurry. Yet the thing in its beak looked more solid, like a greasy old length of string looping and twisting down to her toes. "Yikes! What is that?"

"Caw! Caw! See! Truth! See! Vision!" The bird flew back to her feet, flapping excitedly.

Vision? Yolanda made her eyes cross on purpose and could see some gray shapes strewn over the blankets. When she relaxed her eyes again, she saw a hundred sticky black webs that crisscrossed her whole body. She looked like a mummy, all wrapped up with barbed wire. Black thorny ropes tied her hands, her arms, her legs and even her chest, holding her down to the bed.

"Oh, my lord in heaven. This isn't any sickness I ever heard of!"

"Caw! Caw! Truth! See!"

The bird darted to Ming, swooped down to peck at her legs, and then flew back up – with a web in its beak.

"No! Ming! They're on you, too..."

Ming was covered with webs, from the high collar of her yellow silk dress down to her tiny red slippers. No wonder she was so slow! Everything except her arms was wrapped tight with thorny black ropes. It must have hurt just to walk with all those webs on her legs. Ming lunged at the bird, and caught its wing.

"Caaa-aaaw!" The bird fought to get away, but Ming held tight. Her hands and arms didn't have the webs holding them down.

Why not?

So she can do her chores, and carry her tray.

Yolanda felt sick to her stomach.

Somebody put these webs on us. Narissa?

"Caw, caw. Look." The bird could barely croak. It hung limp from its hurt wing.

"Let it go," Yolanda said, and Ming opened her hand.

The poor bird fell to the bed, squawked a couple of times and hopped to a corner of the curtains, dragging its wing behind. It shivered and bobbed its head back toward Ming. "Caw... Look. Vision. See truth."

"I can see the webs on Ming," Yolanda said.

"Caw...caw...Truth..."

"You want me to see something else?" Yolanda didn't feel like looking again, but she squinted at Ming, blurring her eyes.

She caught the hint of a faint shine glowing behind the black webs. "What's that?"

"Caw...see..."

Yolanda let her eyes relax, trying not to try. The webs faded into wispy gray threads. She could see right through them to Ming's dress underneath. She took a breath and let the easy feeling move through her. Ming's dress faded away and she could see her pale golden skin beneath. It was like looking through the layers of an onion. She could see past her skin to her insides: red muscles, blue blood vessels, and gray bones.

As she saw through the layers, amazed, she saw a faint shape, almost like another body, hovering even deeper inside Ming. This one bent in a crouch, legs and arms all tensed and ready for battle. A fighter!

Yolanda blinked. On the outside, Ming looked as dull and calm as a china doll, but the person inside her was as fierce as a firecracker.

Warrior. The word popped into Yolanda's head.

Ming is a warrior.

"What the heck is going on around here?" she cried.

Ming just stood there with her usual expression: dead-as-a-doorknob. Yolanda wanted to jump out of bed and tear the webs off her, but she couldn't even raise her chest.

"We've got to do something!"

The bird squawked from the corner of the bed. "See. Truth."

"I see it, darn it!" but she looked again. The bird tore a small piece of the stuff away from her leg. It hung in its beak like yarn or rope.

"That's it! The webs can be cut."

"Ming, come closer," she said. "Listen. You and me, we're all tied up with these crazy black webs. They're invisible, but I can see them. They're all over me, holding me down so I can't move, and they're on you, too! Really nasty black things, wrapped tight all around your legs and chest."

Ming didn't say anything.

"Can't you feel it? Do you know what I'm saying? Nod if you do."

Ming's head bowed a little.

"Good." Yolanda took a breath. "There's something else. You're not really a servant. You're a fighter. A warrior."

For the first time Ming looked directly into Yolanda's eyes. Yolanda could see a small spark of the fire that burned inside, behind her calm face. That fighter wanted to bust out.

"Ming, we've got to get away. I can't move my hands, but you can. You're strong. The webs can be cut. And you can do it!"

Ming nodded, very, very slowly.

"Please, Ming. Go get something sharp. Scissors, a kitchen knife, anything. Don't tell anyone. Hurry!"

Ming limped to the door, nearly twice as fast as she usually did, but still awfully slow.

"Ming," Yolanda called after her. "Don't forget. You are strong."

22

*Y*ou are strong."

Ming lurched down the hall to the kitchens, repeating the young mistress's words. Although she could not see the black webs that Miss Yolanda spoke of, she knew their bite. It was as if she walked barefoot on a road paved with brambles. The pain was a good thing now, because it reminded her to stay clear of the mind-numbing fog that pressed in on all sides, tempting her to forget everything with its promise of peace.

"Get a knife. Get something sharp." She whispered the words many times to make sure she didn't lose them.

If any of the guards in the row along the hall heard her, they did not let it show. As she walked past them, a ray of weak sunlight caught the edge of a guardsmen's sword. Something sharp! He stood at the end of the line in front of an alcove, more than two arm's length from the next guard. An easy target. Ming walked a little further, until her body was positioned between him and the others, to block their view.

Her rock-fist punch landed precisely on the bridge of his nose. He slumped, unconscious, and she guided his fall gently into the alcove.

Thank the Four gods, my instincts are still alive.

In one motion she pulled the blade from his hand and tucked it under her sash, inside the folds of her robe. Perhaps the cold sword against her leg would keep her mind awake. She turned to walk back to the young mistress's room.

Keep strong. Keep strong. Each breath was a new chance to remember, to keep strong against the dull fog.

"Stop, there!" The guard leader stepped away from rest of the line. "State your duty."

Ming bowed to him. The sword nicked her left thigh. She took a tiny step forward to release the pressure on the blade. "I return to the young mistress," she said.

"Without food?" He laughed. "The little idiot forgot what she was sent to do. Go to the kitchens!"

Ming bowed again in his direction and slowly turned toward the kitchens. The leader stood only a sword's length away; she could easily silence him, but over a dozen guards lined the hall. She must make a plan before taking action. So hard to push through the dullness clouding her mind, telling her not to worry, to give in.

Keep strong.

How to subdue them all and get back to Miss Yolanda, without alerting all the Palace guards?

Ming held still, trying to imagine step one, step two, step three. By the time she knew step three, step one had sunk back into the soft, cushiony folds in her brain.

Keep strong.

"Do as you are told!" The guard leader said.

Farther down the hall she heard the click-clack of her Mistress's shoes, along with the heavier footfall of the Master. Ming moved out of their path, and slid into a better position among the guardsmen. She prayed the guard leader would not challenge her, with the Master and Mistress coming. She slowed her breath to better hide against the marble.

23

*N*ikolas grew weary of this ancient argument as he and Narissa walked to the girl's room. Of course he was right about the girl; he always was; yet even after a hundred years, his own twin sister still didn't trust the depth of his knowledge. Like a child, she still needed to discover everything on her own. Only after he was proved correct would she come back and say, "Oh, Niko, you were so right," and, "next time I'll believe you, Niko," or, "don't let me do this again, Niko."

But he could never remind her of all those times. She'd sulk and pout and dig her heels even deeper into the shaky ground she stood on. No, the trick was to let her find out on her own that his way was the best way, hopefully before all was lost.

He sighed. If only he didn't need her, for the plan to work.

Narissa chattered on like a monkey. "Niko, now that I've got something to work with, I know I can guide her, influence the direction, like Yakos. So her talents are more useful to us."

Hmph, Nikolas grunted.

"Don't worry, I'll keep it under control."

"She is under our control now," Nikolas said.

"To stifle her could make it more potent, more dangerous, when it emerges on its own…"

"It's a calculated risk."

Narissa stopped. "Just imagine what Yakos will do when he finds out that you've gone against him. He will, you know."

"Yakos may be the racehorse, but we are still holding the reins," Nikolas said, walking onward. "He should be satisfied; this is the closest we've come to real change."

"Change. Now that's an interesting choice of words," Narissa said, walking again. "Yes, we are here, in the East. Foreigners. Pretenders. Despised conquerors."

"You're getting sensitive again, Narissa. Now is the time to be strong. Think of the future, of all Tessar. Have faith. We just need to make sure that this one piece stays in place."

"You are right about the future. But when I open my eyes, Niko, I do not see change. All I see is stagnation."

As they came to the guards, Nikolas drew a breath and infused them with his gift: just enough to keep order. Narissa stopped beside one guard, pinched his cheek with her long fingers and held it tight. The guard did not flinch, though her grip looked strong enough to bruise him black and blue.

She's trying to prove a point, but what is it?

"They obey us, Niko, but they have no spark of life," she said. "This is not what we were born to do. A child of the gods should not be bound to a bed. We're better than this."

"'This' is only temporary!" Nikolas said. "We must keep the vision of what we are trying to do. Stay the course."

"I am, Niko. It's just that I'd rather keep her in place my own way. I've become like a mother to her these past weeks; she trusts me. It's time to let it emerge, so it can be shaped."

Nikolas sighed. *Once again, do I have to let Narissa find out on her own that I'm right?*

24

From the corner of her eye, Ming saw the Master and Mistress stop beside a guardsman only a few paces down the line, speaking in urgent tones. The Mistress reached out to pinch the guard's cheek. When she finally let go and began walking toward Ming, her heels sharp against the stone floor, Ming tightened her mental grip on the sword under her robe.

Keep – strong –

"I will speak to the girl myself." The Master frowned as he passed directly in front of Ming.

The pain tightened around her legs. At the same time the dreamy fog billowed deeper into her mind, drawing her into its comforts. With such sweet feelings of peace, numbing the pain, she could forget what Miss Yolanda had told her. She could let go of trying to be strong, and sink into the dream. But there was something important, something to hold --

"Ming, why are you here, dallying with the guard? Is the young mistress awake?" Mistress Narissa said.

"I go to her now," Ming said.

As she bowed deeply to the Mistress and Master, she felt a cold sword's edge slice her just above the knee, a different sensation than the constant wrenching pain around her legs. As a trickle of blood slid down her thigh, she knew what she must remember. She heard a distant voice in her memory, calling through miles of fog: "get something sharp!"

"Yes, Ming, you will go to her now," Master Nikolas said. The dream cloud rose higher now, nearly drowning her.

Keep – strong – !

With her last bit of concentration Ming squeezed her strength into a hard nugget that could not be destroyed or forgotten. She hid it in the very center of her body where her instincts lived, a place so deep and private it could not betray her. Bowing again to the Master and Mistress, she followed them, six paces behind, to Miss Yolanda's room.

25

*P*lease, Ming, hurry.

It seemed like forever since she'd left. While Yolanda waited she practiced letting her eyes go blurry so she could find the weak spots in the webs. They were so twisted and horrible. Especially the big, thick knot over her chest.

As she looked closely at herself, she remembered more and more: seeing her twin's face in her reflection; following him into Hanging Lake; losing him in a ball of light, and finding him again in a bathtub at the Palace. She couldn't believe that she'd forgotten all about him. How long had she been in that bed? Days? Weeks? Months? All that time, Narissa – and Nikolas – had been telling her that she was sick, that she would get better.

Why did they do this to me? How could I be so stupid, to think they actually cared?

What about Yakos? Is he part of it, too?

No. He wouldn't have led me here, just to let me rot on this fancy bed. He needs me.

"Caw...caw." The black bird huddled in the corner of her bed, shaking. Was it trying to tell her something? All she heard was its pain.

"Poor thing," Yolanda whispered. "When Ming comes back and gets these webs off me, I'll help you, I promise."

The door opened. Instead of Ming, Narissa and Nikolas walked in. Yolanda wanted to scream. Instead, she pretended to be asleep, her eyes mostly closed, so she could see their shadowy shapes through the bed curtains. In fact, her special way of seeing seemed even better with her eyes half closed.

"Good morning, Yolanda! Aren't you awake yet, my darling?" Narissa's high voice didn't sound so nice anymore. "My, but it's windy in here!"

Nikolas walked to the broken window, looking like a general in his blue coat with gold buttons. "There's been an intruder. Something with claws."

"Claws?!" Narissa screeched. "Ming, get in here!"

Ming lagged through the door, struggling against the black webs. They looked thicker now around her waist and legs, and her eyes looked duller, too.

Oh no...! Did she get a blade, to cut the webs?

Nikolas threw open the bed curtains. He loomed over Yolanda and studied her with cold eyes before he spotted the bird trembling in the corner of the bed. "By the Four gods, it's a crow," he said. "It's hurt."

Narissa yanked the curtains to the side. "Loathsome creature. Get rid of it, Ming."

Ming bowed and started walking to the bed. With all those webs around her legs, it was going to take a while.

"Yolanda, darling, wake up." Narissa stroked Yolanda's cheek.

She let her eyelids open, and saw Narissa more clearly. Her smile was too wide, like an overgrown doll, and her skin was pulled too tight across her face. She looked like a Hollywood actress who'd had too many surgeries. How old was she? Yolanda wanted to bite her hand, so cold and fake!

"Oh, thank goodness, you're all right. That disgusting bird didn't hurt you, did it? I'd have to kill anyone – or any thing – that hurt you."

Yeah, right. You liar.

Narissa frowned at Ming, still fifteen feet away. "Never mind, I'll take care of it myself."

Narissa pointed her perfect, blood-red nails at the bird. A thick string of sticky black stuff leapt out of her fingertips, shot across the bed and lashed around the bird's foot.

What in the holy –!?

Yolanda held her breath as the bird squawked and flapped up out of the curtains, with a rope of webs, and its hurt wing, dangling behind.

Narissa slunk around the bed like a stalking tiger and flung her wrist back and then forward again. Another stream of barbed ropes shot out from the ends of her fingers and knocked the bird against the wall, pinning its good wing down with the sticky black webs.

Yolanda gasped, and then wished she could take it back.

"What is it, my sweet? Did that awful bird scare you?"

"Don't worry," Nikolas folded his arms across his chest. "It won't live."

Somehow the bird tore itself away, leaving a smear of blood on the wall in the shape of a 'v.' It circled the room on one wing, yet managed to dodge most of the webs Narissa shot at it.

Nikolas laughed. "Clearly you've lost your touch. Shall I give it a try?"

"No! Leave it to me."

"Caw! Caw! Now! Move!" The bird cawed as it zigzagged into the marble bathroom. Narissa leapt after it, and Nikolas followed, still chuckling.

It took Yolanda a second to realize that the bird had flown in there to get Narissa and Nikolas out of the way. Ming finally made it to the bed, praise Jesus. But she stood there with her old slack expression, not much of a warrior.

"Did you get something sharp?" Yolanda whispered hoarsely.

Ming bowed forward about half an inch, stuck her hand into her robe and pulled out a 2-foot long sword.

"Do it, Ming, now! Cut the webs."

Yolanda wanted to whoop for joy, but Narissa and Nikolas might hear, even with all the bird-squawking and screeching in the bathroom.

"Cut 'em off your own legs first. There, straight down the middle!" Yolanda nodded toward the right place.

As Ming raised the sword over the line between her thighs, Yolanda realized that she couldn't even see the webs, to know what she was cutting into! Luckily, her aim was good.

Ming's calm face broke into a grimace. She slashed the webs all the way down to her feet. Most of the webs shriveled up and fell into a pile of old gristle on the marble floor.

"Cut mine now! Hurry!"

Ming raised her sword high over Yolanda's waist. Yolanda shut her eyes, just in case, but Ming's blade came down true. A sticky tangle of webbing fell to both sides of her legs, and the awful weight was lessened.

"Thanks!" she murmured. "Now, cut along my arms and hands."

Ming was great with that sword; her cuts were perfect, and she left all of Yolanda's fingers and toes intact.

"Now, let's get out of here!" Yolanda tried to roll her legs off the bed and get up, but everything below the waist was totally numb. Her legs had more pins and needles than a sewing kit. She forced both legs over the side, ignored the shooting pains that leapt up her calves when her feet touched the floor. She grabbed the curtains to pull herself up the rest of the way.

"Caw! Caw!" The bird careened back into the bedroom and toward the door, festooned with black webs and dripping blood.

Not yet, dang it!

Narissa followed the bird, pointing her long, thin fingers in its direction. A thick streak of web shot out all the way across the room. The webs pinned the poor bird into an alcove near the door. When Narissa put down her hand, the bird was nearly smothered under crisscrossed ropes, still, it managed to make a weak croaking sound, "caw...see..."

"You're really not the average crow, are you?" Narissa said. "Fascinating. I will speak with you later, my friend. Then we shall see what you are made of."

"Stop babbling at that bird and look at this," Nikolas' blue eyes stared at Yolanda as she hung on to the curtains. Ming stood by her side with the sword.

Narissa froze, and pointed to the frayed webs. One eyebrow arched up, and her smile curled into a nasty grin. "Nikolas, you know how much I hate to admit this. It appears that you were right. Her powers have emerged. And to think I wanted to let her find the way on her own."

Narissa lifted both of her bejeweled hands in the air, pointed one at Yolanda and the other at Ming. "I don't think you've had quite enough rest, Yolanda, my darling. And Ming, surely you are aware that servants are forbidden to touch such a weapon."

Yolanda felt a stab of hunger in her gut as Narissa's hand reached out toward her belly. The webbing shot out from her fingers, just like before, but then, she saw a shadowy black rope twist up and out of Yolanda's own belly button.

Oh my lord. That stuff is inside me!

It twisted across the room like a jumpy, black umbilical cord, heading back to Narissa's hand.

How in creation did she do that? What is it?!

Yolanda looked over at Ming. The exact same black stuff leapt out of her stomach, too.

The two ropes reached Narissa's hands. She drew her wrists back, and then pointed both hands again at Yolanda and Ming. The ropes doubled back through the air, twice as thick as before. The first web knocked Ming backwards and lashed around her fighting arm. The sword clanked to the floor. The other web shot back into Yolanda's stomach like a bullet. She doubled over in agony.

"caw... see..."

Yolanda could barely hear the bird through the pain that hammered up her spine and into her brain. What was it trying to say? She looked up just in time to see another black web hurtling right for her head.

Something rose up from her insides, a raw power that surged up from the pain in her belly and flowed through her like liquid silver. It shot out of her eyes and went straight for Narissa and the webs that connected them.

It's the vision!

In that instant she knew what Narissa's webs truly were: pain. The black ropes coming out of Yolanda's belly were a twisted mass of pain. Her own pain.

The truth stabbed like a knife. She crumpled into the pain, feeling the hurt.

Her vision closed down to a trickle. The webs looked like only a trace of shadow. Pain tightened around her chest. The weight got so heavy her knees buckled and her legs swayed. She gripped the bed curtains to keep from falling.

"caw… see…"

The bird! Still alive! If it can take it, so can I.

Yolanda stopped clenching her gut around the pain and took a breath. She let her face and eyes soften, and only opened her eyes partway. Bit by bit the vision opened wider. Now she could see even more detail: the webs had barbs of thorns that dug into her flesh.

She let the vision go stronger and deeper. Narissa lifted her wrists higher. Now she could see how her hands sucked up pain and suffering like a vacuum and twisted it into an invisible rope, a rope that could bind.

The heavy black weight — so tight in her chest — that was only her heart, all tied up with the pain of old wounds.

She looked down at her heart, and let the vision flow. She could see all the strands of hurt that knotted there, and the cause of each and every one: the stab of Mama's doubts and judgments; the sting of the town kids' taunts and teases; the slow burn of being so alone.

"No!" she screamed.

Yolanda's voice didn't sound like herself. It was raw and powerful, and it came out of her heart, and the hurt.

At the same moment her vision blasted out of her eyes like an angry bullhorn. It met the black rope that was still streaming out of Narissa's hand. The web hung mid-air for a second, coiling, and then it jerked backwards toward Narissa.

"Nooo!" Narissa staggered against the wall, screaming.

Yolanda stared wide-eyed. Her vision still flowed as strong as a fire hose, forcing the webs back into Narissa's hands.

Narissa's elegant face became a mask of horror, her eyes and mouth screaming wide. The webs pushed her backward, and pinned her arms, legs and chest to the wall with thick black ropes. As the webs finally smothered her face and neck in black pain, Narissa's screams stopped.

Yolanda let her eyelids close, slowing down the flow of vision to a trickle. She gripped the curtain, her knees weak and wobbly.

"Impressive," Nikolas said quietly.

26

When Nikolas spoke, Yolanda jumped as if an alarm went off, but she felt completely drained, with no will left to do anything. The webs that had come up from her own insides were strewn like rags on the floor; yet the pain – what they were made of – still lay heavy on her heart. Now that she remembered all the old stings and aches, they didn't go away so easily. And Ming looked like a zombie again. What could she do?

Nikolas stared at Yolanda, his arms across his chest. A warm feeling seeped into her, as if she had just drank a big mug of hot cocoa that soothed all the old hurts and made her forget they ever happened. She closed her eyes for a moment. It felt so good. When she opened them again, everything seemed better.

There's Narissa up against the wall; how did she get there? Where did Ming get that big sword? Why am I standing here holding these curtains, when the bed looks so cozy?

Yolanda let go and lay back into the cushions. All she wanted – all she had ever wanted – was to lie down and take a little five-minute nap. That's all.

"Caw. See..." A bird called weakly from across the room. Its tone didn't fit with the buttery taste in Yolanda's mouth.

Leave me be. Just let me lie down for a minute...

She sunk into her bed of soft, feathery goose down. The lazy curtains drifted in the wind.

It's nice here. Very, very nice.

Just as her eyelids were about to close, the door opened and someone came in. Jade. Nikolas turned to look, and for a second the haze in Yolanda's mind cleared, just a little.

"Caw. Wake up...Wake up!"

It felt much better not to worry, to let it all go, but some part of her listened to the bird. That small part knew something wasn't right. She lifted her chin to look around.

"Caw. Wake up."

"Be still," Nikolas snapped at the bird.

"Caaaawgh, wake..." the bird's call muffled into quiet.

Yolanda mustered her last ounce of willpower and sat up. The room looked cloudy and everything wavered as if she were underwater. She fought to stay awake. Her eyes crossed a little, and her vision cleared up. She remembered what she could do!

She saw Ming leaning on the bedpost, head down, barely able to stand. Narissa was slumped against the wall, all tied up in black ropes. The bird hung from a tangle of black webs on the far wall. Jade was near the door. Nikolas stood in the center looking at her, his forehead frowned with concentration. A deep wave of sleepiness washed over her again.

I can do it. I can.

Yolanda took a breath and braced herself against the tide. She let her eyes get soft again, and felt the surge rise up again inside her. Without looking right at him, she pointed her vision toward Nikolas. His ice-blue eyes searched her whole body like a magnifying glass, looking for something.

What is he doing?

Nikolas shifted his gaze to Ming. Yolanda relaxed her eyes even more, and saw a soft puffy cloud around Ming's head, like cotton candy or whipped cream.

What in creation is that stuff?

She looked closer and saw the fog flowing in and around small empty spaces in Ming's body. She wasn't nearly as solid as she looked; the pores of her skin were wide open. Like water to a sponge, the fog found all the tiny holes and filled them.

Is that what Nikolas is looking for? Holes?

Yolanda looked deeper. The holes in Ming's skin were passages into larger, empty places inside her. Yolanda's vision went inside the openings. She sensed that they were weak spots created by something Ming needed but didn't get: cravings, wants, and desires that didn't get satisfied; people she loved that abandoned her; fears that didn't get comforted. Yolanda could see them all, gaping like hungry mouths.

Oh, Ming!

The fog covered the holes like a soft layer of creamy frosting, but it didn't really fill them, or fix them.

"Yolanda. Don't fight it," Nikolas said like a command.

A blast of fog came after her now, softly pushing to get inside. She turned the vision on herself and found the same holes that she'd seen in Ming. Her sight dove deeper into one of the biggest holes. It was empty, except for a trace of memory of when she was a baby. Her mother rocked her and held her close to her bosom, sweet with the scent of milk. She sang a lullaby in a low voice: "Two babes in the woods, poor babes in the woods..."

Then something changed. Mama got sick. She didn't pick up Yolanda any more. Her tender touch and soothing song were gone forever. That left an awfully big hole, as big as a crater. Yolanda wanted to cry.

A cloud of fog drifted into that empty hole. It warmed her like a hug of suntanned skin. It smelled like home-baked goodness and was full of everything she could ever want. As the fog deepened Yolanda heard strains of that old lullaby in Mama's voice. She wanted that feeling again. She closed her eyes and fell back into her bed, rocking gently to the rhythm of Mama's sweet breath: in, out, in, out.

27

I am strong.

Ming gripped the single thought tightly in her mind as the fog of forgetting pressed in from every side. She'd held just the one thought for a long time, ever since Miss Yolanda told her to keep strong. She had waited for a sign or a call to action, but when the young mistress Yolanda fell back on her bed, as if she would sleep for a thousand years, Ming repeated it again: Hold – strong!

Master Nikolas turned his attention back to her. She drew another breath to strengthen her will, but the fog piled deeper. She heard the sound of metal clattering to the floor at her feet. A sword? It was far away, and had nothing to do with her.

The fog thickened with the promise of happiness. A silky veil of serenity fell around her shoulders. The silhouette of a very great man came toward her with open arms. The cloud of comfort rose higher and deeper, burying the one kernel of strength under layers of dreams.

I – am – strong –

Ming could still control one thing: her breath. Cool morning air filled her nostrils, flowed into her chest and fed the seed of power. She held the breath as long as she could. When she let it go, she released some of the poisonous clouds of weakness, too.

The tiny seed of strength grew into a tender shoot that pushed up through the fog. A rush of memories came back: slashing the webs with the sword; many days of pain and numbness; traveling with Jade to meet her father, but instead finding three Northerners at the Palace: Nikolas, Narissa, and another.

Ming turned her mind to the present, to this room. The cloud still pressed against her, but she could resist it.

I – am – strong!

Master Nikolas smiled. How far to where he stood? No more than ten paces. Ming took a deep inhale. Though her chest did not rise even a millimeter, the breath fueled a great leap that carried her over the edge of the wide bed. Her foot grazed the curtains. With a powerful ki-yai in her throat, Ming lunged for Master Nikolas.

A wall of fog rose up like a tidal wave to block her. It provided everything she'd ever longed for: peace, harmony, and all the fresh dumplings she could eat.

Keep – strong –

Ming called upon the teachings she'd worked hard to learn, knowledge of spirit, mind and body. She needed all her chi to resist him, but her legs and feet were rusty from lack of use. She took another breath and directed the energy into her limbs.

"Aieeee-ya!"

In one motion Ming leapt up, bent one leg back into her left haunch, and thrust her forward leg into the air. She sailed high into the Flying Horse Kick.

The ball of her foot struck Master Nikolas at the seat of his soul, just below his breastbone. He reeled back into the furniture, eyes wide with shock, and his head struck a statue of a monkey on the chest. He slumped against the wall beside Mistress Narissa. Together they looked as peaceful as a pair of nestling birds.

28

*Y*olanda heard a wild yell and a dull thump that broke through the strains of her lullaby. She blinked her eyes open, sat up and looked around the yellow room. She felt slow and thick, as if she'd been sleeping since last Thursday.

"Caw," a bird called weakly from near the door. "See."

Oh, yeah! That poor bird. It's telling me to use the vision again.

Yolanda let her eyes cross and felt it flow. She remembered why Narissa was against the wall, all tied up in black webs, but how did Nikolas get into such a sorry pile beside the monkey's table? Neither one of them looked as if they'd be getting up any time soon.

Ming and Jade talked in a hush, not at all like the slow zombies they had been before. Yolanda got up off the bed and wobbled to them on weak legs, ignoring the stabbing pins and needles in her feet.

"What happened to Nikolas?" she whispered.

"I kicked him," Ming said, matter-of-factly.

"Please, hurry." Jade's face crinkled into a new expression that Yolanda had not seen before: kind, tough and worried. "You better go, now, before the Masters get better. Ming, go to the place of your ancestors. You know the way?"

Ming nodded, and took Jade's arm. "Come with us."

"I will not leave until your father comes back."

"But they'll punish you. Or kill you," Ming said.

Jade bowed to Ming as if she were the Mistress. "No matter, I was born to die. I must stay, to make sure the guards do not follow you. And to tell the Masters which way you went," She winked twice and bowed again.

Ming returned the bow and said, "Ever faithful."

Jade opened the door wide enough to poke her head out, and looked down the hall both ways. "The West gate is good. Hurry."

Yolanda almost tripped over Ming's sword. "Hey, we might need this!"

"A warrior's spirit is her steel," Ming said.

"Huh?"

"I don't fight with weapons." Ming's eyes flared.

Yolanda hurried to the door and saw the black bird huddled in the alcove, shaking. Black webs still pinned its wings down.

"Ming, can you use that sword one more time, to cut the bird free?"

Ming grabbed the sword and sliced through the last of the webs. With a weak squawk the bird careened across the room and out through the rip in the paper window.

"Wait!" Yolanda called, but it had already disappeared into the fog. "Thank you...for everything."

Ming ran out the door. Yolanda hurried to keep up, her legs still aching. She glanced down the hall to the right and saw the guards starting to move slowly, like toy soldiers with worn-down batteries. She followed Ming out the huge door and into the fog that swirled around the Palace.

29

*T*he yellow fog was so thick that Yolanda could only see the very tip of Ming's two-foot long braid as it flicked from left to right up ahead. Though her legs wobbled and her feet stung like nettles, Yolanda made them run faster to keep up: Come on!

Her toes caught on something hard, and she fell against a cold, lumpy shape. It was one of the stone statues she'd seen when she first came to the Palace, a fairy with long, trailing ruffles that looked like water. Perfect for tripping over.

"Ming!" Yolanda called out in a loud whisper. "Wait!"

Ming came back through the fog and touched the statue's robe. Her face still looked like a mask with no expression; only her forehead creased a tiny bit, as if she was sad or worried.

"What is it?" Yolanda asked.

"It's a water spirit. But so hard. Not flowing."

"Spirit? I thought it was a statue. There's tons of them out here," Yolanda said, then got an idea.

She stood on the ruffle and crossed her eyes a little, to see the statue with the vision. Though the fog was everywhere, she could see another kind of fog swirling around the spirit statue, like an extra layer of frosting.

"She's got a cloud on her. Nikolas made those clouds on us, too. To make us forget. To keep us from knowing things."

"Ah yes," Ming nodded. "I know of what you say, but did not know it was from Master Nikolas. How can you see it?"

"It's – it's a long story. Shouldn't we keep going?"

"Yes!" Ming bowed to the water spirit statue, and then took off running again.

Yolanda followed as closely as she could, dodging statues and dead willows all the way to the stone wall that surrounded the

Palace grounds. Ming climbed to the top of the wall, knelt on the clay tiles and helped Yolanda up and over.

Once outside, Ming ran even faster. Yolanda's chest burned and her feet blistered in her tiny satin shoes. She prayed Ming would take a break so she could catch her breath, but she only slowed the pace to a constant jog. Gradually she got used to it.

After what felt like hours, a lot of haze had burned off and the path was much easier to see. But that meant they would be easier to find, too. Nikolas and Narissa could be recovered by now. What would they do? As she ran, Yolanda twisted around to see if anybody followed on the trail. She thought she saw a dark shape high above in the wispy fog.

Could it be the black bird from the Palace? Probably not. That bird could barely fly.

To think that a bird showed me to use the vision.

It was amazing, but scary, to see that way. To see all that pain inside, feel all those old memories. To see what Narissa and Nikolas could do.

She remembered Yakos, his strong face, calling her name.

He left me with them.

No. He's not like them. He couldn't be...

30

*N*ikolas' head pounded like a jungle drum. He opened his eyes to see the hideous monkey spirit, the so-called Monkey King, teetering on his side on a table's edge just inches from his face. Nikolas himself was wedged between the table and against the wall. As he surveyed the situation, the monkey's mouth curled into a wide grin, as if he was about to laugh.

Damn! The creature is waking up.

Nikolas took a breath and sent a cloud of sleep into the monkey's mind. His grin froze into place, like stone. Nikolas winced from the effort. Hard to do anything when it feels like half your head has been blown off. Still, it was worth it, not to hear that blasted monkey laugh at him.

He sat up to gather his wits, his head thundering louder. What in blazes had happened? The curtains drifted slowly in the breeze from the torn window. The bed was empty. Yolanda and the servant girl were both gone.

"Narissa!" It hurt to speak.

She didn't answer. She lay sprawled up against the wall on the other side of the table, unconscious.

Nikolas made himself stand up. His brain exploded all over again, with shooting stars of pain.

"Narissa!" He prodded her foot. "Get up. Time to see the results of your experiment."

Her eyes fluttered open. "What in the Four are you going on about?" She struggled to sit up, then fell back down. "What's – going – on here!?"

"It's only a taste of your own medicine," he said.

"No. Impossible!" Narissa grimaced, showing her age.

"Lift your leg," he said.

"I can't. It hurts!"

"Don't you remember? The girl got up while we were chasing that damn bird. You tried to restrain her. It backfired. When you lifted your hand, you —"

Jade came in, bowed. "Master, a messenger comes," she said.

Her step was too fast, her eyes a little too bright, her face too alert. The controls must have weakened while Nikolas was unconscious. He gave Jade a gentle boost, enough so she could still talk. "Where are they?" he demanded.

"I — don't know…" Jade looked down, her face softening. Still, Nikolas could plainly see that she was lying.

"You will tell me." Nikolas sought her spirit with his mind, to deepen the controls, when a Yellow guardsman came in behind her.

"Who are you?" Nikolas said, irritated.

The messenger bowed sharply, strong and alert, a contrast to the Palace guard. "I am Yinto, sent by the Master Yakos."

Narissa managed to kneel. "How is he —?"

"More importantly, what is the progress on the Red maneuvers?" Nikolas said.

"Master Yakos requests a report on his sister's training. He asks when she will join him in the West."

Nikolas sighed. "Tell him that his sister is far from ready. Tell him he must trust us to determine the timing. And that we expect an update on his status."

"Yes, sir." Yinto bowed his head. "Master Yakos also asks that I speak with her myself."

Nikolas pondered this turn of events. If only Yakos would do as he was told. Stay within the strategy. Stop acting on his own, going off half-cocked. Still, this problem — the girl — it was all Narissa's doing.

"Mistress Narissa will answer your questions." Nikolas gestured to his sister, who was still on the floor trying to gather up her wits.

"What? I've no idea —" Narissa's hands curled like claws, to retract her own restraints. She managed to stand, but leaned on the monkey's table, a bit wobbly. "I've no idea when the young mistress will be ready to see anyone. Her training has been, well, beyond challenging."

"I must see the young mistress," the messenger said. "To complete my duty."

"She's not able to see you now!" Narissa said curtly.

"What shall I tell Master Yakos?"

Yinto was a persistent young man. Nikolas probed his body for weakness and found a typical pattern: a cave of abandonment that formed when Yinto was a baby, when his mother turned her face away each time he cried, to toughen him; the many wounds caused by his father, who berated and beat him for any small mistake. These injuries created another opening: a constant need for approval, to always be both strong and perfect. The ideal soldier. Nikolas filled these wounds with a partial dose of comfort. Yinto's face and bearing relaxed considerably.

"Tell Yakos we will send our own messenger with a complete training and deployment schedule," Nikolas said.

Yinto nodded slowly.

"Now, follow me to my quarters. You will pinpoint Master Yakos' position on my maps, his base camp in the West."

Yinto solemnly followed. Nikolas' headache began to ease. He turned to Narissa as they left. "If you can manage it, please speak with Jade about the missing items we discussed earlier. And send out the guard. Now."

31

*Y*olanda ran to catch up with Ming. She determined herself not to think about her twin or what she would do next, not until they were safe. They pushed on and on for many miles, sometimes walking, sometimes stumbling. Just when she was nearly out of steam to keep going they came upon a trickling stream, stopped for a few quick handfuls of murky water, and found some dried mulberries to chew along the way.

"At least nobody is following us so far," Yolanda said. "I've been checking."

Ming nodded, and then took off running again.

The late afternoon sun shone golden as they came to a wide field of yellow millet with a stand of trees along one side. Ming slowed to a walk then bent to touch a fallen stalk of dried grain. A tiny frown wrinkled her forehead.

"What's wrong?" Yolanda said between catches of breath.

"The grasses are not green, as they should be in spring." Ming looked out across the field.

"That's strange," Yolanda said. "And that statue back in the Palace garden. You seemed upset about that, too."

"It's the spirits," Ming murmured. "Something is wrong."

Spirits. When she was little Yolanda asked Mrs. Weaver, her Sunday school teacher, all about God and the Holy Spirit. The Spirit was supposed be invisible, but if you were really good, he would walk beside you and tell you what to do. Yolanda had wished so hard for the Holy Spirit to walk beside her, and especially to tell her what to do. No matter how hard she tried to be good, it never happened, so she gave up believing.

"What are spirits, anyway?" Yolanda asked. "Nikolas and Narissa said something about Tessar being full of them."

"They know them, but they do not understand," Ming said with a bitter tone in her voice. "Every pool, every stream of water, has a spirit. Every tree, rock and stone, every hill or mountain has a spirit. All the beings that ever lived have a spirit."

"So, these spirits...they're really real?" Yolanda said as they left the field and walked into the trees. She was wondering if maybe Yakos was just a spirit. "I mean, can you see them and touch them and everything?"

"They are not flesh and blood like us, but they can take a physical form."

"Like the statues?" Yolanda said.

"No. Spirits take many shapes, but they are always fluid. The spirits in the garden are cold, unmoving. It's wrong."

"Well, we know what happened to them. Nikolas."

"Yes, but there's something else, too." Ming picked up the pace, walking faster into the forest. She stopped every so often to touch a scraggly branch or pick up a fallen leaf. "I don't know – even the forest is dry."

Though Yolanda had never been there before, something about these woods didn't seem right. The air felt warm as spring; the forest should be leafy and green, buzzing with bugs and birds. Maybe something – or someone – had sucked all the life out of it.

32

ecca knew that her bird body wouldn't last long. She struggled to keep up with the two girls running on the path below. The fight against the Northern woman had injured her more than she knew when she flew from the Palace window. One wing was bent back so badly it took all her concentration not to let it pull her down. The other wing could not carry her alone; updrafts and air currents kept her from falling out of the sky. Her small heart beat fast to stay alive, but it was not enough. She felt faint and weak-headed.

not enough strength
can't – change –
back

Becca's spirit longed to leave the physical world where staying alive – time, place, and motion – was so important. She could easily slip into the comfort of the void, where, in the arms of the Great Mother and Father, she could await rebirth. But Yolanda was too important. She would not abandon this lifetime yet.

A sudden downdraft thrust her weak body into the branches of a tall pine. She flopped down from branch to branch, unable to stop herself. Falling like a stone, fast.

got to
let – go –
now.

Becca's spirit burst free just before her body smashed into the forest floor. She looked down on it from above and gave thanks for serving her so well. Though all her pain was gone, she was not at peace. She wanted to fly, to go home, but was too weak to make another body. She rose up to float among the many lost and bewildered spirits of the East, and prayed for signs of the red-haired girl in the world below.

33

*A*s the sun sank behind the bare trees, Ming kept a brisk pace through the forest. Yolanda walked several paces behind. She thankfully did not complain, although she must feel just as tired, hungry and thirsty.

Ming caught a whiff of smoke in the air. She peered through the woods for signs of people, of possible danger. Soon they came to a cliff overlooking a small stream with a bridge arched like a half-moon over it. On the other side, about thirty cone-shaped huts squatted along the water's edge. A village, thank the gods. Ming stopped until Yolanda caught up. "This may be the place Jade told me about," she said.

"Praise the Lord. Maybe we could stop and rest our feet a bit?" Yolanda said.

Ming nodded, and hurried down the steep precipice toward the bridge. The village was very small, with only a tiny dirt road. Blue smoke curled from holes in straw roofs. She heard the clang of wooden spoons and iron pots. Hearth fires glowed in the dusky light, welcoming and warm. Thankfully, few villagers moved about outside.

On the bridge, an old fisherman hunched over a bamboo pole, mumbling to himself. Ming motioned for Yolanda to wait, then went forward and bowed to him. The man didn't acknowledge that she was there; was he blind?

"A thousand pardons, Grandfather," Ming said. "We are humble travelers, in need of shelter and protection."

He snorted, but didn't look up from the trickle of a stream.

"I am not worthy to ask, but it is the tradition of our ancestors, to help those in need…"

"Bah! We help. If we have something to give." His voice was rough, like gravel.

"I beg your patience, Grandfather. What do you mean?"

The old man finally turned to look at Ming, and gave her a slight nod for a bow. "I come here to fish, every dawn and every sunset, all of my days. Now I stand here with this useless pole, though not one fish has been caught – or even seen – in over a month. Nothing grows, nothing sings. We eat last year's grain. When that is gone, we will turn to dust." He spat into the water.

"Have you asked the water spirits, the fish?" Ming asked.

"Gone," he said gravely. "The spirits are all gone. Even the great god Ching. We thought he was a friend to our village, but he's gone, too. Just like everything else."

Ming bowed her head. All day, as they ran through the dry fields and forests, she'd worried that such a thing had happened. Where is Ching? How will I ever find him? Clearly the fisherman did not know.

"I am so very sorry about your troubles. Please, give us shelter for one night," she said.

The fisherman eyed Yolanda, who stood farther back. "That one is very strange to look at."

Ming ignored the urge to give the fisherman a quick chop on his neck and put him out for a while. "She is only a Northerner. We need help. Will you take us to someone who will?" she said.

The old man shrugged, shouldered his pole and headed down the bridge and along the stream. Ming was grateful for the cover of darkness as they followed him past many huts. He stopped at the last one, a small, round house with a straw roof like the others, but with a square shed attached to the side and a long wooden plank for a stoop.

"Heya, Chua Sung," the fisherman shouted.

"Heya! The door is open." A voice called from inside.

The fisherman bowed a little, then gestured for them to go in before he scurried away, mumbling.

"Many thanks for all your help, Grandfather." Ming bowed, slipped off her sandals and laid them on the stoop.

97

34

*Y*olanda also pulled off her slippers. Her feet were blistered and bruised, but it felt great to get those tiny shoes off. She followed Ming and ducked under the green curtain into the hut.

The hut was just one room, filled with so much swirling smoke she could barely see. A wire lantern held a thick candle above the fire pit, which was just a circle of black stones in the dirt floor. A hole in the roof let out some of the smoke; still, Yolanda couldn't keep from coughing. Through watering eyes she saw a middle-aged man and woman crouching near the pit beside a short table with a few small bowls. They kept waving their hands furiously away from them, as if they were shooing flies.

"Ming, I think they want us to go," Yolanda whispered.

"That means 'come here,'" Ming said, then bowed low to the couple. "Please forgive my manners. I am Ming, and this is Mistress — Miss Yolanda. We are in need of one night's shelter and food, if you can spare it."

The man stood up and bowed over and over. He wore baggy blue clothes like pajamas, and his hair and eyes were dark like all the Easterners Yolanda had seen. "I am Sung. My wife, Cha. This miserable meal is not good enough for guests, but you must join us."

"Husband!" Cha whispered, frowning. Yolanda figured she didn't want them there.

"Shush, woman," Sung said.

"I thank you a hundred times, for your kindness." Ming bowed again, and then sat cross-legged on the floor near the small table. Yolanda copied everything Ming did, bowing and sitting.

Cha stood up to get two bowls from a shelf along the wall, dipped a rough-cut wooden ladle into an iron pot, and filled the bowls with steamy broth. She handed one each to Yolanda and Ming, grinning through a row of half-broken teeth. Ming slurped the thin reddish-yellow soup right from her bowl, so Yolanda did, too. Even without meat or vegetables it tasted salty and good. She drank it all at once, and Cha offered her another bowl.

"Thanks." Yolanda nodded her head up and down like Ming.

Sung and Cha looked at her, then at each other, and then whispered to Ming, so low that Yolanda couldn't hear.

"What did they say?" she leaned to ask in Ming's ear.

"They beg your pardon, but the Chuas are curious where you came from, with your green eyes and red hair. And how did you come here, to the East?" Ming looked down. "I am curious, too."

It was hard to explain since it didn't make much sense. Yolanda took a breath and told them how she saw her twin in a reflection, and then went through the lake after him, but could not find him on the windy plains of the East.

Sung and Cha didn't laugh at her, like she thought they might. "Ohhh," Cha murmured. "Such a story!"

"Yes, very interesting. About your brother." Ming's eyes opened wide and her forehead creased a little.

Yolanda leaned back on her heels and closed her eyes against the smoke, thinking of where he might be and how in the world she could find him now.

"Miss Cha would also like to know how you learned to speak the Eastern tongue so well?" Ming said.

"I never did learn your language. But I can understand you. And you understand me too?"

They nodded slowly. Ming took up the rest of the story. "Miss Yolanda came to the Palace of the Ten Thousand Things."

Sung and Cha both nodded. "The Palace!"

"Yes. But there is bad news there. Two demons from the North have taken over. They enslaved me and Miss Jade, my companion, and they captured Miss Yolanda, too. We escaped this morning. That's why we humbly beg a place under your roof for one night."

"Hmmm. It is the custom –" Sung began.

"But so dangerous, husband!" Cha whispered.

"No one followed us in the fog..." Yolanda said.

"My father stayed here, in this village, long ago." Ming's voice cracked a bit. "His name is Ching."

"Oh, mercy!" Cha swayed like she might faint.

"Such an honored guest! Daughter of a god-king! That makes you – a princess?" Sung jumped up and bowed to Ming again and again. "We do not deserve to sit with you."

Yolanda looked at Ming. So she's not just a warrior, but a princess? She didn't behave like a princess in a fairy tale, all proud and stuck up. Instead, she kept bowing to the Chuas over and over, and then they bowed back. It was like a contest to see who could bow more.

"No, no. Please, sit down," Ming said. "I do not deserve to sit here with you. I owe a thousand thanks to the Chuas, for helping my father so long ago, when he was in need."

"It was an honor for our clan to give shelter to your father. We'll help you in every way we can, Miss Ming," Sung said proudly. "It is our duty."

Cha bowed too, but gestured to the empty pot. "We have so little to give you and your Northern friend, Miss Ming. It is a bad time. Nothing grows. Although my husband does not like me to say it, some in the village say your father, Ching, is dead. He does not hear our prayers –"

Suddenly a pack of barking dogs broke the quiet of the night. Clanging bells and wild shouts rang through the village. Without a word Cha jumped up, pulled aside one of the bamboo mats that hung over all the walls, and waved them through a tiny square door.

Ming went first. Yolanda crawled on hands and knees behind her, her heart beating fast. A pair of skinny cows stood in the dark shed that reeked of hay, manure and animal sweat. They crouched down beside the cows. Ming peeked outside through a crack in the wallboards. Yolanda heard galloping hoofbeats that came to a stop, not too far from the shed.

"Attention!" A gruff voice rose above the villagers' shouts. Even the dogs stopped barking. "Two princesses from the Palace of the Ten Thousand Things were lost in the fog this morning. One is an Easterner, the other is a green-eye from the North lands. Anyone who saw them, come forward."

35

*M*ing held her breath as the guard dogs sniffed the dirt where she and Yolanda had just walked. Sung and Cha had gone outside to join the other townspeople in the village center. They hunched and bowed and held their lanterns just high enough to get a good look at the four guards on their big horses. The leader wore a red padded silk jacket with black and silver armor. He was a high ranking officer, with cold eyes, gray skin, and jerky movements, one of Nikolas and Narissa's servants.

Only a few hours ago, I was just like him.

"Look here! Live prawns! Enough for everybody, if you tell us where the two princesses are." The leader raised a large mesh basket crawling with pink shrimp.

Ming prayed that no one but the fisherman and the Chuas had seen them come into the village. The Chuas – so loyal to her father – would not say anything. But would the villagers' empty bellies tempt them to speak out? Though the crowd jostled and elbowed each other to get a better look, no one came forward, thank the Four gods and the ten thousand spirits.

"Will no one speak? Come on, you fools! We know they came this way!"

Ming held her breath as the officer rattled the shrimp cage high above the villagers' heads. The basket lid slid to one side and a few prawns fell on the dirt. The villagers groaned as ravenous dogs snapped them up.

"These idiots don't like the taste of prawns," the leader laughed to the guards. "Let's go on to the next village." With a snort of disgust, the guard leader led his cavalry back toward the bridge.

"What are a few prawns to us? Our bellies will be empty again come morning," a lone voice shouted.

"What?" The leader snapped. "Who's that?"

The old fisherman they'd met on the bridge stepped out of the pine shadows. Ming clenched her teeth.

"Where did those prawns come from?" the fisherman said. "There are no fish, or anything else, swimming in our river."

Emboldened by the fisherman, the villagers jeered and shouted. "He's right! We have no fish, no rice – nothing!"

"Nothing grows! And no blossoms on the fruit trees!"

"Where are the mushrooms?"

"Quiet!" The leader bellowed. He turned his horse around and spoke to the villagers as if they were children. "As everyone knows, Ching controls the cycles. He is responsible for all your troubles. But if you tell me where the two princesses are, fisherman, we will speak to him for you. Maybe a few fat trout will swim your way." The guards exchanged winks.

Ming shrunk back into the shadows and rested her cheek against the rough shed wall, but then she had to look again. The fisherman only walked back into the forest, grumbling to himself.

"Don't you people have any sense? I'll give you one last chance. Where are they?" The officer demanded.

The crowd hushed. A child whimpered. No one spoke.

The leader swung the basket high over his head, then unlatched the lid and tossed the shrimp to the dogs. The whole village gasped with one voice. A few brave souls rushed in to try and snatch a piece, but the dog's fangs scared them off. Ming watched the poor villagers rake the dirt with their fingers until they gave up and went back into their huts. The guards' laughter echoed through the forest as their horses clip-clopped back over the bridge.

Ming felt an urgent tap on her shoulder.

"What happened? I couldn't see. What did they do?" Yolanda whispered. Even in the dark Ming saw fear in her eyes.

"They tried to bait our fisherman into telling them about us, but they didn't catch him," she said.

Mother Cha pulled the mat aside and motioned them back into the hut with quick, brown arms.

"It's not safe for you here," Sung said. "Next time they'll bring more guards instead of prawns. But I have an idea. Even better, I have a brother with an ox-cart! And a nephew to drive it. You can hide in the back, get out of town quick!" He smiled very wide, showing the gaps in his teeth.

"Your offer is most generous," Ming chose her words slowly, taking care not to hurt his pride. "You tell me that my father is dead, but I believe he is only missing. I must find him. But how can I search for him, hiding in the back of an ox-cart?"

Sung frowned. "A princess like you shouldn't ride in an ox-cart, true, true. But Chua clan oxen are not like other dumb ox. Best in the East, a special breed. Strong and fast!"

"But, I —" Ming began, searching for the right words.

"You will not look for Ching yourself. You will go to Zching City and ask about him there," Sung said. "City folk know more than us villagers. The ox-cart is the best and fastest way."

Ming released the fists she had made without even noticing, and slowly placed her palms on her thighs. This was an argument she could not win, not with Sung's honor at stake.

Cha nodded. "You are in great danger, Miss Ming and Miss Yo-lan-da. It is our duty to protect you."

"The cart leaves at dawn." Sung bowed as he left.

Ming bowed in return. Even a warrior must respect her elders.

36

*T*ea, then sleep." Cha bustled around the hut, gathering stuff from baskets and filling an ancient kettle from a clay jug.

Yolanda rocked on her heels and wished she were back in Huskaloosa. She watched Cha drop a handful of tea leaves from a clay jar into four chipped bowls, and pour water over the leaves. She gave one to each, steaming hot.

Yolanda cupped hers to her lips and blew on it. The surface swirled like a miniature whirlpool, and then Yakos' face appeared in the middle, small but unmistakable.

"Holy crimeny," Yolanda stared into the dark water.

"So very sorry, Miss." Cha bowed, frowning. "This tea is very bad. Tastes like dirt. It isn't fit for princesses like you –"

"No! I'm not a princess! I mean, the tea is fine." Yolanda cupped the tea to her chest and made her way to the door. "'Scuse me, I've got to go outside."

Ming's eyes narrowed at her over her teacup.

Only a few stars twinkled above the village. Yolanda crept into the trees and knelt to see him, careful not to spill a drop. Even in the black of night, even in a cup of tea, she couldn't help but stare at Yakos' glittering green eyes.

"Yolanda...where are you?" he said.

"In a village," she whispered.

"What?" His eyes opened wide. "You're not at the Palace?"

"No," she said. "Can't you tell where I am?"

"Of course not," he answered. "That's not my talent."

Yolanda shrugged. "Well, what is your talent, then? Can't you get me out of here? There's a bunch of guards after us and –"

Yakos shook his head. "Us? Please, tell me everything that's happened, since we last spoke."

"Oh, yeah, in the bathtub. You disappeared. Again."

"Yolanda, I am sorry, I was called to –"

"Never mind," she snapped. "You said Narissa and Nikolas would tell me everything. Well, they treated me pretty good at first. Only I couldn't get out of bed, and I didn't remember a thing, like why I was even there. But then this bird flew through the window and told me to see, with my power, as you call it."

"A bird?"

"Yeah, a bird! And then I saw it all, how it really was. Lying on that pretty bed, trussed up and tied down, like a Christmas pig."

"No! They didn't!" Yakos' eyes flared like fireworks. "Nikolas and Narissa were supposed to teach you, nothing more."

Yolanda wanted to believe him so much. "Well, that didn't happen. When I saw those black webs all over me, and on Ming too, I knew we had to get out of there."

"Ming? Who is Ming?"

"In the Palace she was a servant, but she's a princess – and a fighter."

"How did you –?"

"Well, Ming's hands were free, so I got her to cut the webs off both of us, but then Narissa and Nikolas came in and chased the black bird, and I used the vis – my power – to stop them –"

"You stopped Narissa and Nikolas?" Yakos blinked.

"Yup. I took care of Narissa and then Ming got Nikolas. They were in pretty bad shape when we left, all slumped up against the wall. Served 'em right. We ran in the fog all day 'til we got to this village. Some people took us in, but now the guards are after us. So you'd better come get me."

"Yolanda, that's impossible." He shook his head. "As much as I want to, the situation here, in the West, it's very complicated."

"Well, things are getting complicated around here, too! The guards have horses and big, nasty dogs. Maybe you can have

Narissa and Nikolas call 'em off, since they're such good friends of yours."

"They are not my friends. And it's not possible for me to contact them right now."

Yolanda's cheeks flushed. "What's to stop you from popping up in their teacups? Or, next time they're taking a bath, or looking in a mirror? You can just drop in and say howdy!"

"They can't see me," he shook his head. "Only you can do that. That's your gift, your power. You would have known as much if they had taught you."

Yolanda heard sounds near the hut. Probably Ming was looking for her. "I've got to go now," she said.

"Trust me, Yolanda. I'll find a way to help you. In the meantime, don't let anyone see you. Cover your hair, hide your eyes. I will find you again, very soon, I promise." Yakos smiled, and then his face swirled back into the dark tea.

37

*H*ello, Miss Yo-Lan-Da," Cha bowed as Yolanda came in. "Miss Ming was outside worrying for you. She's in the shed now. It's not a palace, but you'll be warm and safe with the cows."

Cha gathered some hot rocks from the fire pit with a pair of tongs. Yolanda followed her under the grass mat into the shed, where Ming spread some blankets over some hay laid down between the two knobby cows. She didn't look up at Yolanda.

Cha rubbed the stones between the thin blankets to heat them up.

Ming bowed from a kneeling position. "Mother Cha, a thousand thanks. We do not deserve such kindness."

"Shhh! Now sleep," Cha covered her mouth. "Oh! So sorry! I shouldn't talk to princesses the same as my good-for-nothing nieces."

"It's all right." Ming slipped under her blanket with her robes still on, and Yolanda did the same.

"Good night." Cha took the lantern back into the hut. A tiny slit of light fell across Yolanda's cheek. Half of her was squished against the knobby old cow's back and the other half lay on the rock-hard ground. She was tired, but everything that happened ran circles in her head: Yakos in her teacup; the guards that could show up any minute; Nikolas' dream cloud and Narissa's black webs; the vision that rose up from her insides and showed her things that she didn't always want to see.

"Ming," she whispered. "You still awake?"

"Umh," Ming grunted.

"What'll we do if they catch us?"

Ming didn't hesitate. "I will fight them. I'd rather die than be a prisoner again...I must be free, to find my father."

"Who is he anyway? He sounds like — well, is he God?"

"Ching is one of Four gods of Tessar, a very great spirit."

"Where I come from, there's only one, and he's in Heaven."

"In Tessar, one god in each land must master its ways of knowledge. He or she rules for a hundred years until the next generation."

"She?"

"Yes, we have female gods, called goddesses."

"What about Ching, what is he like?"

"Ching is responsible for the wheel of change. Everything that lives by a season or cycle depends on him. Now that he is gone, the rains don't know when to come. Plants wither. Everything is dying. I must find him, so the wheel of change can turn again."

Ming the slow servant girl was gone. The new Ming sounded very serious and important, with a lot of important problems.

Yolanda had problems of her own: to find Yakos, and get back home. But she couldn't just strike out on her own, the way she'd always done things. Not here. Everything was too different.

"I've got to find my brother, too," she murmured. "He's in the West." Yolanda didn't want to say any more. After all, he was still only a reflection.

38

*M*ing saw the same longing in Yolanda's eyes, the way that she probably looked when she thought about her father.

She remembered the red-haired, round-eyed young man she'd seen for only a moment at the Palace, just before she became Nikolas' prisoner. Was he Yolanda's twin? What does he have to do with all that's happened in the East? With the Northerners who took the Palace? With Ching? She did not know. She could not say anything to Yolanda.

"My teachers, Ting and Tan, live in the Fung Mountains, the borderlands to the West," she said. "It's just beyond Zching City, where Chua Sung said I must go to look for Ching."

"So you are going near the West?" Yolanda said.

"Yes, but it's a long way from here. A dangerous journey."

"So I have to go the same way as you!" Yolanda sat up on her elbow. "That's good. We could help each other out, you know, getting there. You're awful good in a fight."

"And you are a very fine seer."

"Then it's a deal. We'll go West." Yolanda thrust out her hand toward Ming's side.

Ming looked down at her outstretched palm, wondering what she should do, and nodded her head toward it.

"Oh, I keep forgetting. I'm not in Kansas anymore," Yolanda said.

"Kan-sas? Is that where you came from?"

"Nope." Yolanda laughed with her mouth wide open, a bit too loud but it sounded pleasant. "I'm from Huskaloosa. I've got a small place, out in the middle of nowhere. Where did you come from? Some fancy Palace?"

Yolanda was always so direct. Ming shook her head. "No, not a palace. I come from a crowded city, in another world."

"Holy moly! You mean there's another world besides Tessar?"

Ming nodded slowly. "The same one you came from."

"Jeez, Ming! Why didn't you say so before?"

"I am sorry. It is not our way — my way — to speak as freely as you do..."

"Yeah, that's ok. You don't have to tell me anything." Yolanda lay back down and closed her eyes.

Ming drew a breath for courage, and then began. "My mother was a lady of the night, in a slum of Taipei."

Yolanda nodded a little.

"I have ten brothers and sisters, all with different fathers. We never knew them. My brothers left by age eight to join gangs. I always wanted to get away, too, to be on my own, but the only way for a poor girl was my mother's way. I vowed I would not be like her."

Yolanda rolled on to her side, facing Ming again.

"I shared a bed with my seven half-sisters. One night when I was eleven, one of Ma's rich customers came into our room. When I saw his shriveled old face grinning over my sister with only one tooth, I leapt out of bed like a demon whirlwind and beat on him with both fists."

Yolanda's eyes were wide open now, and as green as jade in the thin light from the hut. It was not so hard as she'd imagined, to tell the story to her. Ming took another breath and went on.

"I jumped down the fire escape and never went back. If my brothers could survive on the streets, so would I. I was tougher than most men, and could win a fight against anybody. 'The ferocious fighting girl of Taipei,' they called me. Important people bet real money on me. I made a lot, too. I had my own room behind a brothel, and all the clothes and whiskey I wanted."

"Really!" Yolanda grinned.

"One day an old fortune-teller came after a fight. Though he had only gray marbles for eyes, he said my chi was stronger than any he'd ever seen. He said I was wasting my talent in this world, and that I belonged in another. I thought he was crazy."

"That's what Miz Becca said! That I should come to Tessar. I thought she was crazy, too," Yolanda said. "So, how did you end up here?"

"The next day I passed an alley I'd never seen before. It was full of steam, like every other back street with a laundry, but when I walked through it, I felt weightless, like I was flying in a cloud. I saw a ball of light up ahead, but could never touch it. After a while I started to fall, a long, long way. Then I landed on the ground, but couldn't see or hear anything. The fog was too thick."

"Just like me! I mean, it was foggy." Yolanda said. "And I saw that light, too!"

Ming nodded. "I think all the gateways are like that."

"There are more?"

"My teachers told me there are many in our world, and here in Tessar, but they are hidden. You have to know where."

"Your teachers, how did you meet them?"

"When the fog lifted, I saw two people walking toward me. They were waiting for me."

"There was nobody waiting for me." Yolanda frowned.

"Ting and Tan keep an eye on the gateways around the Fung Mountains, in case someone comes through. They didn't expect to find a foul-mouthed kid in a green satin jumpsuit, looking for a fight. They made me go with them to their hut, kicking and screaming. It took a while to understand they wouldn't hurt me or use me for profit. Instead, they taught me to use my strength and to speak and move in harmony with the Way."

"The Way!" Yolanda started to laugh.

"Yes, the Way," Ming said.

"I just remembered. I did meet somebody near the gateway. A little talking monkey. He kept blabbering about the Way."

"Wasn't there a monkey in your room at the Palace?"

"Oh yeah!" Yolanda yawned. "Wow, I can't believe we busted out of there this morning. It seems like a week ago."

"We should sleep now."

"Yup." Before she settled into her blanket, Yolanda bowed her head slowly toward Ming. "Is that how you say 'thank you?'"

"Yes," Ming bowed her head, smiling. "And good night."

39

*M*iss Yo-lan-da. Wake now. Miss Ming is up, making ready." Cha poked Yolanda in the shoulder until she roused.

It was still dark, and a cold wind whistled through the shed. Cha held out a pair of baggy blue pants and shirt, exactly like the clothes she and Sung and the others villagers wore. Shivering, Yolanda slipped out of her silk robe, pulled the new clothes on and crawled into the hut. Ming wore the same outfit; she nodded to Yolanda as she made loosely tied bundles of dried plums and millet cakes, and stuffed them into rough cloth bags.

Sung came in carrying two leather bags dripping with water. "Rice this morning, eh, Mother Cha?" he said. "In honor of the princess' journey."

Cha grunted, reached to the bottom of a big clay jar and tossed a handful of kernels into a boiling pot.

Ming put her hand out over the pot. "Please. We cannot eat rice while your people starve."

Cha threw in three more handfuls. "Princess Ming does not think our rice is good enough."

"No, no!" Ming protested. "Your rice is very good, too good for Ching's worthless daughter."

Sung winked at Yolanda. A few minutes later Cha put four bowls of steaming rice on the table, and they all dove into it with chopsticks. Yolanda dropped only a few grains on her shirt.

"Time to go," Sung said as the pale morning light seeped under the door. "The guards will be back here, sure thing."

"Wait," Yolanda grabbed a round, flat hat of woven grass down from the wall. "Can I borrow this?"

"Good idea," Ming said.

Cha nodded. Yolanda tied it under her chin, and tried to stuff her wild red hair under the brim.

"Tsk, tsk, such hair!" Cha took the hat off and wrapped Yolanda's hair close to her head with a thin rag first, and then shoved the hat back down over it. She tipped the brim down low in front so Yolanda could only see her own feet, nothing else.

"Better," Ming said. "We'll still have to be careful."

Sung shooed them all into the shed. The cows were gone. A pair of bony oxen was hitched to a small wooden cart strewn with hay. A skinny boy held the reins from the driver's seat, trying to look taller than he was. He didn't look at them.

"This is my brother's good-for-nothing first son, Chen. He takes our grain to market – when we have any to sell, that is. But I say he drives too fast!" Sung yanked the boy's ear and he looked down, blushing.

"Don't worry," Cha said. "Chen is a good driver. He will protect you with his life."

"Yes. And now it is good-bye." Sung bowed so low that his forehead nearly touched his knees. "A great honor to meet you, Miss Princess Ming, and Miss Yo-lan-da. I pray good fortune rides with you."

"We can never repay your kindness. Perhaps someday, when my father –" Ming bowed to both Sung and Cha.

"Thanks a lot," Yolanda bowed like Ming, but her hat slid down over her eyes. Cha reached up to straighten it.

They climbed into the cart and lay down in the straw. Sung piled big burlap sacks over them, with heavier bags on top. Cha tucked the water and food bags within reach, then arranged Yolanda's hat over her face so she'd be well hidden, and finally threw down a final layer of straw.

Cha leaned over the cart. "Don't drink too much water," she said.

Yolanda could hardly breathe, and something made her nose and throat tickle like crazy. "What is in these bags?"

"Grass and pine needles. Only a few on top are grain."

"AAA-choo!" Yolanda couldn't help but sneeze.

115

"Shhh!" Sung's voice sounded muffled. "We can hear you!"

"Ya!" Chen cracked the reins, and the cart groaned out of the shed.

The cart lurched from side to side behind the oxen, who ran amazingly fast. Their endless clopping hoofs made Yolanda's head ache. Her bones bounced against the hard wooden cart. After an hour or two the suffocating sacks grew hotter and heavier. A dangerous tickle crawled up her throat. She swallowed to keep from coughing, but her mouth was as dry as dust.

I'd give anything for a drink right now. I can't help it if I'm allergic. I'm not getting enough air. I could die of thirst before we stop to rest. If we're gonna stop at all.

Finally she just couldn't stand it. The water bag was buried under a ton of straw. She dragged it closer, up to her lips, and took a couple of big swallows. She could almost feel Ming staring at her through the hay, but took another gulp, then another.

"Ho, Chen," a man's voice called out from beside the road, rough but friendly. "Where you headed?"

"Hiyah," Chen said to the oxen. The cart slowed then jerked to a stop. Ming let out a long slow breath, while Yolanda almost choked on a big guzzle of water.

"To market," Chen's voice cracked a little.

"Shame on you Chuas, selling what's left of our grain to rich folks in the city. What're you trading for?" The man's voice sounded awfully familiar.

"Tools, and a little fish."

"Tools! What do you need tools for? Can't eat tools."

It was the fisherman, the one that spoke out to the guards last night!

"I do as my elders tell me."

"You're a good boy. But you'd better go back home. It's not safe on the roads. Ku-zin bandits. One farmer in Aya, I heard they burned his house, his fields and barn. Took his wife and daughters. All for a few kernels of rice at the bottom of a jar."

"I can handle them," Chen said, rustling the reins.

Yolanda clenched her teeth. Was Chen like the boys in the valley, the ones that talked big when they got scared, but couldn't live up to their talk?

She heard the fisherman's sandals flip-flop to the back of the cart. Through a tiny crack in the bags she saw him stick a weathered finger into one of the sacks. Grains of millet poured right onto her foot.

Can he see my toes? Or hear my heart beating?

He padded around to the front. "You take care of the two of them, now. Don't let the ku-zin get 'em," he said.

Chen didn't answer.

"I mean your oxen, boy." The fisherman laughed.

"Yes, uncle. I will take good care of them." Chen cracked the reins and the cart took off.

Yolanda let out a sigh of relief, and then took another drink. What if he saw them? What if he tells the guards? Ming can't fight all of them. We'll be dragged back to the Palace. This time we won't be so lucky.

Just thinking about what could happen made Yolanda's throat burn even more. She reached for the water bag again and again.

As the late afternoon sun beat down on the cart, the sacks of grain and hay got heavier and hotter. Sweat ran rivers down her sides and back. Her belly rumbled with hunger, but now she had another problem: a totally full bladder. If the cart hit one more bump she was sure it would burst. Yolanda wriggled her arm up and knocked on the wooden driver's seat just behind her head.

"Chen! We gotta stop!" she whispered.

"We'll be at the village soon," Chen tried to sound like he was talking to the oxen. "Keep strong for me, eh?"

Yolanda's hope sank. She couldn't even cross her legs under the bags of grain. She waited as long as she could. Finally she knocked on Chen's seat again, twice as hard. She felt Ming's body tensing near her. "Chen! Stop! Please…"

"Up ahead," he hissed. "I see some trees. Whoa…" Chen finally slowed the cart and pulled to the right.

Yolanda was just about to kick the sacks off and run to the woods when a gruff voice called out. "Hai-ya! Get down!" She froze, praying the bags still covered her legs.

"I am only a poor farmer. I have nothing…" Chen stammered.

"Get down, I said!"

She heard metal scrape on metal – a sword? – and then dozens of feet crunching around the cart. Was it the bandits that the fisherman warned Chen about?

"If you don't get down NOW we'll take everything you have, including your worthless life."

The wooden seat groaned. Chen was getting up.

We're goners.

it's your fault, it's all because of you

Oh, God. Mama.

"Get down!"

"Ch'aaaaaaaa!!!" Yolanda heard the sharp smack of Chen's leather whip. The oxen jerked into a hard gallop. She was thrown first against the side, and then into Ming, who lay as still as a piece of wood. A few sacks of grain lurched off their legs and nearly fell out the back.

The bandits ran after them, whooping mad. So close! It sounded like they were just a few short steps behind.

The cart wobbled and creaked like it might split in two any minute. Yolanda's bladder felt the same way. She squeezed her eyes tight to make it all go away.

Either the ku-zin would catch up, or the cart would fall apart, whichever came first.

40

*C*hen relaxed his jaw as the ku-zin's shouts faded away behind the cart. He thanked the Four gods that the bandits had only their miserable feet to carry them, while he had Ping and Peng. The Chua's secret breed, a mix of oxen and Northern yak, were by far the best in the East. All the other animals in the village had become so skinny and weak that their bones stuck out like insects. Not Ping and Peng. Chen always gave them part of his food ration, even now, when there wasn't enough.

"You idiot!" the villagers had jeered at him. "You'll starve like a rat, bring dishonor to your family."

Ha! They are the idiots, Chen thought. Ping and Peng saved the princesses from disaster!

"Hai-za!" Chen drove them on while he searched for the path to the haunted cave. They wouldn't be truly safe from the Ku-zin until he found it, but the trees and vines along the road were so dry and dead that he barely recognized the place. Finally he spotted the twisted double tree that marked the trail and jerked the reins. Ping and Peng just made the turn, the cart careening behind them.

Chen counted on the giant ferns to cover their tracks. Before, the fronds had been so thick and tall that the trail below was completely hidden under a green canopy, but now the leaves had shriveled so they barely camouflaged the cart. Just one more thing that wasn't right anymore. He prayed silently: Oh great fern spirits, I wish you had not left us. If you could hear me, I would ask you to bless us who pass below, and to hide us from the ones who may follow.

Ping and Peng ran strong, deeper into the forest. When they came to the rock face of the lesser mountain, Chen bade them to stop under the thick slab of stone that partly hid the mouth of the cave. He jumped down and led them inside the cave, stroking their necks to soothe their fear of the dark. They snorted and shook beads of sweat into the cool, dank air.

"Shhhh," he murmured, straining to hear any possible sounds of the ku-zin coming through the brush. All he heard was the low moan of the wind blowing across the mouth of the cave. Although the bandits might know of this place and come here looking, Chen would stay alert and listen for them all night, until they left.

He hurried to the back of the cart and rolled the heavy sacks off both princesses. The round-eyed one, Miss Yolanda, jumped down fast and limped behind a rock. Chen tried not to hear the sound of the rushing stream and her long sighs of relief.

He gave Ping and Peng a bundle of hay and his own ration of water, then gathered some food and led the princesses through the darkness to a rough circle of boulders at the back of the cave. He started a small, smoky fire as the princesses ate Aunt Cha's best dried plums and fish. Chen's belly rumbled with hunger, but he did not know the right thing to do: take a share, or let the princesses have it all?

Miss Ming dug into the bundle and frowned as she pulled out three sticky rice balls, the best of the food. "Mother Cha should have saved her rice for her people."

It had been many long weeks since Chen had tasted rice. Miss Ming offered one glistening white ball, the largest, to him. Her face was round and pretty, yet there was power in it, too.

"I am not hungry," he said, looking down.

"You kept us safe from the ku-zin," she said. "Please, take it."

He had no choice. He accepted the rice ball and bowed his head to her. "I beg your pardon, Miss. It was Ping and Peng who saved you. They are strong and fast."

"It's all my fault," Miss Yolanda hung her head in shame. "I shouldn't have drunk the water. If we hadn't stopped –"

"No, no. It was only my lazy eyes. They don't work so well. I should have seen the stinking ku-zin hiding in the bamboo." Chen wanted her to save face, to feel better about what happened.

"What are the ku-zin, anyway?" she asked.

"They are thieves, and worse," Chen said. "Every day, more and more people starve. They are so hungry, young men will even trade their family honor for the stinking ku-zin's food. They join the gangs and then they go crazy for power. Nobody is safe."

"What would they do to us if they got us?" Yolanda shivered.

"Take everything, kill us, maybe." Chen did not say the other things they might do. "But if they're smart, they'll give you to the guards for ransom. It's a lot of silver. Fifty cash, I heard."

"Where is this cave? Are we safe here?" Ming asked.

"We are near K'o, the village of my eldest uncle, K'an." Chen said. "Nobody ever comes to this cave. K'o people say it's haunted by bad-hearted spirits, but I say it's a good place to hide or keep the rain off your head."

"Haunted?" Yolanda's eyes opened wide.

Chen wasn't sure how much he should say. "Uncle K'an says it's just a legend that only fools believe."

"Tell us!" Miss Yolanda said.

Chen looked uneasily toward the cave mouth. "If Miss Ming will please keep watch for the ku-zin, I will tell the tale."

Ming nodded and he began:

"An old man had three daughters. Number One Daughter was beautiful and Number Two Daughter was a very good cook. But Number Three Daughter was not only ugly, she was sly and lazy, too. Because she'd never bring a dowry, she had to work in the rice fields for her keep. One day she stole some coins from her father and went to the matchmaker's to beg her to find her a husband."

"It was very bad manners to go without her father, when her older sisters had not yet married. But the matchmaker took her money, and said she knew an old widow with three sons. Number One Son was very smart, and Number Two Son was good with his hands, but Number Three Son was so weak-minded that he could not even carry water. He hid under the kitchen table all day long, catching the table scraps that happened to fall."

"Number Three Daughter would have married the sluggard under the table, but for the dishonor of having to fight him for some of the scraps that happened to fall. So she had an idea. She arranged to meet in secret with Number Three Son in this very cave. She said, 'If our sisters and brothers are gone, then our parents will stop treating us so badly. We'll be the only ones left, so they will love us! We'll have an honorable marriage, and get all the inheritance, too.'"

"Number Three Son liked the idea. 'We'll trick them into this cave, and roll this big rock in front of the door. Then we'll be rid of them for good.'"

"Everybody knows how easy it is to offend cave spirits, but Number Three Daughter and son were so stupid, they didn't even worry about talking that way in a cave filled with spirits! All of them were angry, but the spirit of the biggest boulder in the cave decided to teach them a lesson. 'Ha, ha ha,' he laughed. 'A weakling like you can't move a huge boulder like me!'"

"When Number Three Son heard that, he had to prove his worth. He pushed and pushed against the rock with all his might, but nothing happened."

"I'll show you how it's done," Number Three Daughter said, and gave the rock a heave. It lurched a little, then a little more, and then it kept on rolling, all by itself, until it stuck right in the mouth of the cave, blocking the only way out.

"Number Three Son and Number Three Daughter were never seen again in K'o village, but they were not missed. Eventually the huge rock rolled back inside the cave. People said that the ghosts of the dishonored son and daughter moved it, so they could get out and haunt their elder brothers and sisters. Some people say they are still in this cave, still trying to move these rocks.

"The funny thing is," Chen rubbed his chin. "Every time I come here, the boulders are in a different place. Is it the rock spirits, or the ghosts?"

A low rumble came from the back of the cave.

Yolanda looked over her shoulder. "Do we have to stay in here all night?" she said.

"We have too many worries already, to be afraid of ghosts or rock spirits," Ming chided.

Chen's face grew hot with shame. "So sorry, princess! I should not have told you the ghost story. Rest now, and I'll stand watch. We leave before dawn, while the stinking ku-zin sleep off their drunkenness."

"You may call me Ming. I do not deserve to be called a princess. And please, wake me after three hours to take over the watch. You can't stay awake all night and drive the cart all day."

41

*Y*olanda wrestled with her scrap of burlap to try and make it big enough. No matter what position she tried, her butt was hanging out on the bumpy, cold floor. She heard a constant drip-drip-drip at the back of the cave, and then Ming started to snore. She wondered what Ming had meant when she said, 'don't deserve to be called a princess?'

It was hard to know what Ming was thinking. Back in Huskaloosa, Yolanda could figure people out just by watching them: how they walked, whether or not they whispered during church, or how they did their hair. She pictured the church ladies in the Kmart parking lot, talking about everybody else's business but their own, and the old men jawing over coffee in the cafe, or spitting chaw at the feed store. Thoughts of home reminded her of Mama, and the MacGroders, her neighbors. Did they miss her? She sat right up when she remembered Jimson, the orange and black and white kitten she left behind.

He could have starved to death by now! Or got run over by a truck, or eaten by coyotes. That little runt depended on me. Look what he got for it.

you didn't know where you was going, how long you'd be

Yolanda lay back down and tried to sleep for at least an hour, but she had to empty her bladder again. Damn all that water. She dreaded creeping to the back of the cave to do it. Finally she pulled a stick of wood from the fire to light her way, and crept behind the big boulders. They seemed to rise up and down a little, as if they were breathing.

that's crazy. it's just your imagination

On the way back Yolanda accidentally stepped into a small pool of freezing water. Damn! She looked down to see how wet her pants were. Her reflection swirled into a familiar pattern, and then she saw him.

"Yakos!" she whispered, trying not to wake Ming.

"Yolanda..." His voice echoed off the rocks as if he was right there in the cave. "Thank the Four, you're safe."

"But we've got killer bandits chasing us, and we're in a cave with creepy ghosts and boulders that move. And that's not even counting the guards. So, when are you gonna come get me?"

"Yolanda. This is very difficult..."

"What do you mean, 'difficult?!' I thought you wanted me here!" Yolanda hissed.

"I do, Yolanda, I want you with me, very much. More than you know. But this is war, in the West, and I am the leader. We've been fighting for unity, to put an end to our differences and join together as one. If I leave now -"

Yolanda hung her head. Yakos was trying to save the whole world, just like Ming, while she was just feeling sorry for herself. "Well, - so it's not worth it, to come for me."

"You are worth it, Yolanda. I've agonized over this. If I leave now, the future of all Tessar is in the balance. Still, I could not live with myself if anything happened to you. So tell me. Is it so dangerous for you that I should come now?"

Yolanda's chest could have burst. This was the brother she'd longed for, one who cared. Although he was still just a reflection, he finally felt real.

"It's okay. You don't have to. We decided to go west. So I'll come to you!" She smiled bravely.

"I'm not sure that's a good idea," he paused. "I've sent an army to the Palace to stop Narissa and Nikolas and call off the guards, but it will take time. Until then, promise you'll stay out of sight and off the roads. Don't let anyone see you."

"Don't worry! We'll be fine!" Yolanda sounded much more sure than she felt. As she started to say goodbye, the water swirled again. The hard edge of his jaw softened, and that wild eyebrow – the one that wouldn't stay put – slipped down.

"When will I see you again?" she whispered, but she was only talking to herself.

42

*G*ood morning, my good beasts." Shafts of pale morning light slipped into the cave like thieves as Chen harnessed Ping and Peng. Out of the corner of his eye, the round-eyed princess tripped over a boulder on her way to the cart.

"Owwww! That rock wasn't there last night, I swear it!" she said.

"You're right," Ming said. "We can take hope. Not all the spirits of the East are gone."

Chen hurried to help the two princesses into the cart. As he piled the bags of millet and hay over them, Yolanda said, "I'm not touching a drop of water today," and Ming smiled.

He led Ping and Peng out, into the thickest yellow fog he'd seen in many seasons. Thank heaven that he knew the back trails to K'o better than the wrinkles on his own mother's face.

"Don't worry, it's the same path we've taken before," he whispered to the oxen. "Run like the dragonwinds. Quiet and quick. Jihah!"

By mid-morning the sun burned through the haze and they were out of the woods in open country. Chen searched the fields for signs of the ku-zin. He only saw twisted stacks of hay dotting the pasture lands, last year's harvest. It was bad enough that the soil had turned gray, the color of rotten turnips, but where were the birds and butterflies, the foxes and moles?

Mostly he missed the spirits that used to be along this road, shimmering playful beings that hid in every flower and cloud and tree. Sometimes they leapt out and showed themselves only to him, made faces, teased him, and danced around him like fireflies. They showed him how good this life really is, made him laugh and forget his worries.

In the distance he spotted the cone-shaped farmhouses of K'o, but no farmers in the fields. He usually met women carrying baskets and kids chasing cows with sticks, but today, the road was empty, all the way into K'o.

Where was the pretty noodle house girl who always waved shyly? The noodle shop sign flapped in the wind, torn from its post. Broken crates lay in front of the barrel maker's. The tea shop stools lay in a reckless pile. Every house and shop was shuttered and locked.

He thought he saw eyes, peering out between the slats. What were they afraid of? The ku-zin?

On the other side of the village, Uncle K'an's farm looked as if a tsunami wind had blown through. Tools, hay and splintered wood were scattered everywhere. He drove Ping and Peng into the barn, next to the cows that should have been out to pasture.

"Shhh," he whispered back to the princesses. "It's not safe yet. Please, stay hidden in the cart while I find Uncle."

The house was shut as tight as the rest of the village. Chen pried a loose board off the door and stuck his head in.

"Hullo? Uncle —"

Chen saw a dark round shape coming toward his head, then smack! The lights of heaven whirled past his eyes. Darkness overtook him as he slumped into the doorway. When he came back to this world, partway, he felt a lump the size of a peach pit on his head. A woman slapped both his cheeks and screeched in his ear.

"Oh! Chen! It's Chen! Worthless nephew, wake up! Wake up! So sorry! Are you dead?"

Chen opened his eyes. "Please stop, Aunt Mai! I'm alive!"

She dragged him into the house, bolted the door, and hung the big iron spoon back on its hook above the fire.

"So sorry, nephew. We thought you were another one."

"One of the ku-zin?"

"No, no, no. Worse than ku-zin! Palace guards." Uncle K'an crawled out of the shadows and looked out the broken door and windows, as jumpy as a tree frog.

"They kicked Grandmother Bo in the stomach," Aunt Mai said.

"They held a sword to Ha Fung's neck. Rode in at dawn, breaking into honorable law-abiding houses, throwing things around!" Uncle K'an clenched his fists at the sight of the strewn-open storage boxes, the torn mats and broken dishes.

"What do they want?" Chen thought he already knew.

"They were looking for two princesses. We could have been killed! Over a couple of giggling girls, lost in the woods."

"Uncle, those princesses are not lost."

K'an peered at him suspiciously. "How do you know so much?"

"Uncle Sung hid them in the ox-cart. He sent me to drive them to safety." Chen stood a little taller, proud to be chosen for such an important duty.

"You brought them here? You bring disgrace to this house!" K'an's face puffed up, berry red, at the same time his hand flew. He would have slapped Chen on the head, right on his lump, but the boy ducked under it. "You're an idiot, to bring us such a disaster! What have these princesses done, that guards will beat poor villagers to find them?"

"They've done nothing, Uncle! One is Ching's daughter and the other is a round-eye, from the North."

"Ching's daughter, eh? And a round-eye?" Uncle K'an's face brightened, then narrowed. "Where are they?"

"In the barn."

"Fetch them, boy. And be quick!"

43

*A*s if to answer Ming's prayers, Chen came back in a few minutes' time unhurt. She began to help him, to move the heavy bags, but he put out his hand to refuse. So much pride in such a skinny boy.

"The guards just left," he whispered as he led them into the house. "They tore the village apart looking for you. Uncle K'an is hopping mad, but he'll decide what to do."

Ming stood in the doorway of a disaster. Uncle Chua K'an resembled his brother Sung, but his hair was thinner and his face was fatter. He didn't see them come into his hut, and was too busy huffing and puffing and shaking his fists at the mess to help the woman who stooped to gather up the broken pottery.

"Such a shame," she muttered. "Our best bowls, all broken. Ah well. We have no rice to put in them."

"And who is the cause of that? The girl's father, Ching!"

"Excuse me, Uncle K'an, Aunt Mai, this is Miss Ming and Miss Yo-lan-da."

Ming winced at the way Chen announced them like royalty.

"Come in, come." Aunt Mai bowed to them and gestured to some pillows on the floor. She helped K'an lower himself to a pillow and scurried to the back of the house.

Ming approached Chua K'an very slowly, then bowed deep enough to touch her toes before sitting. "Thank you. We have traveled far."

"So I hear. We have no time for idle talk," Uncle K'an grunted. With a wave of his hand he rudely dispensed with the usual courtesies, the seemingly meaningless small talk that greased the way for more difficult conversations. "You are Ching's daughter, eh? Why does trouble follow you, and why do you bring it here to us?"

K'an thrust his chin at Yolanda, glaring at her as if she were the cause of all his problems.

Ming shot Yolanda a glance as if to say: stay quiet, don't draw his notice, don't look at him directly or let him see how odd you are. Thank the Four gods, Yolanda seemed to shrink a little under her hat, and took up less space on her pillow.

Ming bowed her head, too, so her eyes did not meet his. "A hundred pardons, but we hate to bring the Chuas any hardship. We owe our very lives to your clan."

"Then tell me why you are here, in my house, with over a hundred guards chasing you."

Ming took a breath. "Yesterday morning, we escaped from the Palace of the Ten Thousand Things, where we'd —"

"They say it's made of gold and jade, pearl and ivory," he interrupted. "Is it true?"

"Yes, the Palace is lovely, but a pair of round-eyed demons from the North have taken it. They tricked us, with —"

"Round eyes. Like her?" He jerked his thumb Yolanda's way.

"She is nothing like them. If it weren't for Miss Yolanda, I would still be their slave."

"I knew it! You are escaped servants! You should be whipped a hundred times and sent back to your masters."

"But, Uncle, she is Ching's daughter!" Chen said.

"How do we know? She has told me nothing of him yet."

"Perhaps you should let her get a word in, Husband." Aunt Mai brought a pot of jasmine tea. K'an glared as she poured his cup first, then the others.

Ming sipped her tea, knowing she must choose her words carefully. It wouldn't do for Chua K'an to know the truth. "I came to the Palace for my father, but he was gone. I believe the demons tricked him somehow. They are very powerful. They took our spirits, and our memories. They tied us with invisible rope. I heard them plotting to take all four lands under their control."

"All of Tessar!" K'an slapped the table, making the teacups jump. "That's ridiculous. The Four gods won't allow it."

"But look at what's happened in the East, to the grain, the fish, the trees? My father's disappeared."

K'an waved his hands in the air, and his face reddened. "Some say Ching is a false god, to punish his people this way. Some say there will be a new god to take his place – a real god that wouldn't get tricked by a pair of ordinary demons!"

"Narissa and Nikolas are not ordinary demons," Ming said. "They have the power of the gods in them. They could destroy the Balance. I must find Ching – not only to restore the cycles in the East, but for the Balance of all the Four."

"I don't waste my time worrying about the red, black and white. I just want the grain to grow! And you still have not told me why you are here, in my house."

"We are going to Zching city, to seek Ching there. We beg protection, for just one night."

Chen approached the table, his head very low. "Pardon me, Uncle, I am only the son of your younger brother and know nothing of value..."

"Yes, yes," K'an said.

"...but if a person were to help the daughter of a god, wouldn't that person be well rewarded for their trouble, when Ching comes back?"

"A reward, eh? How much will Ching give? The guards will give me 50 cash for them."

"No!" Yolanda said.

Ming spoke quickly. "I cannot speak for my father, but it is said that he makes the grain grow."

"He could double the Chua harvest for 50 years!" Chen said.

K'an frowned. "It's a gamble."

"You love to gamble, Husband!"

"Hmmmm. Chen may be right, for the first time in his worthless young life. They may stay, for one night. When the morning light comes, I will drive the cart myself. I'll hitch my four cows next to the oxen."

"But, Uncle –" Chen's face flushed hot.

"Eh?" the old man frowned at him.

"Uncle K'an, it is my duty! To keep them safe, and to help them find Ching."

"This is not a game for children, with armed guards and kuzin at every bend in the road."

"That's why they need a strong young man to protect them." Chen puffed out his puny chest like a bird.

"Ha, ha! Do you dare question me? I will drive them. You, will stay here."

Chen could not completely hide his shame. "Yes, Uncle."

Ming's heart sank. She could not refute her elder directly, but let her voice carry just a hint of irony. "Chen has been very loyal and brave. Will you take us all the way to the borderlands, Chua K'an? It's likely we may be killed or captured."

K'an stood up suddenly. "We'll go by night then, instead, and we'll hide in the day. We leave as soon as the sun sets."

44

*W*hoa, you dumb ox. You'll trample my cows. Whoa, I say!"

Yolanda heard Uncle K'an crack the whip again and again over Ping and Peng and his cows. The cart lurched like a two-headed animal, pulling in opposite directions, so it seemed like they hadn't gotten anywhere. She couldn't sleep and her whole body felt black and blue. It wasn't right for K'an to take over and make Chen go home, after he'd worked so hard to keep them safe. Yolanda gripped her jaw, determined to change things. But how?

When the sun started to rise Uncle K'an stopped the cart. He didn't even help move the sacks. Yolanda glared at him from under her hat while she and Ming rolled the heavy bags over to the side so they could get out. They crouched beside the cart in a grove of yellowing trees on the crest of a gray-brown hill. The banyan trees here were even more dried out than in the grove where she'd met that talking monkey.

"It's stupid to stop up here, where anybody on the road could see us," she whispered to Ming.

Ming frowned. "Excuse me, Uncle K'an, a hundred pardons for asking, but is it wise to hide on the top of a hill?"

"I say this is good, Princess." K'an tied Ping and Peng to a tree. "I'm tired. Nobody's going to bother an old farmer taking a nap. You can hide up in those trees. If you can climb, that is."

"She's a heck of a lot stronger than you," Yolanda muttered.

K'an sat down against a gnarled trunk and pulled an old straw hat down over his eyes.

Ming climbed halfway up a tree on the other side of the grove and scowled. "I'll keep a look out for a while."

Yolanda found a sturdy branch near her and watched the daylight spill pink and yellow over the plains for a long while.

She dozed until noon or later. It was good to hang around up there with Ming, almost like in her climbing tree back home, except it was hard not to think about Uncle K'an, the guards, the ku-zin. And Yakos, fighting a war.

"How long does it take to get to the West?" she whispered.

Before Ming could answer they heard a roar like thunder in the distance. A big cloud rolled along the horizon, but it wasn't rain. Yolanda leaned out to see better. "Somebody's coming!"

A long line of horses rode fast up the dusty road, stopped at a fork, and then took the way that led to the hill and the grove.

"Uncle K'an!" Yolanda said as she and Ming scampered down.

"Wake up! It's the guard! Coming this way!" Ming added.

"Ai-ee-ya!" Uncle K'an jumped up and ran around like a headless chicken, just like when Mama butchered the hens. He got his foot all tangled up in Ping and Peng's harness, and then it was too late to get away.

Yolanda and Ming scrambled back up to the highest branches that still had a few broad leaves and peered down as the horses came to a stop just outside the grove, snorting.

The guard leader walked stiffly to the tree where K'an pretended to sleep. "Kowtow, you lazy old beggar! Don't you know the law?" He sounded just like the one back at Chen's village.

K'an dropped to the ground and put his face in the dirt. "Please...have pity on a poor farmer!"

"Quiet! What is this worthless hunk of junk? An ox-cart with cows?"

"Y-yes, sir. It's mine."

"No longer. Tie 'em up."

"No!" K'an wailed.

"My ears must be filled with dirt. What did you say, old man?" The leader pulled his sword from his belt.

"No, – ah – what I mean to say is, please, we will starve without the cows and ox-cart! Listen. My wife and I have many children. I'll give you my strongest boy for your personal bond servant. I beg you. Take him instead of the cart!"

The leader's laughter echoed through the grove. "You are a man of honor, to trade a son for a broken-down cart and a few half-dead animals!"

"I've got two young girls, if that's your pleasure."

Yolanda's heart almost stopped beating. Does he mean us?

"We do like the young ladies, don't we, men?"

The guards hooted and hollered.

"But we don't want any horse-lipped, radish-leg daughters of yours!" The guard leader walked toward K'an with jerky steps. "We want two princesses, lost on a pleasure-outing several days ago. Have you seen them, old man?"

"No, but –"

Yolanda's breath caught in her chest.

"But what? Speak or I'll cut out your miserable throat!"

"I'll help you look if you let me keep my cart and cows. I'll hunt high and low for them, Master, I will!"

The commander pointed to the cart. "Search it."

The guards split the bags open. Grain spilled onto the dust. "Master! Some are stuffed with hay," one shouted.

"Hey, farmer," the leader laughed. "That's a good trick, selling the city folk hay for millet. You are my kind of man."

K'an bowed so his forehead touched his knees. "Thank you."

"Lieutenant. We found three bags with food, water and clothes."

"Three bags? For one farmer?"

"I – I am visiting my poor sister and brother on the way to the city. There is nothing to eat in Sambah-la."

"Or water? Or clothes? Whose bags are these?!" He flashed his sword near K'an's neck.

"Well, since you force me to tell you, I'm an old man, can't hold my water anymore. Sometimes I mess my clothes, have to carry fresh ones. Have to drink all the time. Look in my throat. It's dry as a desert!" K'an opened his jaw wide.

The guard brought the tip of the sword right up under K'an's chin. Yolanda saw Ming grip the tree like a cat ready to pounce, when a huge blast rocked the hill like an earthquake.

45

Chen crouched in the dirt at the edge of a deep grotto, not half a mile from the hill where Uncle K'an had foolishly stopped his family's ox-cart. He'd followed all night on foot. Uncle K'an would flay him when he found out; still, it was more important to keep the princesses safe. It had been easy to keep up, since the dumb cows were so slow. They were not fit to share a yoke with Ping and Peng! They'd barely made it out of K'o province.

When Chen saw the guard's horses on the road only a few miles behind, he hatched a plan to divert them. He'd run to the quarry, taken off all of his clothes, stuffed them with dried leaves and threw the bundle into the deep pit.

Now he leaned his bare shoulder against a giant rock that sat near the edge of the grotto. "Please, oh great spirit of stone, I have a favor to ask of you. If you would kindly roll off the edge of this cliff, then I can save two princesses from disaster."

The boulder was a lot heavier than Chen guessed. He leaned against it and pushed, praying that the spirit inside had heard him. "Please, I beg you, roll! Just a tiny bit, you're so close."

He had a way with most spirits, even rock spirits, which were known to be the hardest to communicate with. Time to try another way. "I know your brothers in the cave near K'o," he said. I'll tell them of your greatness, your sparkling granite, your solid round shape, your perfect command over the quarry."

Nothing. Not even a twitch. Maybe the fisherman was right. All the spirits are gone. It's useless to try.

"All right then, great boulder, if you will give me this one small request, I will make a promise to all the rock spirits. I will kiss one of your kind every day, for the rest of my lifetime!"

The stone didn't budge.

"Please?"

46

$\mathcal{T}$he spirit that was Becca soared high above the lands of the K'o province, floating with the other spirits: sky, river, birds, grain, fish, turtles, ferns.

So many. Usually not so many here.

Then, something pulled her to the world below.

The girl. Yolanda. Below.

Fear clutched at her heart.

A road. Horses.

Far, but not too far.

Clouds of dust, hooves.

Another thing, pulling.

A boy, praying.

A rock spirit. Asleep for a thousand years.

Spirit so deep, so slow, barely hearing.

The boy, frantic. Praying.

Please.

Why?

Not clear. Something to do with the girl.

Becca drifted down to probe the spirit,

spirit touching spirit.

Light touch. Wind on water.

Wake up wake up wake up

47

*C*hen leaned his bare chest and arms against the stone and heaved again and again until he couldn't push any harder. He'd about given up when he felt the giant rock groan under him and roll the tiniest bit.

"You are alive! Ka-sha! Show me how mighty you are!"

Chen put his back to the rock, and pushed with every muscle in his body. It moved a hand's width, then more, and then a bit more. The boulder lurched forward and gathered speed until it crashed over the edge, taking many of its brothers along for the ride. When it hit bottom, it shook the canyon like a real quake, and made a huge roar, louder than dragon thunder.

That will bring them! Chen leapt for joy. "Thank you, o great one. I praise the Four gods and all the rock family!"

When the dust settled, he picked up the first rock he saw and kissed it. Then he looked down into the quarry. From that height the fake body he'd tossed in actually looked real, and the bright red handkerchief he'd tied on looked enough like blood.

Those guards will want to take a look at that; you can't keep them away from a dead body.

Chen crouched behind a row of brambles that scratched his skin and waited for the guard. Just as he'd hoped, they rode up the other side of the quarry, paused at the edge to point and shout, and started down the steep quarry walls.

Ka-shaa! The trick worked.

Chen took off running down the road to the hill. He'd get the princesses safely away in the cart before the guard could climb back out of the quarry and catch up with them.

Uncle K'an'll be hotter than a boiling teapot. And me with a bare backside! Ach!

That was the only flaw in his perfect plan. How could he face the princesses this way, as naked as the day he was born?

All his hopes of glory and of taking his honor back from Uncle K'an vanished. He pictured coming into their camp without a scrap of decency to cover himself. Miss Ming would have the good manners to hide her smile behind her hands, but Miss Yolanda would probably laugh at him, her round eyes wide.

Wahhhh! Chen's face burned with shame. This punishment was far worse than a whipping.

As he sprinted the last bit up the hill and into the banyan grove, he was tempted to run back, but he must carry out the plan, to save them. Then he saw Uncle K'an slumped against a tree, as pale as a shroud, his hand over his heart. Chen forgot his nakedness and ran to him. He knelt to gently shake K'an's shoulder. "Uncle! Wake up! Are you all right?"

K'an's eyes flickered, and then closed again as his head rolled to the side. Chen listened to his heartbeat. Weak, but alive.

Miss Yolanda suddenly stood up from behind the cart. "Chen! Thank goodness you're here. We're leaving. The guards came. But K'an, he's – not –. What happened to your clothes?"

She didn't laugh or smile. Her brow was frowned with worry.

Miss Ming stepped out from behind a tree with the food bags. She looked down when she saw Chen. He felt his skin flush hot from his forehead to his toes and wished a hole would appear so he could fall into it. Then he spotted Uncle's K'an's quilted silk jacket on the ground, and tied it around his own waist.

When he lifted Uncle K'an into his arms, princess Ming ran to pick up the old man's feet. Miss Yolanda spread hay in the cart for Uncle K'an. He moaned a little when they set him down, and she lay down next to him. After Miss Ming helped Chen pile the bags over Yolanda and Uncle, she jumped into the driver's seat and lowered her farmer's hat over her eyes.

"I'll ride with you, Chua Chen, if you put those clothes on." She pointed to the blue trousers and tunic in the dirt.

Chen hurried to put the clothes on, and then hitched Ping and Peng to the cart. Uncle K'an's cows were too far away to round up, and too slow, besides. Probably food for the ku-zin, now. He murmured a small prayer and smacked the reins. "Ji-yahhh!"

48

$\mathcal{I}$n the back of the bouncing cart, Yolanda watched K'an's face for signs of life. She knew how to take care of sick folks, having watched over Mama for years. Every now and then he gasped for breath, wagging his jaw as if he wanted to say something, but no sound came out.

"It's going to be okay. Just hold tight."

K'an's eyelids flickered. "Mon–a–" He tried to talk again, but the rickety cart was too loud.

"What? Can you say that again?"

"Mo–na–mona–"

It sounded like gibberish. Still, maybe it was his last words. Mama never did say good-bye or anything. Yolanda tried harder to hear Uncle K'an, but his lips opened and closed like a fish with no sound coming out. How to make him talk better?

Something clicked inside, as if the black bird had come back to tell her something. She looked through a crack in the bags to see the sky, but could see no birds flying in all the pale blue.

Instead of making him talk better, I've got to listen better. Not with my ears. With the vision.

Yolanda remembered how to relax her eyes and let the vision open up. At first it was only a trickle, but then she saw K'an's body begin to pulse and glow with a faint yellow light.

She let herself sink down into the feeling, to let the vision flow stronger until she could see under his skin, to his lungs, stomach, heart. She let the vision go deeper and noticed a strange gap that went right through his heart, like the holes that she'd seen in herself and Ming back at the Palace. It seemed to make his heart work too hard. Yolanda felt bad for him.

Maybe that's why Uncle K'an acts the way he does, always trying to get something, not believing or trusting anybody.

"Mon–a–" K'an's moaned again. "Mon-a-shurry!"

"I hear you, Uncle K'an."

Yolanda opened her vision further to try and understand him. She heard the cart wheels rubbing the axle, flaking tiny bits of metal on to the road. She heard the wind in the distant trees of a nearby mountain. And she heard horse's hooves, pounding on the road behind them.

Yolanda reached up and tugged the reigns until Chen slowed.

"Your uncle keeps saying 'mona-shery...'" she yelled. "And the guards are coming!"

"What?"

"K'an says MON-A-SHER-Y!"

"Ah-ha!" Chen cried. "The monastery! The monastery of Kua-ma will give us sanctuary. Ji-hahhhh!"

49

C hen drove harder as twilight fell. He remembered that the monastery was high on the small mountain to the north. He winced as he cracked the whip again and again, but Ping and Peng had to move faster, and they had to get off the road before the guard caught up. When he saw the shortcut that went straight up the mountain, he pulled the reins sharply and nearly knocked Miss Ming off the seat.

The hill was steep from the start. The oxen panted, sweating, as the climb got even steeper. The road was rutted, too, and filled with deep dust from the long dry spell. Ping and Peng kept pulling, harder than they ever had before. The wooden cart groaned, until he felt it slip backwards and lurch to the left.

Oh no!

Both oxen bayed, a terrible sound.

With the back end sunk deep in a ditch, the cart tilted worse than a sinking ship. Miss Ming jumped down to lift Ping's yoke. He was still standing, but the weight of the whole cart had fallen on Peng.

Even in the dim light of the moon, Chen could see the ugly white bone that stuck out of her front leg, crumpled under her where she fell. The broken edge of the bone stabbed into her chest. A dark stain trickled down the dusty ground.

Peng's eyes searched the sky and trees, frantic, and her skin heaved.

Yolanda slipped out of the back of the cart, and it shifted a bit, but was stable. She stood watching, glistening tears on her cheek. "Oh, Peng –"

Chen bent down to his knees beside Peng's head, to stroke her brow and whisper into her ear.

"I love you, Peng, and you are among the best of all the oxen that have ever lived, even among all the ancestors of all the oxen.

I am to blame. I shouldn't have taken this back road to the monastery. I am a worthless young fool and will never be able to repay the life that was so blessed and is now cut short by my stupidity. You were brave and strong and true and you will be double-blessed in your next lifetime."

Peng heaved one last sighing gasp.

"Go now, sweet Peng, and do not fear."

50

ing bent to Peng's side and bowed her head. "I'm so sorry, Chen… But we must try to get moving again…the guards…"

"They are past us now, but they are looking," Yolanda said.

How in the four worlds can she know these things?

Chen stood up in the moonlight, his cheeks wet with tears. Each of them seemed to know what must be done, as hard as it was. There was a steep ravine beside the road. They all crouched beside poor Peng and gave her a heave downhill, away from the broken yoke and tangled harness. She weighed more than a hundred-stone sack of grain, but together they made enough momentum. Ming said a silent prayer of thanks, and then picked up the wooden yoke.

Thank the Four gods. Though the end was sheared and ragged, it might hold together well enough to pull the cart. Ming knelt under the beam and lifted it squarely onto her own shoulders.

"I'll help," Yolanda said. Ming moved closer to Ping to make room for her. Ping's eyes rolled partway back, and he snorted.

"Peng is gone," Yolanda said. "You are sad and afraid, but you are still strong. Please help us pull the cart out of the ditch so we can get to a safe place."

Chen went to the side to push. "We will all help."

Ming took a deep inhale, the way Ting and Tan had taught her. As the cool breath penetrated every pore of her lungs she felt the power of chi – the life force – coursing through her body, drawing energy from the ground, the sky, and everything in between. Balancing her strength equally on both legs, she waited until Ping's breath – his chi – was aligned with her own, and with Yolanda's and Chen's.

A wave of strength pulsed through her arms, back and legs and into the yoke. Ming released the energy with an outburst that leapt from the deepest center of her being: "Ki-yai!"

The beam thrust forward as if under its own power. The wheels of the cart wobbled out of the rut, as smoothly as water flowing around a rock, and rolled over the hump.

Ming stopped to take another breath.

"Did you take extra vitamins today or what?" Yolanda said.

"What?"

"You sure are strong, Ming."

"But a princess – like an animal –" Chen stammered.

"You are brave, Chua Chen, but you need my help. I mean, our help." She looked over at Yolanda, smiling.

"All right." Ming took another deep breath. "Push, now!"

Slowly, steadily, through the darkness of the forest they climbed toward the top of the hill, resting only a little as they went. Pearls of sweat flew from Ping's neck and onto Ming's shoulders as the cart slowly creaked up the trail.

Near dawn, as they inched slowly forward, the sound of a gong reverberated down through the trees.

"What's that?" Yolanda asked.

"The monastery bell. We're close," Chen said.

Before long they came to a stone wall about six feet tall with a weathered wooden door.

"Thank the Four gods," Ming said, and they all put down the yoke.

Chen went to the door, hesitated, and then knocked politely. No one came. K'an moaned from the back of the cart.

"He's getting weaker," Yolanda said. "We've got to get him inside! Knock a little harder."

"We must wait."

"But what if they didn't hear you? Maybe they're asleep."

"We must wait until the next temple bell rings," Chen's voice was firm.

"But how long will that be!" Yolanda sounded more tired than they all felt.

"Remember the gong we heard?" Ming said. "Monks live each day by the time of bells. At dawn they sit morning meditation. We must respect their way, and wait until their meditation ends."

"The way again! What's meditation? What if the guards come up here? I'd rather stay alive than be polite!"

Yolanda walked to the door with a frown. Chen stepped aside, his face very red. Just as she lifted her fist to knock, a second bell rang. Thank heaven.

Chen came forward to knock again.

A shaven monk's head appeared at the door. "Who comes to the Temple of Kua-ma?"

Chen bowed. "Four travelers, one hurt."

The monk looked past Yolanda and Ming to see K'an lying in the cart. "You and the old man may come inside, but females are not allowed."

"Please! We can't leave them out here —"

"So sorry. Temple rules."

The door slammed shut.

51

*C*hen paced around the cart as the sun slowly rose behind the trees. Uncle K'an's moans grew weaker each minute that passed. He needed help, soon. And the guard could be climbing the mountain now. No time to find another hiding spot.

Miss Yolanda comforted K'an, then gave Chen a stare. Her green eyes seemed to say, "do something now."

Honorable uncle is tyrant and a fool, and he's a boil on the neck of our family, but I would rather offend the temple of Kuama than allow him to die in the back of an ox-cart.

Chen unhitched Ping and led him to the wall. "Stay strong and quiet. We will climb on you to get over this wall."

He clambered onto the oxen's bony back and up to the stone ledge, then called down to Miss Yolanda. "Take my hand. I'll pull you up, then Miss Ming, and then I will carry Uncle over."

"I can do it myself," Yolanda said.

"I will lift you. Much better. No trouble for me."

Chen pulled her arms. Miss Yolanda weighed a lot more than a bag of millet. Although his arms shook like red bean jelly, he hefted her over the top of the wall and she jumped down.

When he turned back, Miss Ming had already brought Uncle K'an to Ping's back. She hoisted him up to Chen, and then leapt up herself. Together they lifted his weight over and down to the other side. Thank the Four gods he was so skinny now.

"That tree looks big enough to hide us," Yolanda pointed to a tall pine tree with thick boughs that spread wide to the ground like a tunic. Once they'd carried K'an inside, she pushed together a bed of pine needles for him, and gave him some of her water. She treated him as well as Aunt Mai did.

"We can't leave Ping and the cart by the temple gate," Miss Ming said. "If the guards come, they'll know we're here."

"I was, eh, planning to hide them, don't worry." Chen hated to leave the princesses alone, even for a minute, but climbed over the wall to the outside. He led Ping into the woods, hid the cart under some branches and gave him some of their precious millet and water. Ping's eyes roamed, searching for something.

"You miss Peng, eh? I do too. I'll be back soon."

The third gong sounded. As he scrambled back over the wall with the food bundles, he saw a bald monk with a large mole on his cheek slip under the boughs of the big pine tree.

Chen flushed with excitement. He crouched under the branches, edging in slowly, ready to fight him if necessary. He saw the monk and sprang up to face him, but instead of making a bold impression, he cracked his head on a branch.

"I beg your pardon, Master Monk," he said, rubbing his skull as he bowed.

The monk bowed to Chen. His smile was bigger than his mole, thank the Four gods. "Not to worry, my son. I like surprises, and puzzles, too. Why does a young man and two young ladies, one a foreigner, crouch under a pine tree with a sick man?"

"We're hiding," Miss Yolanda said.

Chen gulped. Why did the green-eyed princess speak so boldly?

"Hiding? From whom?" the monk asked.

"The palace guard, the ku-zin – you name it, everybody's after us. Even the monks don't want us here. Do you?" she said.

"That depends." The monk's eyes sparkled. "Who are you?"

"I'm Yolanda. One of the two lost princesses from the Palace of the Ten Thousand Things. Haven't you heard of us?"

Miss Yolanda's talk made Chen's face burn. He could see Miss Ming tense, too. "What Miss Yolanda means to say is –"

"No, I've not heard of lost princesses. We don't get much news from the world of dust. Ho is my name, a monk in the service of Kua-ma. You must be the other lost princess," he bowed to Ming.

Unlike the round-eye one who simply bent forward, Miss Ming bowed gracefully, in the way of a princess, daughter of a god. "I am Ming."

"And you?" The monk nodded in Chen's direction.

Chen stood as tall as he could under the pine boughs. "My name is Chua Chen, and this is my uncle, Chua K'an. He needs help, but the monk at the gate –"

"Did not let you in. No females allowed. Monastery rules."

Chen's heart fell. Now they'd all be thrown out.

"But Uncle K'an's heart is bad, and the Palace guard will take us back if they find us, maybe even kill us. Please don't let them – please!" Miss Yolanda said.

Her terrible manners – the way she looked right at the monk and spoke so directly – would only make things worse.

"Don't worry. Though I am just a gardener here at the temple of Kua-ma, I will see what can be done for you. Come."

52

*Y*olanda stayed close to the gardener as he led them down a stone path overgrown with moss, evergreen boughs and ferns. A sweet smoke drifted through the morning fog: jasmine flower incense. Even without any birds or bugs in the greenery, the monastery seemed to have more life than the dry fields below.

Ho came to a tall building with thick timbers and a grass roof. He kicked off his sandals and rinsed both feet in a shallow tub of water near the entry. He bowed deeply before bending under a purple cloth that hung for a door. Yolanda and the others followed him, leaving their sandals in a row outside.

The large room had a shiny wood floor and at first glance seemed empty, except for the many purple cushions that lined the walls. Half in shadow against the back, there was a huge wooden statue of a woman sitting on a platform.

"She's beautiful," Yolanda murmured. In her mind she knew she was Kua-ma, the one the temple was named after.

A single stream of morning light poured through a hole in the roof to light her face. With her half-closed eyes, moon-shaped face and perfectly carved nose and lips, she looked like an angel of the East. One giant leg was bent underneath her and the other barely touched the floor. Candles and incense flickered in small jars on her platform.

Ho knelt to the floor and laid his forehead on the ground in front of the great wooden lady. Yolanda did the same, bowing as low and as long as she could.

Chen and Ming laid Uncle K'an down in front of Kua-ma, then kowtowed to her, too. The old man's skin was pale whitish gray and his breathing was very slow, but Yolanda wasn't as worried about him. She didn't care that the guards still chased them, or that she might not ever find her way back home.

Somehow the peace and quiet in Kua-ma's temple made her feel as if all the problems in the world would take care of themselves, sooner or later.

"Kua-ma knows this man's fate, so he will remain. You two ladies shouldn't be here. The head abbot won't like it. All of you, please follow me."

Though she hated to leave the temple, Yolanda bowed good-bye to Kua-ma, then followed Ho and the others through a side door.

The monk hurried down a narrow path between a row of small bamboo huts. He rounded the last hut into a tiny yard with a low stone wall. A thick patch of bamboo shaded the ground covered with moss and smooth stones. Motioning for them to stay outside, Ho bent low under an arched door into the hut. He came back out with four purple pillows and put them carefully on the stones.

"Please, sit. The monks are all at morning meal, so you are safe here. I'll get whatever food is left and bring it for you."

"You are very kind," Ming said, bowing.

Nobody said a word or even looked at each other until Ho came back carrying a tray with millet cakes, bowls of hot tea and broth with dried radishes on top. The food tasted so good. Although they hadn't eaten since K'o, they sipped and chewed as slow as Sunday.

"Thank you once for your kindness, and twice for this food." Ming bowed again. "But I must warn you. The palace guard may come here to look for us."

"Hmmph. Palace guard should look after the Palace. You don't look like dangerous thieves to me."

"We're not!" Yolanda said. "We escaped."

Ho frowned as she told him about Narissa and Nikolas, and Ming told the part about Ching's disappearance from the East.

"I am only a gardener. But I have lately wondered why spring is so long upon the hill. Without change of season, there can be no dying back. Without dying, there can be nothing new. Ching can put the cycles right again. You must find him."

"We may not get far," Ming said. "There is a huge reward for our capture. Innocent people have already been hurt. One of our oxen died on the way here, and Chua K'an is so ill."

The gardener sat quietly, his palms on his knees. "You may stay here, in my hut, until your uncle is better. But the abbot is very strict. Everyone – the men – must contribute. Chua Chen, you will shave your head and work alongside the monks. And the young ladies will stay out of sight. Do you agree?"

Everyone nodded, and Ho led them all into his hut. It was smaller than Mama's chicken shed, with only a bedroll and a wooden box with a candle, a jug of water and a bowl on top. Ho carefully moved the items to the floor, took a roll of cloth out of the box, unwrapped it and handed a long razor to Chen.

"Please, shave your entire head. I'll fetch robes from the wash-house." Ho bowed slightly and left the hut.

"I can help," Ming said. "I've done it before."

Chen frowned but gave her the razor. Ming poured water from the jug into the bowl. She scraped his scalp with short strokes, dipping the blade in the water each time to get rid of the hair.

"Doesn't that hurt?" Yolanda asked.

"Of course not," Chen said.

His scalp wasn't totally round. Yolanda was surprised to see a couple of bumps and valleys that were hidden when he had hair. His naked head reminded her of something. "Chen, whatever happened to your clothes, back at the grove?"

Chen's scalp turned red and his jaw muscles clenched, but then he told them how he'd bundled his clothes and threw them into the quarry to look like a dead body. "I pushed a boulder over the edge, to make a big boom that would tempt the guards down into the quarry, and get them away from you. The rock spirit wouldn't budge at first, but I begged and pleaded, and finally it rolled in."

Sometimes the East seemed pretty much like home, and other times it was totally crazy. "You asked the rock to move, and it did?" Yolanda asked.

"Spirits will sometimes help us if we ask the right way. That boulder made a huge crash when it fell in!" Chen's face lit up like fireworks, and then he frowned. "I did not think of Uncle, how jumpy he is. I never thought a loud noise could scare so much, or hurt his heart. I am a worthless excuse for a nephew."

"No blame," Ming said. "If it wasn't for you, and the rock spirit, we might all be dead."

"And besides, it wasn't your fault," Yolanda added. "He's got a weak spot through his heart."

"How do you know?" Chen asked.

Before Yolanda thought of a simple way to explain, Ho came back carrying a stack of bright yellow robes.

Chen put on his robe, and then bowed to the gardener, hands in prayer. "Thank you. I am now a monk in K'ua-ma's service. Before I start work, may I tend to Ping, my ox? He's outside the wall."

"Bring the ox and the cart to the shed behind the temple. If anyone asks, bow and say my name." Ho nodded to Chen, then to Ming and Yolanda. "Do not leave the hut until the fifth bell. After that, you may go out, but only in my courtyard."

Yolanda and Ming bowed in agreement, and they left.

As Ming began to put away the blade and bowl, an idea came into Yolanda's head. "Hey! What if we were monks, too?"

Ming stared at her as if she was nuts.

"Never mind. It's a stupid idea. I should keep my fool mouth shut."

"It's not a bad idea. It's only your eyes," she said. "Wrong color, wrong shape."

"But I could wear Mai's hat, keep it low, and keep my head down. I wouldn't look at anybody, no matter what." Yolanda felt a tingle of excitement. "Think about it. We could ride in the cart, instead of hiding under those rotten bags."

"If you were very, very careful, we might get past the guards," Ming nodded slowly. "The ku-zin would never bother us — monks have nothing to steal. And there is a tradition, to give them food and shelter. But shaving your head like a monk is a big step. It would be as if we are taking a vow of honor, to live and behave as a monk. Can you do that? And lose all your hair?"

Yolanda picked up the razor. "I never liked it. 'So red, it runs right over you like a freight train.' That's what Mama used to say. Go ahead and shave it off. Then I'll do yours."

As Ming scraped her head, the blade tickled and the water dripped cold down her neck. Yolanda reached up to feel her naked scalp – so fuzzy! When it was Ming's turn, she first cut off her long braid at the nape of her neck, tied off the end and tucked it into her bundle, to keep it. Then Yolanda slid the blade against her scalp, careful to tilt it just right, so her hair fell off in rows.

I've never touched anyone like this. Feels nice.

As she dipped the blade into the water, it began to swirl with the tiny hair cuttings floating on top.

Yakos! Not now...

She looked away, and concentrated on scraping the last bits of black hair from Ming's head. After it was done they both put the monk's robes over their peasant tunic and trousers.

"Ming, you actually look good like a monk! Being bald makes your face stand out even more. Your head is so round and smooth."

Ming blushed, and the fifth gong sounded. "I would go outside for t'ai chi practice. Would you join me?" Ming asked.

"I'll clean up first. You go ahead."

Yolanda was glad to be alone with the bowl of water. Maybe she could contact Yakos when she wanted to, not just by accident. She scooped up the cuttings to take outside later. Her hair looked pretty all mixed up together with Ming's, maple red and midnight black. She gathered a few locks and rolled them up into a bit of cloth in her bundle. Then she sat cross-legged on the floor and looked into the bowl. When she saw a bald girl staring up at herself, she almost dropped it.

God in heaven, I look like an alien!

The water swirled, and it looked as if her hair was growing back, but short, with stiff curls. Yolanda's heart beat faster and her palms sweat, the way they always did when she saw him.

"Yolanda? Is that you?" he said.

"'Course it's me. Just a bit different." she laughed.

"Where are you? Are you all right?"

"I'm okay. Except one of our oxen died, poor thing! The guards almost got us, too, but we got away to a safe place. We're resting here for a bit, but we'll be heading to the West soon. I can't wait to see you!"

Yakos was quiet.

I said the wrong thing. Again.

Finally he said, "It's not wise for you to come here now. The battle here is – it's very risky – and I cannot be distracted."

"Distracted? If you didn't want to be distracted, why did you even call me here then!"

"I don't have time to explain everything to you now! Trust me, it's important. Very important. Not just for me, but for both of us. For all of us."

"'Important.' Why does everything around here always have to be so damn important! Well, so am I! I'm –"

The water swirled, and he was gone. "Wait...Please!"

Yolanda clenched her jaw. "Okay, fine. Go away. Just like you always do. Just like everybody does. I don't need you! I don't need anybody."

53

*W*hen Ming walked out to the courtyard for t'ai chi, the wind felt cold on her newly bare scalp. She soon found that she felt lighter, more free, without her hair, and moved like water through the first sequence. Focus on breath, body and the movements. Not on the guards, Ching, K'an, Yolanda's brother.

She thought she heard Yolanda talking to someone in Ho's hut, and then she came outside, looking like a monk in her saffron robes. She tossed the water and hair cuttings under some bushes with an angry frown on her face.

Yolanda was generally very positive minded. What was wrong?

"I don't see how you can feel like dancing – or exercising, whatever that is," Yolanda said.

"T'ai chi actually gives me energy. Would you like to try?"

"Tie-what?" Yolanda asked.

"T'ai chi is a martial art – a fighting style that teaches us to feel and work with our chi."

"Chi. Is that energy?" Yolanda asked.

"Yes. It's the life force that's everywhere, in every thing." Ming gently moved into the next posture.

"I could never do that. I'm about a graceful as an ox."

"Yes, you could. Come."

Yolanda shrugged and stood beside Ming. "What do I do?"

Ming showed her to balance both feet on the ground, then to slowly stretch her arms out and then up to the sky. Next, both arms spread downward and out to align with the shoulders.

"Keep your knees gently bent and your eyes focused straight ahead. Take a gentle, long breath as you begin each motion. The chi will flow from where your feet meet the ground, up through the center of your body, and out to your fingers, like this –"

Ming shifted her weight from one foot to the other. She moved slowly through the set of simple postures so Yolanda could follow. Yolanda got frustrated when one arm went the opposite way as Ming's, and went to sit on a low wall. "I can't do it."

"You did very well!' Ming said. "Could you feel the chi?"

"I guess so," she said.

Ming continued the sequence. "You can practice t'ai chi for a lifetime and never master it completely. I'm still a beginner. My teachers, Ting and Tan, have trained me since I came to Tessar."

"Do your teachers know how to get back, to our world?"

"Probably. They are full of knowledge."

"Well, I might want to go back." Yolanda kicked a small stone into the garden. "Yakos doesn't want me to go to the West."

Ah. So that was the reason for Yolanda's bad temper. Ming brought her movements to a close. "How do you know?"

"I can see him. In reflections. The same way I could see the webs and everything. So, I just talked to him, in the hut."

Ming sat next to Yolanda. "What did he say to you?"

"He's in a war. Says it's too dangerous for me to go there."

Ming took in a sharp breath. A war in the Red lands? What was he doing there? A shot of fire coursed through her heart. "I must – there's something I should tell you about your brother."

"What is it?" Yolanda looked at her with the same piercing green eyes as his. She seemed desperate for any knowledge about him.

"When I first came to the Palace, I saw someone with Nikolas and Narissa. He looked like you, green hair, red eyes."

"Really? What did he do?"

"He did nothing to me." Ming could not bring herself to say more. She did not know more; she had only a fear about what he had done or what he could do. Nothing worth speaking about.

"Well, that's good." Yolanda's face relaxed. "I wanted to find him so bad, but now, I'm not sure. Seems like it would be good to figure out how to get back."

"Ting and Tan will help you. If not, perhaps my father —" Ming bowed her head.

"Don't worry. You'll find him." Yolanda smiled.

"I've waited so long to meet him. Ting and Tan said it was time for my father to continue my training. That's why Jade and I went to the Palace, but Ching was not there."

Yolanda stared. "You mean you've never even MET him?"

"No."

"But you said — he's a god and all."

"I am his daughter. I've just never seen him."

"How do you know that he's your father?" Yolanda looked away over the wall. "Never mind. You don't have to prove anything to me. I was just — upset."

Ming wanted to help her feel better, to let her know that she did not keep anything back intentionally. But she was so used to being strong. And silent.

One of Tan's teachings came into her mind: 'Grace is half of your strength. When it comes to people, bend like the willow.' Easy to say, but hard to do. Ming took a deep breath.

"I should have told you about my father before, but I didn't know —" Ming took another breath. "Back at the Palace, I was a prisoner. You saved me, Yolanda. That makes you my — a trusted friend."

The sixth bell rang.

Yolanda stood up fast, as if she'd like to run away.

54

*Y*olanda's legs felt jumpy. She paced around the courtyard and tried to make sense out of things. She finally got it through her head that Yakos didn't really care that much, and then Ming reminded her that she didn't even have a father. Or anybody else.

She wanted to believe the part about being Ming's friend, but it came hard. Nobody had ever wanted to be friends with her. Ming sat on the wall and looked down at her hands. They were trembling a little. Yolanda sat down next to her.

"Hey, Ming. Thanks. I want to be your friend, too."

Ming didn't smile that much, so Yolanda didn't even know that she had dimples until she grinned, very wide, just as Ho came back into the courtyard.

He stepped back in shock. "What's this? Two new monks?"

"It's only us, Yolanda and Ming," Yolanda said.

"Females, shaving their heads to impersonate monks of this temple? The head abbot would be very upset to hear of this. I can only hope that it is not an offense to Kua-ma."

Ming's smile melted and her face burned red.

"Oh, I'm sorry! I didn't think of that! We figured it would be a good disguise, keep us safer from the guards," Yolanda bowed.

"Very well. Since you are monks now, it soon will be time for meditation. Much better to sit together, here, in the courtyard."

"Umm, what is meditation? What do you do?"

"Meditation is not about doing, it is about being. It is a quiet time when we simply sit and breathe and let our chi flow."

Yolanda was tempted to laugh, but Ming looked serious as Ho laid three purple pillows on the courtyard and beckoned them to come and sit with him, cross-legged.

"Anyone can sit on a pillow, but very few can quiet their minds," he said. "Shhh. Can you hear it?"

"Umm, hear what?"

"The chatter in your head. It never goes away, does it? Try, now. Close your eyes and clear your mind of all thoughts."

Yolanda closed her eyes, but it wasn't quiet in there. She couldn't stop thinking about Yakos, and about Ming and how they made Ho mad and what would happen.

Clear your mind, darnit!

clear your mind, ha! might as well clear the table!

mama just leave me alone, I'm supposed to be calm, does ming really like me? yakos is such a rotten brother I hate him I'm sick of all this running, what if they catch us, I can't stop my brain from talking, when do I go home?

"Wow," Yolanda let her eyes open. "I can't do it."

"The secret is the breath. As each breath enters and leaves your body, let the thoughts flow through your mind, drifting like clouds in a peaceful sky. Soon you may hear only the flow of chi inside you."

ha! breathing in and out. now that's special, ain't it?

I'm ignoring you, Mama. And I'm gonna do this.

Ming and Ho closed their eyes and put their hands, palms-out, on top of their knees. Breathing. Ok. Yolanda closed her eyes and took a breath. Keep going. No thoughts, only breath.

my scalp is naked, the wind feels weird, what if the head abbot comes, what if they find out I'm a girl, what if the guards come and the ku-zin too, that's not a bunch we want to run into again, how is uncle k'an doing? what a jerk, he's so mean to chen but it's not his fault, it's only his heart

Back to the breathing, darnit!

In, out, in and out: Yolanda concentrated on each breath, just like Ho said. It was so simple, but somehow it was so hard. Her brain was such a motor mouth. Shut up!

When she finally stopped trying to stop thinking, and just let her thoughts float past as if they didn't matter, her brain calmed down and there was space between them. She started to feel tingly inside, more alive. Maybe it was all that breathing, making her dizzy, but with each breath she felt it pulsing, not just inside her but all around, too. Got to be that chi stuff.

She wasn't thinking anymore; she was sensing. It grew stronger, like at the Palace when her vision first opened. Although her eyes were closed she could sense many things around her. Everything glowed with its own shape: Ming, Ho, and other monks that meditated on their cushions in nearby huts. She could feel their chi, even at a distance.

The circle of what she sensed with her vision and chi kept getting wider and wider, like ripples on water, until she became aware of all the living things all over the monastery grounds. Even the trees and plants shimmered and pulsed with chi. But the really big waves of chi came from the temple. With her vision she reached out toward it, like a new shoot growing toward the sun. It was like she was actually there.

In her mind's eye, Yolanda saw the beautiful statue of Kua-ma. A hundred bald men sat in front of her, cross-legged, palms on their knees, eyes closed. Though from the outside it looked like they weren't doing anything, an electric charge pulsed between them, like invisible threads of lightening. Everybody was connected to everybody else. At the same time she heard a strange song or a vibration in her inner ear. It grew louder, so loud she thought the temple roof might blow sky high. Was it their chi?

I can hear it! she felt like shouting. Then she heard horses' hooves, thundering up the hill. She wanted to stand up and scream, to warn everyone, but another part of her said to wait, and listen. The power of the chi was stronger.

She took another breath.

Yolanda waited and listened, even when she heard angry shouts and the clang of metal at the gate. She heard a big booming thump, as if a huge door – the main door – had hit the ground. Her palms got clammy. She tried to breathe and clear her head, but couldn't stop her brain from racing again.

stop it just breathe don't let it end, it's nothing just ignore it stop! it's the guards can't let them get us!

She peeked out of the corner of her eye. Ming and Ho sat as peacefully as before.

Then she heard shouts of victory and heavy footsteps on the path. Didn't Ming and Ho hear them, too? It was driving her crazy. She just couldn't sit there for one more second.

"The guards are here!" she cried, opening her eyes. "Shouldn't we run, or hide, or do something?"

"We will wait," Ho said. He did not even open his eyes.

wait for what? to get slaughtered?

55

*A*ngry voices broke the peace on the top of the hill. Kua-ma sensed the disturbance at the monastery gate, even through the depths of her thousand-year meditation. Through closed, wooden eyes her spirit watched the band of soldiers knock down the gate and rush into the sacred gardens.

Who are these people? Clearly they have not come to follow the Way.

The chi was very great in the temple hall at that moment, or she would not have been able to calm the hundred and one monks who joined her in meditation. Her mind was linked with theirs in a bond that the soldiers could not break. One mind.

"Wait," she said to her devotees, not with words, but in the way the wind speaks to the pines. The monks continued to sit on their cushions when the soldiers burst into the temple, swaggering like stiff toys.

Something is terribly wrong with these men. Do they not know they are in the presence of a deity?

"Hey!" one of them, the leader, shouted. "Wake up! Are all you monks made of wood, like the big lady here?"

"Wait," Kua-ma whispered to the minds of her devotees.

The monks did not so much as open their eyes as the soldiers slashed the silk temple banners with their swords. They did not waver when the guards kicked over the bronze incense burners, scattering smoking lumps of jasmine. They did not rise up when they grabbed precious offerings from the altar to stuff their pockets, or when one tossed a small clay turtle to another, and missed. The effigy fell and broke into a hundred pieces.

The leader stooped beside the sick man who had been placed at Kua-ma's feet to heal, and nudged his ribs with a filthy boot.

"Here's that old farmer! How did he get up here? He knows more than he told us yesterday, I reckon. Get up, old man."

Though Chua K'an's body still lived, his spirit wandered between the physical plane and the next. He could not answer.

The others circled, prodding him with blunt wooden swords. "The lieutenant said to get up! He doesn't care how sick you are." Still, Chua K'an did not move.

"He's dead already." The lieutenant then faced the two young acolytes who sat in deep meditation beside Chua K'an. "Wake up!"

"Wait," Kua-ma whispered to the two boys.

The lieutenant kicked them. The boys did not flinch.

"These monks have been away from the world too long," one jeered. "They don't know a real master when they see one."

"Then let them feel a real sword!" The lieutenant lifted his blade high over the boys' heads, the wide side facing down.

Kua-ma reached out to the acolytes' spirits, to soothe and prepare them for the suffering to come. "Be at one with me, and with the Way," she whispered. "Accept what is."

They did not cry out, even as the leader's sword came down on their heads. They did not falter, though ribbons of crimson, their life's blood, ran down their faces. Then they slumped forward and fell to the stone floor.

Kua-ma was deeply moved by their profound devotion, by their unwavering meditation on the patterns of life and its inevitable partner, death. She vowed to reward them with deep spiritual insight and inner peace in their next lifetimes.

Still, their sacrifice was abhorrent! A deliberate, tragic waste of two precious lives. How could this happen here?

"Stupid monks!" the murderer laughed as he wiped his blade. "Don't even wake up to die."

She looked into his heart, and found only a shriveled nugget of pain, crisscrossed with a black, thorny kind of rope. The rest of the soldiers' hearts were the same. She wondered what manner of unnatural force had done this. What had happened to her people, to cause them to stray so far from the Way?

Regardless of the cause, every action has a consequence, in this lifetime or the next. The killing of two beautiful, innocent boys was beyond cruelty. These guards would experience the consequence for their actions, right now, in the flesh.

Kua-ma's spirit penetrated the fine old wood that embodied her. She extended her knotted wooden knee, the one that had been bent under her body for a millennium, and put her giant wooden foot down on the temple floor. Slowly, slowly, she rose up to stand on her platform. The ancient supports creaked and groaned under her great weight.

"Who comes here to desecrate my temple?" Her voice thundered through the space, surprisingly clear after so many centuries.

The soldiers' eyes opened as big as rice bowls. Every one of them dropped to the floor to kowtow, while the hundred monks sat, silent, waiting.

The lieutenant alone stood, trembling. "Oh Great Mother of mercy, I beg you to hear me. This old man here, this farmer. He lied to us!"

"Who dares to judge any of my devotees?" she said.

"Captain of the Palace Guard, third rank."

"I care nothing for your earthly rank!" Kua-ma took a step down and towered directly over him.

Several guards crawled toward the door, but it slammed in their faces with the force of a gale wind. They mumbled an endless stream of prayers, whimpering and begging for mercy.

"Silence! Your words mean nothing. Your actions have already spoken." Kua-ma's voice took on the edge of a sword. "Though this day comes long before your natural deaths, when all lives are weighed for the balance of good and cruel deeds, today you have been judged."

The men sobbed and prayed. "Spare us, please, we beg you!"

"Do not fear. I will not banish your souls to the place of everlasting waiting, never to be re-born in this, or any other world. Instead, you will receive an earthly reward for your deeds in this life. First, worms will crawl through your bowels, as your victims have been made to crawl on their knees for mercy."

"Aaa-eee-aaa!" they moaned, clutching their bellies.

"Fevers will rage through you, as you have raged against the innocent. You'll be tormented by chills, as your hearts have become frozen to the pain of others. And your minds will be tortured and mad, as you have forgotten the Way and the sanctity of all life."

"No! Please! Have mercy on us!" One by one, the soldiers fell, stricken. They shook and quivered, rolled on the ground and tore out their hair. They called their mothers' names, and filled the temple with their wails of despair.

The lieutenant struggled to draw his sword out of its sheath. He pointed it against his own throat, but it fell away, skittering across the floor.

"Your reward is not so easily avoided," Kua-ma said. "You must live out your full time on this earth."

"But I cannot live with this pain!" he cried. For all his bluster, he was the weakest of all the soldiers.

"Your suffering is a great gift. You now have the chance to learn the secrets of many, many lifetimes. Endure this pain, so you may feel compassion for the pain of others. This is the key to all spiritual understanding. When you feel true empathy for all the creatures that inhabit this world, you will be healed of all that pains you. Go now, and seek your enlightenment."

Once the guards had hobbled out, Kua-ma stepped back one pace and lowered her great wooden body back down to the platform. She smiled upon the two young acolytes, blessing them once more, and then returned to the peace of the spirit world.

56

*A*s Yolanda unfolded her legs and slowly opened her eyes, she noticed a bunch of tiny things that she normally would have missed: a bead of sweat forming on Ming's upper lip; the steady plop-plop of water falling through a bamboo chute onto a mossy stone; the flutter of a single eyelash as the wind blew across Ho's face. Everything vibrated with chi.

She had just witnessed – at a distance - so many amazing and terrible things in the temple, and yet she felt calm. She didn't go crazy when the guards busted in, kicked Uncle K'an, or even when the leader whacked those two young monks on the head. She'd just breathed and took everything as it came, even when the huge wooden statue of Kua-ma came to life.

Ho slowly unfolded his legs and opened his eyes, sad and yet not sad. She barely noticed the big mole on his left cheek now.

"The guards are gone," she said.

"Yes." Ho stood up, bowed and padded toward the temple.

Ming blinked and straightened her back. "I heard the guards, but not anymore. It's strange. Somehow I sense that much has happened, but all is well now. I wonder how Chua K'an is."

At that moment Uncle K'an himself walked into the courtyard, leaning on Chen's shoulder, his face a ruddy shade of tan. "What have you done with my princesses?"

"Chua K'an! You're all right!" Ming smiled.

He peered into her eyes. "Is it you, daughter of Ching?"

"Yes," she bowed. "And Miss Yolanda, too."

"But these rotten monks, they shaved your heads!" he said.

"We did it ourselves," Yolanda said. "It's a disguise, so we could get around better."

"I never thought I'd see this," he snorted. "Never thought I'd see anything again. I thought I was dead! But then that great lady

K'ua Ma stood up! She punished those murdering soldiers. Taught them a lesson!"

"What?" Ming asked.

Chen's eyes burned like fire. "While we sat meditation in the temple, the guards broke in and killed two acolytes. It was terrible! But Kua-ma's spirit stood up, as big as a tree, and sent them crawling away. They'll be in pain forever. Or at least until they learn compassion. In this lifetime, or the next."

"The next lifetime?" Yolanda asked. "You said that to Peng, when she was dying. It was so sweet, but I didn't know what you meant. So, you believe in... what's it called? Re-carnation?"

"Yes, we believe in Reincarnation," Chen said. "Death is not just an ending. It is also the beginning of something. In nature, nothing goes away forever."

Uncle K'an smiled, nodding. He sure seemed different. Nicer.

"Like the millet," Chen continued. "It's born in the spring, grows tall in the summer, is harvested in the fall, and in the winter, it dies. But it always sows new seed. That way the millet always comes back again. Ching's wheel of change —" Chen looked over his shoulder at Ming, who sat very quiet. "Sorry, Miss Ming."

"So if nothing goes away forever, and Peng and those two boys aren't really dead, why were you so sad?" Yolanda asked.

"Because their flesh is gone now, and we'll miss them. But, after a time, their spirits will be reborn into a new body: a person, a god, an animal – or even an insect. A fly, maybe."

"A fly!" Such a thing had never crossed Yolanda's mind.

Ho had come back to the courtyard. "Ah yes, the endless cycle of death and rebirth. You make a good monk, Chua Chen."

"When I was five, I killed a fly in our hut. My ma scolded me, said the fly could have been her in its last lifetime. She taught me not to hurt anything that lives. Not even a fly."

Yolanda smiled to think of Mama as a fly, one that still bugged her. "What if the fly bites you first? Can't you kill it?"

"It is the natural way of the fly to bite. The fly is only doing its best to live, just as we do. All actions have a consequence, in this life or another, so we avoid killing if possible."

"But everybody kills things. I mean, we all kill things, to eat. Even bugs kill things!"

"We can choose to eat only vegetables, as we do at this monastery," Ho said. "We believe we have a greater mind and can rise above violence."

"But, what if guards or bandits try to kill you? Can't you do anything to defend yourself?"

"Don't worry, Miss Yolanda," Chen set his jaw firm and stood a bit taller. "I will protect you."

Yolanda smiled. Chen was a good guy to have around.

Ho put his palms together. "We mourn the passing of the young monks. But today we saw a great miracle: Kua-ma stood and spoke! It has never happened, not in a thousand years since the monastery was built."

"Who is she?" Yolanda asked.

"A spirit, one of the oldest and greatest. She keeps the destiny of all of our souls."

"My destiny took a turn," K'an said. "When Kua-ma stood above me, my heart felt strong as an ox. I knew I would stay here in the monastery and devote the rest of my days to her, if the monks will have an old man like me." He bowed to Ho.

"Any man who has been touched by Kua-ma belongs with her." Ho stood. "Come. There is much to be done. Once you are shaved and robed you can help put the temple in order and prepare for the ceremony." Ho turned to the others. "What will you do now?"

"I am anxious to get to the city," Ming said. "We'll leave tonight."

"With only one ox?" Chen asked. "Ping is strong, but not that strong."

"We have an extra ox in the shed. Take her with you. Her name is Pong."

"Ping and Pong?!" Yolanda giggled. "Thank you, Ho."

"At least those guards won't give us any more trouble," Chen said. "They could barely drag themselves out of the temple."

"No, but there are many more devils like them," K'an added.

"Don't worry about us, Uncle K'an," Ming smiled. "Once you take your vows, you'll have millions of souls to worry about."

"You are right. I've got to meditate on that." K'an made a little bow. "It was an honor to know you. I hope we meet again in this lifetime, or the next."

Ming rose to her feet and bowed deeply to K'an. Yolanda gave his leathery cheek a light peck and whispered in his ear before he left with Ho. "Your heart is getting stronger now. Take care."

"Good-bye, and safe journey to all." Ho bowed.

"Your kindness is beyond measuring," Ming said.

"Thanks for helping us!" Yolanda bowed low beside Chen.

They packed up their bundles and left. Yolanda was careful to lower her hat over her eyes, but it was great to walk out in the open instead of sneaking around. On their way to the monastery gate they passed the temple door, hung with long purple banners. The sweet smell of incense drifted down the path. Yolanda wanted to see Kua-ma one last time. She slipped off her sandals and ducked inside before Chen or Ming could try to talk her out of it.

Once her eyes got used to the smoke and the dim candlelight she saw two long shapes laid out in the middle of the room with purple covers over them. The hundred and one monks – including K'an – sat cross-legged around the poor acolytes, praying. Kua-ma smiled down on them all, her smile so tender and compassionate.

One of the monks stood and walked between the rows of monks, chiming a small brass gong and chanting. Was he the head abbot – the one who was so strict? He sang in a low, vibrating voice, the same words over and over:

no pain, no suffering, no desire
follow the light, the bright light
the spirits will guide you
Kua-ma will lead you
follow the light, the bright rainbow light
that leads to the pure land

The abbot slowly made his way around the two figures. When he turned to face the door, Yolanda gasped. He had a large, unusual mole on his left cheek. She backed into the doorway to slip out, but Ho caught her eye and winked. The head abbot of the monastery of Kua-ma bowed to Yolanda once more, and she bowed back.

57

*I*sn't Lieutenant Sun back yet, Niko?" Narissa curled herself on his favorite chair, and tucked her long legs under the pink kimono. "I wonder what's happened to him. They should be here by now, don't you think?"

Nikolas paced the thickly patterned carpet, his eyebrows furrowed. It was not like him to show so much emotion. "Do you imagine our young trainee has done him in? I think not."

"It's been six days since they ran. Yakos will not be pleased to hear of it. If you are lucky, his anger will be tempered by his victories in the West."

"Victory? How do you know so much?" Niko shot her a glance that would have stung, if she cared what he thought.

"His messenger arrived this morning."

"Why wasn't I told?"

"I got to him first." Narissa flashed a smile. "Yakos is absolutely brilliant. He's convinced all the young warriors to run right off the edge of those famous red cliffs. The goddess of the West must give in to him soon, before all of her tribespeople follow. Imagine, all of them running as fast as gazelles to jump off a cliff. Aren't you proud?"

Nikolas was saved from comment by a knock at the door. "Come in."

A soldier of the blue guard entered and bowed for nearly a full minute.

"What is it?" Nikolas hissed. "Speak."

"It's Lieutenant Sun, Master."

"Where is he?"

"He is – he won't –"

"Speak up, man!"

"Lieutenant Sun is at the gate, sir, but he will not come any closer. He and his men are very sick."

Narissa raised an eyebrow. I knew it. That girl is powerful.

"He's a worm and a weakling. He should come here himself."

"But he – they – cannot walk, Master. They say that their insides burn like fire, that they have never known such pain. All they can do is writhe on the ground and moan."

"Well, man, what happened to them?"

"They found a suspicious cart and followed it to the monastery of Kua-ma. Two young monks were accidentally killed during the interrogation. They say Kua-ma herself punished them for it."

"K'ua ma? Who is she?" Narissa said.

"Never mind that. What about Lt. Sun's orders. Did he find the princesses?"

"I-I don't know any more than that, Master."

"Where exactly is this monastery?"

"In Sung province, Sir. In the hills west of K'o, I believe. Five days' journey east of Harbor City."

"It's your lucky day, Lieutenant – what is your name? No matter. You are now in command of the Palace guard. Your first task is to deliver Lieutenant Sun and his men to the dog pit. Make sure the dogs are hungry. Next, you will find and detain all monks on the road between the monastery and the city."

"Yes, Sir."

Nikolas rustled his maps and pointed to one. "I see there are four gates to enter the city. Make sure all four are impenetrable. If even one monk gets inside, I will hold you responsible. Do you understand?"

The soldier's knees shook, but he bowed and went out.

Narissa followed the poor man into the hall, and smiled over her shoulder at Niko as she delivered the tastiest bit of news. "By the way, Yakos is very concerned about what happened to Yolanda while she was in our care. His messenger wants a full report by noon."

58

The cart creaked heavily down the moonlit road, heading toward Zching City. Yolanda was happy to be out in the starry night air instead of under those scratchy burlap bags. Soon she fell asleep, and didn't realize until the sun rose that she'd been leaning against Ming half the night.

Being a monk was fine, except for her infernally itchy scalp. She took pains to scratch her head without knocking off her hat, because they passed a lot more people on the main road to the city: sunburnt farmers, suckling mothers, dirty kids, old people bent over walking sticks. They all squinted in the hot sun reflected on the yellow plains.

At sunset Chen stopped at a few huts to ask for shelter for the night, but came back surprised. The people either shut their doors in his face, or didn't bother to answer.

"It's very bad. Monks have depended on the kindness of those along the roadways, for thousands of years," Ming said.

"Too many thieves these days," Chen shrugged.

Around midnight he spotted a small hut with a lantern still burning. A middle-aged woman appeared at the door.

"It's late, but don't see any harm in letting a few monks stay the night, if you'll do something for me in return," she said. Yolanda could hear from the cart.

"Surely we can do it," Chen said.

"Carry my incense to the city for me," she held up a few red silk pouches. "Ryuku Temple wants them by the holidays, but it's too hard to travel alone, with the ku-zin and all."

"It's no trouble," Chen bowed up and down, his palms pressed together against his chest. "We will be honored to deliver your incense to the good monks of Ryuku Temple."

After a hard night of sleep on the seamstress' floor, they loaded ten small crates of incense into the cart.

"Many thanks for your kindness," Ming said. "Kua-ma smiles on you."

"Don't forget, you're giving me something in exchange. But take care," the woman wagged her finger at them. "I heard there are over three hundred soldiers at the gate. Don't let them touch my incense! They shouldn't bother monks like you. They're only looking for some escaped princesses."

"Don't worry." Chen bowed. "We'll keep your goods safe."

59

*Y*olanda. I've never seen a monk scratch so much." Ming tried to let her friend save face, to not be embarrassed.

"I can't help it! My head itches like crazy," Yolanda said, rubbing under her hat. "But don't you think you should call me something else? Something like a real monk."

"Hmm. How about Yo Yo?" Ming smiled.

Yolanda looked as if she'd just eaten a pickled radish that was too long in the brine, then Chen jerked the reins and the cart thudded to a stop on the crest of a small hill.

Ping and Pong nearly trampled into a small knot of travelers stopped in the middle of the road. As they hobbled to the side to make way for the cart, Ming saw that they were sick, old or lame. One man was so bowlegged that he had to swing his hips in a wide half-circle just to get one foot in front of the other. A little blind woman with white hair reached ahead with a willow branch to find her way. But the worst was a boy of six or seven, his legs so twisted with palsy that he could only drag himself through the dirt.

Ming could not understand why the great Creator allowed such suffering. Why can't pain be stopped forever?

I'll ask my father, when I find him.

"These poor folks should be riding in the cart instead of us," Yolanda whispered.

Ming nodded, though it was risky. "Good idea. Ting and Tan always say, 'Compassion in the heart is good, but even better in the hands.'" Chen, may we sit with you so these travelers may ride?"

"It would be an honor," Chen bowed his head.

Yolanda climbed to the front and held the reins while Chen and Ming jumped down.

"You look very tired," Ming said. "There is room in our cart for you." She lowered her voice to that of a male monk.

"If it's not too much trouble," the bowlegged man said.

"No trouble!" Chen said. He hoisted the man over his shoulders and into the cart, hiding the strain in his face.

Ming piled bags of hay over the incense crates and helped the man get comfortable while Chen lifted the blind lady and the crippled boy in.

"Thank the Four gods that you monks came along," the old woman bowed. "I didn't think I could go another step. And little Tao here, he's got no one. I won't wish you good luck, because monks don't gamble much, but may Kua-ma bring happiness to all your lifetimes."

"We may need your good luck wishes," Ming said as Ping and Pong started off. "The roads are dangerous these days." She turned to the boy. "Where are you going, little one? How did you come to be on the road?"

Tao did not answer quickly. "We had no food," he said.

"You can tell the good monks," the lady encouraged him.

"Papa ran off to join the ku-zin. Mama carried me on her back a long way, to go live with grandfather and grandmother, but she got sick with fever. She fell down beside the road one morning. I stayed by her but she didn't get better. She got so hot. Then she got cold and didn't move. She couldn't talk or sing to me anymore."

"That's a terrible, sad story," Yolanda said from the front seat. Ming was relieved that she deepened her voice, and kept her hat low.

"What did you do then?" Chen asked.

"I cried. A good man came. He said he'd take care of Mama, but I had to keep on going, to my grandparents."

"Where do they live?"

"Ko-ko-ma, Saimin province."

"I can find it. It's not far - and not far out of our way. I'll take you there now, if that's all right with my brothers," Chen said.

"Of course." Ming put her hand on Tao's shoulder. He did not smile.

Though the cart groaned under the extra weight, Ping and Pong managed to keep a good pace all day. Golden light blazed against the western horizon as they reached the outskirts of Ko-ko-ma. Chen inquired at a few huts until they found the right one. A woman with silver hair pulled into a tight bao – a bun – opened the door, with a man, her husband, behind. Tao whimpered and reached out for her.

"Little Tao! How did you – ? Where is your mother?"

Upon hearing his story, both grandparents shed tears. Then Tao's grandfather spoke to them, rubbing his red eyes. "Very bad luck, to be sure. But good luck has smiled on us too. How can we thank you for bringing our little Tao safely here? He is more precious to us than gold."

"It was no trouble! But our oxen are very tired," Chen said. "We need to rest."

"You must all stay the night. Grandmother will make you a feast fit for the great god Ching himself!"

Ming bowed. "Thank you, but we are poor monks, just a little food and water and hay to sleep on – that is enough."

"Nonsense! You'll sleep on our own pallets tonight."

Once Ping and Pong and cart were safely quartered in a neighbor's shed, everyone enjoyed a fine meal of millet cakes, taro roots and dried pears. After Chen and Yolanda and Ming were tucked into pallets in a small sleeping loft, the couple bowed goodnight and lay down on the floor below.

Chen and Yolanda were soon snoring like a couple of old men, but Ming slept lightly, with half her mind awake. Soon she heard a sharp rap on the door. The grandfather got up and put his ear to it. Ming could hear bits and pieces of a rough, snarling voice outside: "Open up! Unholy monks."

The guards! She heard many horse hooves and feet approaching. It could be a whole army.

"I pray you, give us a moment, we are not dressed," Grandfather said.

As Ming readied herself to leap off the loft and attack, she overheard the couple whispering.

"Get the gold coins," the grandfather hissed.

"But husband, those coins are all we have!"

"Now is the time. What better use can they have?"

"We're coming in!" The guards pushed against the door, shaking the little hut. Yolanda and Chen still snored.

"Wah!" The old couple shuffled to the door and lifted the slab lock only part way, just wide enough to drop a few gold coins – probably their life savings – into the guard's palm. The grandfather mumbled, "No monks here."

Ming thanked the Four gods when she heard horses' hooves pounding the road into the distance. The couple lay back down, and her heartbeat gradually returned to normal. Yolanda and Chen and the others still snored soundly, never dreaming how dearly the grandparents had paid to keep them safe.

In the morning, the couple didn't mention it, so Ming could not thank them openly. Finally, Tao's grandfather spoke to Chen as they loaded up the cart with fresh supplies.

"If I were a monk, I wouldn't take the main road to the city. Not unless you like trouble," he said.

"Why is that?" Chen asked.

"Oh, I heard the villagers gossiping at the water hole. Said the palace guards were roaming last night, beating on doors. They were looking for monks."

"Monks?" Chen glanced at Ming and Yolanda, frowning.

"I cannot thank you enough for your many golden kindnesses," Ming said, and her bow was twice as long as it needed to be. The twinkle in the corner of the Grandfather's eye let her know that he understood.

Safe in his grandmother's arms, Tao managed a small smile as they all bowed good-bye.

60

though he'd never been to Saimin province, Chen knew he'd find the way to Zching City. He left the main highway on a crumbling back road that the spirits would like, if only he could catch a glimpse of one. Ping and Pong made him proud and rode hard all day over miles of rough ground without stopping. Luck was with them. No stinking guards or ku-zin were lurking in the dry, dusty fields. Not that he couldn't handle it; he'd fight them, even if a real monk wouldn't.

It was getting on to sunset when the blind woman, whose name was Lu, woke from a nap and rapped his seat. "Thank you for driving, young man. This is a far better way to travel."

"Miss Lu, I am wondering how you came to be on the road alone?" Chen said.

"My husband died eleven years ago, but my seven sons provided for me. Life was good until the drought came and killed the crops. My sons went to find food, but not one of them came back. The ku-zin came one night and stole every grain of rice! So I took my walking stick and left for the city, to sniff for food – and better luck."

"Pardon me for asking, but what do you mean by 'sniff'?"

"Though I was blind from birth, I can smell better than a pig on its third lifetime. I can even smell the perfume of the spirits, though I haven't found any for a long, long time. Speaking of smells, I don't want to be nosy, but what is in these crates we're sitting on?"

"It's incense. We're delivering it to the Ryuku temple in Zching City," Chen said proudly.

"Hmmmm," she shrugged. "Smells like gunpowder to me."

"Oh, I'm sure it's not. It was made by a woman we met," Chen said. "Say, Miss Lu, can you smell water? My oxen, Ping and Pong, are strong, but they can't go too long without it."

The blind woman's gray eyes rolled in her head as she sniffed in all four directions. "There's a river, not five miles that way." She pointed across a wide, rutted field.

Although he couldn't see the river, he decided to trust Miss Lu's nose. "Brace yourselves for some bumps, back there. We're going off the road."

Chen drove down a steep embankment and over the field, slow and steady, not to push the oxen too hard. They came to a small river arched with a high footbridge, like the one in his own village, tall enough to pull the cart under. "This is lucky! Water, and a place to spend the night. Thank you, Miss Lu." He bowed to her even though she couldn't see him.

"You're very welcome. I wish that you were my son, a good boy like you! You wouldn't leave an old woman alone."

"No, I'm not so good – but I wouldn't leave you alone."

Chen drove the cart under the bridge and tied the oxen close so they could not be seen from above. After a long drink and a few rice balls, a gift of Tao's grandmother, they all lay together in the back, like fish in a market stall. Although hoofs pounded above them a few times, and the cart was too small for comfort, everyone got a little sleep – except Miss Yolanda, who took a turn keeping watch.

At sunrise they filled the leather bags with fresh water and started out. Morning deepened into a cloudless blue afternoon. The sun fell as Ping and Pong climbed up and over a steep hill. In the distance, Chen could see the flaming torches that ringed the city walls, and the ten thousand candles that twinkled inside. It was even bigger and more beautiful than he'd imagined, yet he felt a sense of dread.

"Look," he pointed. "It's Zching City."

The bowlegged man, whose name was Ji, said, "If we keep going we'll be there by morning. My son Rika lives in a shanty town just outside the walls. He knows the ways of that city better than anyone. He can get you in."

"We'll take you to him, but then we have a promise to keep," Chen said.

61

olanda was excited to see the torches of the city burning bright against the midnight sky, but the closer they got, the more she worried about the three hundred guards at the gates. At least it kept her mind off Yakos. She was still mad, but wanted to see him again. Wanted to make him feel that she should be there with him, to help him!

Why does he have to be so damn slippery?

She barely slept at all, with the rickety wheels and Miss Lu's snoring. As the sun rose they came to a squatters' village; Yolanda snuck a peek from under her hat. A pink and orange glow fell on rows and rows of makeshift tents and lean-to's. Cozy, except for the smell of rotting trash and all the yelling and crying babies. Women in rags hauled water baskets down the narrow streets. Sad-faced men crouched beside empty bowls. Dirty kids fought over pickings from the garbage, and some ran in front of the cart, begging for food.

"If we had food, we would give it to you," Chen bowed, holding out his empty hands as he drove.

"They're awfully bad off around here," Yolanda said.

"All the hungry people left the country, came to the city. Too many," Ji said, shaking his head. "Then the guards got mean. Rounded up all the beggars and anybody who looked poor, and made them leave. There was nowhere to go but here."

"That's terrible. What about your son?"

"Oh, he does better than most. Turn here." Ji motioned to Chen to drive the cart down a dark narrow alley, and then pointed to a tiny lot tucked between two sheds. "The cart should fit here, but you'd better hide the oxen in this shed or they'll be someone's breakfast in an hour," he laughed.

While Ming helped Ji down, Yolanda took Miss Lu's arm and followed him as he half-rocked, half-limped down the path between the sheds. They picked their way over broken stones and twisted bits of junk to a crude lean-to, cobbled together from odd scraps of wood. Ji threw aside a moth-eaten rug that served as a door, and went in. Yolanda could see a boy sleeping on a pile of brightly colored pillows.

"Rika! Get up, you worthless pile of dung!" Ji shook the boy, and shouted in his ear. "We've got visitors!"

Ji's boy stumbled outside in a ragged gold tunic and too-short silk trousers, a tangle of black hair over his eyes. His skin was darker than Ming and Chen's, and his eyes were more round like Yolanda's, not as pointed.

"Hullo. The name's Rika. Rika Rika. I welcome you to Zching – I mean Shanty Town. Friends of Papa are friends of mine. Even monks, eh?" He put his palms together and bowed to Yolanda, bobbing up and down like a crazy puppet.

She couldn't keep from giggling under her hat. "My name's – umm, Yo Yo, and this is Miss Ju. I'm not really a monk." Damn! Yolanda realized she'd blurted out the truth, too late. "But don't tell them I said so," she whispered, nodding back to Ming and Chen who were locking up the oxen.

"Sure, sure! I won't say a word. Not really monks? That's okay. I'm not really a thief! Monk, thief, all time same same! That's what I always say. Come, into my palace. I'll fix you something nice to eat and drink. Come, come."

They ducked under the rug and Ji beckoned them to sit with him in a corner stacked with pillows. Once Yolanda's eyes had adjusted to the dim light, Rika's 'palace' seemed much bigger than it looked. The crooked walls were hung with dishes and tools, scraps of metal and wood, and baskets overflowing with bright patterned cloth.

When Ming and Chen came in, Rika handed everyone half of a scooped-out melon filled with a delicious, thin juice.

"Thank you. Pardon me, but may I ask where you got this fruit in a hundred-year drought?" Ming asked between slurps.

Rika's eyes sparkled. "We have ways of getting certain luxuries. Enjoy! But are you monks going to the city?"

"Depends on the stinking guards," Yolanda said. "Are there really three hundred at the gate?"

"Ah! An enemy of the guards is an even better friend of Rika's!" His eyes gleamed with excitement.

"I told you Rika would help," Ji said, nodding.

"Any chance I get to break the rules! Let's see, now. Where were you going again?"

"Em -" Chen looked down, frowning and rubbing his chin.

Chen doesn't trust Rika. But if he can get melons in a hundred-year drought, he can get us past the guards.

"First we're heading to the Ryuku Temple, then to the borderlands," Yolanda said. Chen glared at her, and Ming took in a sharp breath, but it was too late.

"Ah, the temple on the hill. A lovely spot for quiet contemplation. Too bad. Haven't you heard? Monks are on the guard's list. You won't get that far, my friends."

"But we must deliver some incense there," Chen said.

"Not to worry! I, Rika, will deliver it for you!"

Chen shook his head. "We made a promise that it would be delivered safely. It's a matter of honor." He said the word as if Rika didn't have any.

"Well then, what you need is a disguise — a better one than that hat. It's begging me to look under, to see what's inside!" He leaned toward Yolanda, close enough to see her eyes. She pulled the hat down over her face, blushing hot.

"How about a beautiful turban?" Rika leaped up to grab a length of purple and gold cloth that hung from a basket on the wall, but the whole thing fell onto Chen's head.

Chen threw off the tattered bits of silk. "This gaudy stuff will only attract more attention, not less."

"Here's a plain white one, then, if you monks don't like my pretty colors." Ji draped a simple scarf around his own head, and then stood up straight, nearly hitting his head on a big pot. "I've got it! We'll wrap you up in bandages, like lepers! Everybody hates the lepers – they are so disgusting, with their poor fingers and toes always falling off! Such a terrible, sad disease. Nobody will come near you. They'll be afraid they might catch it!"

Ming shook her head. "Thank you very much, but if the guards won't allow thieves and beggars into the city, surely they won't let lepers in."

"Don't worry so much! I've got that figured out. We'll go tonight, to the yellow gate. Fewer guards there. The kind that like wine!" he laughed. "Meanwhile, you need a rest?"

"I don't –" Chen began to protest.

"I sure do," Yolanda nodded, yawning.

"You are sure tonight is most favorable?" Ming asked.

"Yes, yes! Rika knows the city better than anyone! Now please. Rest here, without any worries." He jumped up and yanked even more pillows out of hidden corners. He gave two to everybody except Chen, who got three. Chen gave him a tiny nod for thanks. "Everybody, get comfortable. I'll go fetch some linen, take care of business."

Yolanda wondered what Rika's business might be as she drifted into a deep nap. She didn't wake until sunset, when they all took off the yellow monks' robes and put on their baggy farmers' clothes again.

"Will you come with us, Miss Lu?" Ming asked.

"Oh, yes. I'll be good to have along. I'm already so old and withered. And I've always wanted to see the city."

See the city? I thought she was blind.

"It will be dangerous..." Chen took her hand.

"Don't worry!" Rika had slipped in under the door, quiet as a fox. He threw a couple rolls of gauze to Chen and Ming, and then hurried to Yolanda and flipped off her straw hat. He saw her face and the red fuzz starting to grow back on her head.

"Ah!" he nodded, sizing her up with a grin. "You are a very strange monk – a girl? And those eyes, that red hair! So exotic. You'd fetch a good price in the harbor brothels."

Ming glared at Rika. "Not another word of that."

"So sorry. I was only liking her pretty green eyes. Say, are you a lady, too? Are all you monks ladies?"

"No!" Chen growled.

"I beg your pardon. All time same same. No more jokes, no more questions. May I put on the bandages? Yes? Yes!"

Before Ming could say no, Rika's quick fingers had already stretched a layer of linen around Yolanda's head. After a few more wraps her face was almost totally covered

"But I can't see anything!" Yolanda said.

"Here, here, let me fix it. It's too tight, yes, but we must hide those beautiful eyes from the guards."

Had Rika heard about the missing princesses, one a green-eye? What about the reward – would he try to get it?

He opened the wrappings a tiny bit until Yolanda could see him grinning at her, his dark eyes shining. She wasn't used to boys looking at her that way, and never once had a boy touched her. Her cheeks burned hot as he finished wrapping her elbows and knees, one hand and both feet.

"It might work," Ming said. She and Chen wrapped themselves and Miss Ju until they looked like mummies, too.

"I'll stay here. No more excitement for me." Ji said.

"Good! Good! It's time we got to the gate. The guards should have drunk all the wine I gave them by now." Rika spun on his heels like a drunken fool.

"I hope there are not too many," Yolanda said.

"No matter. The captain and his men should be rushing to the eastern quadrant. The fire gong was so loud, even I thought it was real! There's no fire, of course, but it will take them a long time to get back to the gate, with all the roadblocks my friends have fixed up."

"That's my son!" Ji beamed. "He thinks of everything."

"Let's go, lepers!" Rika bowed them out the door.

62

*P*ing and Pong were so glad to see Chen return that they nuzzled his face between his bandages. He was about to climb into the driver's seat when Rika stopped him.

"Lepers don't drive, man! Get in back and start moaning. Don't forget. You're in a lot of pain. Now, for my disguise." Rika flipped Yolanda's hat onto his own head, wrapped a red cloth around his shoulders, and then squirmed down in the seat. He looked just like an old hunchback.

With some envy, Chen saw how fast and easily Rika charmed Ping and Pong into backing out of the alley.

Out on the road they passed drunken, ragged men who shouted insults as the cart rattled by: "Get off the road, you filthy lepers!"

"Here's what I think of you," one of them spat at the cart, close to Miss Lu.

Chen clenched his jaw, barely able to keep himself from leaping up to teach them a lesson. But when one of them flung a clay bottle that shattered against the side of the cart and missed Miss Ming's head by only a hair, he stood up halfway, his bandaged-wrapped fist in the air.

Rika cracked the reins. "Hai-ya!" Ping and Pong took off at a gallop.

Chen fell back down, landing almost on top of Miss Ming. "So sorry," he mumbled, barely hiding his shame.

The hooligans chased them through the shanty town, and all the way to the Yellow gate before they scattered.

Chen looked up in awe at the two great pillars with the curving beam over the top. The door itself was a huge slab of wood, carved with intricate characters.

At least forty guards leaned or crouched near the gate. "You said there were only a few!" he hissed to Rika.

"That's not many. Usually there's over a hundred. Don't worry so much!"

I knew we shouldn't have trusted him! The guards do look drunk, though, propped against the wall or lying on the road.

"Whoa," Rika slowed to a crawl, nodding to them.

One guard strutted over to block their way. "This gate is closed." His voice was harsh but slurred.

Rika jumped down and fell to his knees, kowtowing. He rummaged in his pockets and managed to drop a few coins into the man's hand. "Oh great master, with this offering, we beg your lord's kind permission to pass to the Ryuku temple."

The guard's bloodshot eyes peered into the cart where Chen and the others lay on the crates. He put his hand over his mouth. "Lepers!" he said with disgust.

Rika dropped a few more coins into the guard's purse, left hanging open beside his sword. "Rich lepers, my lord. They pay their way, yes?"

Where did Rika get that money?

The man snorted. "How dare you bring such filth to my gate? You should be whipped and sent to the harbor galleys." But even as he threatened, the guard bent closer to Rika's hand, making sure the pouch was wide open.

"They do no harm, master! They only wish for a final blessing before they leave this world of dust." Rika dropped more coins into the guard's purse. "The Four gods will surely bless you, my master, if you help these poor souls."

"Well, at least they don't stink." The man spat.

Rika made a great motion of digging deep into his pockets, and then put a few more gold coins into the pouch.

Chen had never seen so much money in his life.

While Rika argued the details with the leader, some of the other drunken guards staggered to the cart to see the lepers. They leaned over the side, holding their torches very low, almost close enough to singe the bandages.

"Just look at them. Sickening, isn't it?"

"Ugh. I heard their toes and fingers just fall off."

"And they're covered with oozing sores."

"Disgusting! I want to see it for myself, don't you?"

"Yeah! Take the bandages off!"

Before Chen could think of how to stop them, they grabbed the bandages around Yolanda's head and pulled, hard. She wriggled like a trapped animal, making muffled sounds. Chen and Ming wriggled up and reached out with bandaged arms to stop them, but the guards laughed and thrust their torches in their faces. They had to pull back, or catch on fire.

Chen heard the clanking and scraping of iron hinges. The huge door slowly opened. Yes! But the guards didn't stop tugging Yolanda's bandages. Meanwhile, Rika chatted with the drunken guard leader near the gate entry.

"RIKA!" Chen shouted. He hated to ask him for help.

Rika scurried back to kowtow to the guards. "Please, stop! Something bad could happen. You'll catch the disease!"

The guards were in too much of a frenzy to hear him.

The leader walked over and grabbed the collars of their tunics. "Ku-zin filth! Leave them. Get back to your posts."

They finally backed away, but Yolanda's bandages were shredded. Chen and Ming drew close to shield her. She tried to cover her head with her arms but there was no mistaking the ruddy red color of her scalp.

"Eh? What's this?" The leader bent closer to look.

Rika squeezed in to block his view. "It's nothing, my master, it's only the healing herb, the cherry root that the women rub on the lepers. All time same same. We go now, eh?"

"Get down." The leader had sobered up quick.

"Oh, great Master –" Rika pressed more coins into the man's hand, but he shoved him away. Rika fell to the ground and his coins scattered; the guards scrambled to grab some.

"Get down! All of you!" The leader nudged Yolanda and the others with his blunt sword.

"Ai-eee! I'm old enough to be your great-grandmother. You should show more respect!" Miss Lu wagged her finger.

The guards stormed into the cart, roaring with laughter as they grabbed Miss Lu and Ming and Yolanda. Chen wanted to kill them all, but only watched helplessly as the guards pinned Miss Yolanda against the cart. Chen burned with shame.

I should have stopped them! I must help the princesses... but what can I do, or Miss Ming? Nothing, against so many!

"Let's see what we have here." The leader forced Miss Yolanda's hands behind her back so hard that Chen thought her shoulders might break. She whimpered as he tore the rest of the bandages from her face and arched her backward.

"It's the one!" he shouted. "The princess with the round green eyes!"

63

*A*s the guard leader loosened the last of the gauze around Yolanda's eyes, Ming stealthily unwrapped her own bandages, freeing her arms and legs for battle. When he named Yolanda as the green-eyed princess, she drew a single breath. Chi rose through her chest and out to her toes and fingertips. Her legs, as strong as ironwood, bent slightly. From this position of harmony and power she kicked the leader in a most vulnerable spot, just below his ribs. He doubled over in agony.

"Run!" Ming screamed.

Yolanda only got as far as an arm's length before he grabbed the gauze that trailed from her shoulder and reeled her back in.

"You're worth a lot to me, princess." The leader held her waist and pointed at Ming with his other hand. "Get that one!"

While the drunken guards fumbled with their swords, Ming shouted "Ki-yai-eee!" and knocked three of them to the ground. Only four more. Ming kicked and chopped like a graceful, vicious machine. One after another fell, writhing in pain.

"That leper is making fools of us! Fight!" The leader shouted to another band of unruly guards.

They pulled themselves into a loose line to charge her. Ming knocked their swords from their hands, one by one. As she kicked and punched she kept an eye on Yolanda and the others through a growing crowd of gawkers. The leader held Yolanda's arms in a brutal lock behind her back while he commanded the attack.

Nearby, Rika fought off his attackers with a short knife, and did a pretty good job of keeping them at bay. Where were Chen and Miss Lu? Ming spotted them crouching in the shadows of the stone wall, moving to the huge door that still stood half open.

I hope they get through! she prayed, but then a circle of guards came up behind them, wooden swords high over their heads. Ming leapt over fallen guards toward Chen and Miss Lu. But then she saw the guard leader drag Yolanda in the opposite direction. She stopped, tensed. Which way? To help Chen and Miss Lu, or Yolanda? She could not do both at the same time.

In her moment of hesitation five guards charged her again with blazing torches. Ming contracted her body into a tight ball, and then sprang high over the guards. She landed on her feet and searched for Yolanda. There! On the right side of the door.

Ming leapt past another tangle of guards, but the ring of five closed in again, surrounding her. Unlike most of the drunken soldiers, these guards knew how to fight. Their swords slashed at her ears and toes. Ming shifted her weight to dodge their blades as she sensed the weakest link, the one who feared her most. With one kick she cracked both his kneecaps like two lengths of bamboo, and then sprung high over his fallen body. The four others jumped after her.

As she ran to the wall, a sudden flash of sparks blazed across her path. The ox-cart was on fire! Flames licked high into the night sky, dim with smoke. Stupid guards. Their torches set the incense on fire. But it didn't smell sweet, it smelled like –

Gunpowder! The tops of the crates blew into the sky, spinning crazy. The fireworks explosion was louder than a thousand bolts of thunder. Ping and Pong broke free of their yoke and harness as the cart burst apart. Burning shards of wood careened up into the sky, then fell back down over the heads of the crowd. Hot sparks of color became wild flames.

Ming danced between falling embers, trying to get to the others. She stamped out a small blaze on her trailing bandages. Smoke seared her eyes and panicked guards blocked her path as she searched for Yolanda. There, a reddish head with white bandages!

With arms beating and legs kicking, Yolanda fought like a cat to get away from her captor. Flames shot up around his legs, but still he did not let go. Ming got to the wall just as the guard leader's tunic bloomed into fire, three meters high, and spread to Yolanda's clothes.

Ming took aim at his shoulder and kicked. The man's arm dropped. Yolanda was free to jump back from the fire. Ming's second kick to his temple knocked him against the wall. The leader slumped to the ground. His arms and legs twitched as he continued to burn, a frantic, living torch. Finally he moved no more. A cloud of smoke and ash drifted into the midnight air.

Ming bowed her head. Although he was an enemy, he was only trying to do his job, and he did it very well.

Yolanda fell to her hands and knees, her eyes dull with shock. Her tunic and trousers still smoked and burned. The cloth crumbled in blackened shreds. Underneath, her legs were red and puffy, but she was lucky. The burns could have been much worse.

"Can you walk?" Ming asked.

Yolanda's head rolled to the side like a lifeless doll. Ming caught her up in her arms, lifted her onto her shoulder and crept along the wall to the gate. Rika was there, beckoning.

64

*C*hen held Miss Lu as burning chunks of wood fell around them, thicker than rain. One dropped right in front of them, and Miss Lu almost tripped. She held him tighter, her body trembling.

"I told you it was gunpowder, in those crates," she said.

"Ah yes. So sorry! You were right," Chen said.

"You didn't look inside."

"I should have listened to you. I believed the other lady."

Another stick of fiery wood fell near Chen's foot, and flames burned everywhere. Have to get her to safety.

Rika stood at the wall, waving frantically. Although Chen didn't want to trust him, he'd know a safe place to take her.

A couple of guards near the wall spotted Chen and raised their wooden swords high, leaping out to attack. Chen tensed, ready to fight. But what about Miss Lu? I can't leave her.

Fires raged behind them. Can't go back…

Miss Lu broke away from his arm to stand alone, her balance teetering. "Leave me here. I'm an old woman. I had a full life."

The guards were nearly upon them. Chen picked up a burning torch and started to run to fight them, away from Miss Lu. But he could not leave her there alone. He reached out to hold her again, and waited for them to come, his torch high.

65

*B*ecca's spirit felt the passage of time only through brief awakenings, when called to the world below through a thick veil. She touched ground lightly with her awareness, just enough to know that Yolanda was still moving, still safe. It would be so much easier if they were both on the same plane of existence.

The spirits were also affected by the unrest of the cycles. The scattering of souls roamed around her, confused and bewildered. Below, in the world of dust, Becca sensed more and more destruction and cruelty, especially in the crowded city. She drifted down to the ox-cart with its precious passengers just as they came to a tall gate and were surrounded by men in uniform tunics. The guards' souls seemed wooden, unfeeling. Like those cruel guards at the monastery on the hill.

A blast of fire exploded. Becca reeled from the vibrations of the sound wave. The cart was gone. Where was the girl, Yolanda?

There – one of the guards grabbed her. Her arms behind, hurting. Not using her vision. Too afraid?

What about her friends? The girl Ming fought like a banshee. The boy held an elderly woman. More guards came, swords raised. Another blast. A huge crate flew toward the boy and woman. Breaking shards of wood, sharp as swords. Bodies thrown against the stone wall. Burnt. Bloody.

Becca came down close. Wrapped her spirit self around them like a blanket. Release. The woman's spirit didn't cling to her body for long. She rose up and soared past the embers that flew everywhere.

Welcome, Becca said with her spirit.

But the boy fought to hold on to his body. His spirit seemed to say, "I can't go yet. I've not done my duty here."

"You can," Becca said gently.

"But the princesses –"

"Come. I'll help you. We'll find a way," she said, as if holding out a hand to draw him to the spirit world.

"Oh –" With a burst of energy, the boy Chen made the leap to spirit, and soared above his body.

66

*Y*olanda's eyes burned. She blinked them open and found herself hanging upside down over someone's shoulder, in a dark narrow passage.

Where am I? How did I get here? Oh lord. The guard leader?

Her legs and back throbbed. She lifted her head and scraped her cheek against a stone wall, rough and clammy. "Ow."

"Yolanda? Are you all right?"

Ming. What a relief. "Yeah – I guess so."

"Thank the Four gods. Up a bit farther, I'll put you down."

Yolanda's tongue felt thick and her throat was raw, coated with smoke taste. When she named the flavor, it came back: how the guard's face lit up when he saw her green eyes. He'd twisted her arm behind her back, dragged her away, holding her so tight she thought she'd suffocate. Then, out of nowhere, a blast. Hot sparks fell. She twisted under his grip, fighting him, pounding him, but he wouldn't let go. Flames licking at her neck and legs. She gagged on the sweet smell of burning flesh as the smoke filled her eyes, her mouth, choking out everything.

Yolanda closed her eyes until Ming gently lay her down on a dirt floor. Her head pounded and the skin on her legs felt raw. "Thanks, Ming," she said with a grimace. "If it wasn't for you I'd be dead meat right now."

"Let me look at those burns."

"It'll be hard to see. At least we have lots of bandages."

"Thank the gods, there's water left in my pouch." Ming squatted and gently pulled the tattered bandages and trousers from Yolanda's legs, and dripped water over the red patches.

"Youch!" Yolanda clenched her teeth as pain screeched up her legs. Little by little the water cooled down the burns.

"You need an herb for this, but we can't go out yet." Ming wrapped a length of gauze around both her calves.

"Where are we?"

"Inside the wall. Rika showed me this secret passage. We should be safe, until he comes back for us."

"What about Chen, and Miss Lu?"

Ming re-tied her bundle, but didn't answer.

"What happened?" she asked again, in a shaky voice.

"I don't know. Before the explosion I saw Chen leading Miss Lu to the gate. Some soldiers came up behind them and drew swords, but – I couldn't –" Ming hung her head.

"It's okay, Ming. Please, tell me."

"I tried to go to them, but the leader dragged you the opposite way. Five guards came at me. Then everything went up in flames. I ran to you –" Ming choked back a sob.

"It's all my fault. If I didn't get caught, none of it would have happened!" Yolanda pictured Chen and Miss Lu, hurt, bleeding, maybe even dead. She felt terrible, but Ming seemed to take it even harder. She bent over her folded knees.

"Ming, you couldn't help everybody at the exact same time – "

Ming sighed, long and slow and sad.

Yolanda leaned against the stone wall and closed her eyes, trying to ignore the throbbing pain in her legs. The ache in her heart was worse. Chen was smart. And brave. Maybe he found a way.

After a long while she heard footsteps trudging down the tunnel. Ming sat up fast, ready to pounce.

"Hey, no more kung-fu! It's only your friend, Rika! I come in peace. And with breakfast."

"Did you see Chen?" The name caught in Ming's throat.

"Yes, I did. And Miss Lu, too." Rika hung his head. "I'm sorry. Very, very sorry."

Miss Lu was an old woman, but Chen was so young, and good. Mother Cha and Sung will be so sad to hear the news.

No. It can't be. A storm rose up in Yolanda's chest. Tears blocked her eyelashes. Out of habit she held her breath, to keep the tears from coming.

Ming turned toward the wall, her shoulders shaking, while Rika pretended to rub dust out of his eyes.

Somehow it didn't seem right not to cry. A big fat tear rolled down Yolanda's cheek, and then another. Her throat felt as if a boa constrictor was wrapped around her neck, squeezing it shut. Her choking sobs echoed down the tunnel.

Look. See...

A voice in her ear. It couldn't be the black bird, but the message was the same as before: use the vision.

Her pain was so strong that it was hard to relax, to let the vision come, but slowly it rose up inside her like a wave.

Let go. Let yourself feel.

"Oh –" She took a breath and opened her throat. Tears poured down her cheeks. She didn't worry what Ming and Rika might think. Her chest heaved and her breath came hard. Her eyes burned more than before, but somehow the tears kept coming.

It was hard not knowing what happened. Yolanda wanted to see for herself. She opened the vision further until part of her mind was free to float away from her body, the same way she had at the monastery. She flew back down the musty tunnel. Once outside in the dim morning light, she saw a bunch of guards around a pile of burnt wood, lifting and moving the pieces. She flew in closer.

Chen lay in his torn bandages, one arm draped over Miss Lu. Blood and puffy black burns covered their bodies. Back in the tunnel, Yolanda's throat clenched up again like a fist.

Don't – want – to see!

Her vision turned to go back toward the tunnel, but then she sensed something else hovering near the bodies. It had no shape or color, yet it seemed to be alive. She probed with her vision.

It was Chen! Or some part of him. Was it his soul?

'Spirit doesn't die. It just changes into something new.'

Where did that thought come from? Chen? The spirit-shape seemed peaceful. Yolanda started to feel calmer, too, but she felt the pull of her own body back in the tunnel.

She looked at Chen and Miss Lu one more time. Although his spirit hovered nearby, what about the real Chen? She would never again see the skinny boy who tried to act bigger than he was. The boy who rubbed his chin when he was nervous.

The boy who would do anything to keep us safe.

67

*M*ing took a deep breath, but it only lightened the heaviness in her chest a little. She almost wished she could cry like Yolanda, but a warrior does not reveal emotion that way.

Yolanda had finally stopped. Her green eyes were bloodshot and puffy, but she looked almost peaceful in the dim light.

"It was a beautiful death," Rika said, his voice shaky. "Your friend Chen died protecting the blind lady, like a good son. Lucky that I still had a couple of coins left. I bribed a guard to take them both to the Ryuku temple. Chen wanted to go there, didn't he? He was a very good monk, wasn't he?"

"Yes, he was very good." Ming looked at Yolanda. She nodded.

"He's with Kua-ma now. Probably get a better lifetime next. Life, death, all time same same. Since we are alive, it's time to eat!" Rika spread out a patterned gold cloth and handed each of them a fat rice ball, a dried plum and bits of dried fish.

Ming didn't feel much like eating, but food was scarce and she needed fuel after all the fighting. "Thank you."

Rika turned to Yolanda. "Last time I saw you, you hung over her back like a ten-stone sack of rice. Aren't you better now?"

Yolanda blushed. "Yeah, thanks to Ming. She fixed up my legs with the bandages. They don't hurt so bad."

"Stolen linen, twice used! Very good luck. Here. I brought you also this." He tossed a black thing that looked like a dead rat's tail into her lap.

"What is it?" Yolanda picked up a long black braid fixed to a circle of something like skin.

Ming remembered her own braid in her bundle.

"A wig. Very rare, only the richest can afford. Just this morning that wig belonged to Lord Yung himself."

"Who is he?" Ming asked.

"Regent of the city. He's bald. Needs a wig to keep favor with the ladies."

"Did you steal it?"

"Not exactly. I borrowed it. He has many more!"

"You must steal a lot. I saw you giving the guards a lot of coins," Yolanda said. Ming was amazed at how direct she could be.

"Yes, but that pig of a guard broke his bargain. When he took you, I would have attacked him myself if your friend hadn't beaten me to it. Say," he turned to Ming, "that was some extra nice fighting! You want to work with Rika? Make lots of money!"

Ming smiled and bowed her head. "Thank you, but we should leave the city as soon as possible."

"What about the Ryuku temple? Aren't you going there?"

"The delivery burned up last night. Who would have guessed? A country seamstress and a famous temple, dealing in fireworks."

"Oh, anything can happen, and usually does," Rika shrugged. "Very lucky, that you got out of that cart before it blew up. Still, so terrible for Chen and Miss Lu! Wah!" Rika's eyes welled up with tears that he brushed away, fast. "Ahem. Where will you go next, if I might be so bold to ask the princesses?"

"How do you know who we are?" Ming's face darkened.

"Everybody knows. Very dangerous now. Many eyes are looking for you. That's why I brought the wig. But where to take you?"

"The Fung Mountains," Ming said without hesitation.

"Oh, please, let's don't go there! Mountain climbing in dragonwinds is even more dangerous than sitting on fireworks!"

"My father has disappeared. My teachers live there. They may know how to find him."

"Ah. For an honored father, you must go. Hmmm. But how?" Rika's eyebrows knitted together. "I've got it! You need an imperial rickshaw, or a palanquin, grand gowns. And another wig."

"A rickshaw can't go up those mountains," Ming said.

"No, but it will get you through the city to the Fung gate. It is heavily guarded."

"They will search us. We cannot go that way."

"It's the only way to the Fung territory. But don't worry. The guards will not search if you are imperial consorts. Your palanquin must be very big, very expensive."

Ming frowned. "Maybe something less flamboyant?"

"Ok, ok. It's not as glamorous, but you could be dowagers from Lord Yung's palace. He has so many relatives and hangers-on I'm sure the guards don't know all of them. Hmmm, let's see. You need makeup. Lots of it." Rika's eyes narrowed. "I'll get a rickshaw and take you to the Imperial Opera Theater. I have many friends there, skilled in makeup and wigs. They can even make your green cat eyes disappear." He nodded at Yolanda.

"We can't go in the streets like this. After last night the guards will be looking everywhere for us."

"The ones that were close enough to see you are dead." He spat in the dirt. "Trust me. It's a short trip. But we'd better put some fresh bandages around your face, Miss Yoyo."

68

$\mathcal{A}$s they crept down the narrow passageway Yolanda's legs throbbed again. She hoped Rika's plan would work. But what to do after they got to the Fung mountains? Should I look for Yakos there? Will he even want me?

"When we get outside, watch me and move quick," Rika whispered. "Miss Ming, please hold Miss Yoyo up, like a nurse."

Ming helped Yolanda limp between two high stone walls and climb into the rickshaw, which was only an open black box with two long poles on both sides. Rika held up the front end while another street kid stepped from the shadows to pick up the back.

They ran down the alley and onto a rough cobblestone street with tall pagoda-shaped buildings on either side. Yolanda peeked at the city through her bandages. Colorful, frayed banners flew from small windows. Strings of paper lanterns painted with fading tigers, dragons and dogs hung between makeshift shops – crates half-filled with dried chickens, sandals, you name it. Steaming black pots filled the air with strange smells.

The people rushed through the streets like bugs in a giant hive, scurrying in every direction with bundles, frowning as they looked in the shop baskets. Nobody seemed to buy anything. They wore the same baggy clothes as the farmers and peasants, but with flowers, birds or symbols sewed on their tunics.

They passed the Imperial Opera Theater, a carved pagoda three levels high, and turned down a narrow alley to the side door. Rika helped them out of the rickshaw. A bent old man with a long pointed white beard led them behind a beaded curtain and through a maze of narrow halls and tiny rooms no bigger than closets. In each room sat a beautiful lady, primping at a tiny dressing table. They wore heavy, embroidered costumes of every color. Their pale faces were painted with purple eyebrows, pink cheeks and blood-red lips, and their hair was piled high with trinkets and jewels.

Rika squeezed Yolanda and Ming into a room near the end of a hall, and tugged the curtain closed. The lady put down her hand mirror. "Not now, Rika! Can't you see I'm busy?"

Rika whispered in her ear. She smiled sweetly as he slipped several large coins under her dressing-table cloth.

"Hmmm," Precious Virtue looked them up and down. "This will require my best work."

Rika winked to Ming and Yolanda. "Precious Virtue is the best in the city, so please do as she says! I'll be back soon."

Precious Virtue opened jars of different sizes. Though her hands moved like graceful birds, they looked big. When she spoke her high-pitched voice sounded way too girlish. "Come, sit here. Don't worry. I, Precious Virtue, will make you a dowager in a matter of minutes. Such a pity, to grow old before your time. But at least you can wash it off!"

Precious Virtue threw her head back and laughed. Yolanda saw a lump just above her jeweled neckline. Was it an Adam's apple?

"You first, Ming!" Yolanda pulled Ming's arm toward the dressing table, but she stood so firm that Yolanda lost her balance and fell into Precious Virtue's stool, scraping her burned arm against the table. "Youch!"

"So sorry." Ming bowed to the lady. "Forgive us."

"Dear me! Such a lot of trouble! Your friend Rika Rika will have to pay extra." Precious Virtue clicked her tongue as she scooped a pile of thick gray paste into her fingertips. "Now close those ugly little round eyes for me."

69

*P*recious Virtue smeared mounds of cold, slimy goo over Yolanda's forehead, cheeks and chin. It stank to high heaven. Yolanda flinched when she rubbed it into the folds above her eyes.

"Be still, puppy dog, and keep those eyes closed. This mud could blind you. It's very rare. Expensive. From the Chow river valley. A thousand slaves may have died to bring it for you."

Precious Virtue dabbed over her face with quick fingers. As it dried, the mask felt heavy and pulled Yolanda's skin tight.

Next, she glopped some cold sticky stuff on Yolanda's scalp, rubbed it around, and then set something about as big as a lunch box on top. "All right, peach blossom. You may open your eyes now – slowly. And I do mean slowly. Don't blink."

Yolanda's eyelids weighed a ton, but she got them open.

Ming covered a smile with her hand. "Greetings, Auntie Yoyo!" she said with a deep bow.

"Look in the glass. See how respectable you are." Precious Virtue held a small mirror up to her face.

"Oh, lord!" Yolanda didn't recognize herself under all the deep creases, baggy jowls and heavy folds that hung low over her eyes, hiding the green color under shadows. A huge wig like a pagoda sat on her head. As she stared in the mirror at the old lady – a stranger – the surface began to swirl.

Yakos! She wanted to see him so badly, but not here, not with Ming and Precious Virtue. She jerked her head to look away before the reflection changed. The boxy hairpiece tilted sideways and almost pulled her off the stool.

"That wig cost me 10,000 taels of silver!" Precious Virtue shrieked. "Don't move so much. Bow nice and ladylike, like this." Though her head tilted forward less than an inch, the bow was as convincing as a full kowtow.

"You are more of a lady than I'll ever be." Yolanda said.

Precious Virtue sniffed, and then clapped her hands together three times. A young boy in a white satin robe pulled the curtain aside and bowed. "Take Madame to the costumers," she said, and then nodded to Ming. "You're next, my flower."

"Good luck getting old!" Yolanda smiled at Ming, but her cheeks felt as if they might break off.

The boy helped her get through the narrow doorway and hall without snagging her hairpiece on all the masks that decorated the walls. The costumer's tiny room was jammed with racks of robes, fabric, and shoes. A lively, white-painted face peeked out from behind rows of colored silk with pins in her mouth.

"Ah, that's such a good leper costume! That make-up on your legs, and the bandages – it's so convincing! But which opera has a leper character? I can't think so well in the morning."

"It's not make-up," Yolanda said. "I got burned."

"So sorry. No matter. We'll see what we can do." The costumer stooped to measure her, then stood back up and bowed. "How rude, to think of touching you before we've been introduced. I am Radiant Blossom."

"Pleased to meet you. My name's Yo –"

Before she could finish, the boy interrupted. "My mistress, the esteemed Madame Kuo-fo, of the royal Yung clan."

"I am honored to make your acquaintance," Radiant Blossom bowed again, deeper this time. She hummed a few notes of Eastern music as she pulled down a stiff yellow robe embroidered with peacocks and pheasants from a shelf high over her head. "Symbols of a long and lucky life."

The dress was so big and heavy it looked like it could stand up all by itself. "Won't that be awfully hot?" Yolanda asked.

Radiant Blossom raised an eyebrow. "A well-born lady is never seen without the proper attire. Spring, summer, winter, fall – personal comfort is of no consideration in these matters."

The boy helped the costumer hoist the beast of a dress up and over Yolanda's shoulders, and lay the sleeves over her bandaged arms. Radiant Blossom leaned back to size her up, then rearranged a few tassels and draping scarves. "There. From a leper in rags to a proper lady of the Court! If only it were this simple, to better our position in life."

Yolanda started out as a lost kid in muddy jeans, and then became a princess in a Palace. Since then she'd been a runaway under bales of hay, a monk with a shaved head, a leper, and now a wrinkled old aunt. She missed Chen. What would he say?

"Time to go, Madame," the boy said.

Yolanda took a step toward the door.

"You're not finished!" Radiant Blossom stared at her feet, as if they were ten feet long instead of ten inches. "A proper lady's got to have her feet bound."

"What?" Yolanda leaned on the boy's shoulder while the costumer lifted her calf. A spasm of pain shot up her leg. "Ouch! Those burns are real."

"Forgive me." Radiant Blossom clicked her tongue and wrapped a piece of gauze around her foot, much tighter than a bandage.

"What are you doing? That hurts!"

"Of course it does. That is why ladies never walk. You are very lucky to ride in a fine palanquin and be carried wherever you wish to go." Radiant Blossom reached for her other foot.

"But what if I have to run or –?"

"Pardon my unforgivable intrusion, Madame Yung-Kuo-fo." Rika stepped in from the hallway and bowed to Yolanda.

"Rika, thank goodness you're back. Can you tell her to take that stuff off my feet?"

"Pardon my insolence, Madame. Did I hear you correctly?"

"Psssst! Rika says you're supposed to talk like a lady!" The boy whispered to her from the folds of the costume.

"Yes. Of course my feet will be bound!" Yolanda stifled a moan as the costumer tied her other foot in tightly wrapped knots and then pulled a pair of red slippers over the wrappings.

"Madame Yung-So-Kuo awaits you in the palanquin," Rika said, in a very serious tone.

"Who?" He was talking about Ming. "Oh, yes. Thank you."

Yolanda bowed to Radiant Blossom the way Precious Virtue had showed her, with just a tilt of her head. Radiant Blossom bowed good-bye. Rika lifted her left arm and the boy supported her on the right. Her toes were cramped up worse than in a pair of five-dollar shoes. She groaned as they inched through the main hall of the opera to the waiting palanquin.

70

*M*ing sat on a well-padded seat in Rika's borrowed palanquin, which was gaudy enough for Madame Yung-So-Kuo, her new persona. The makeup was well done. She looked about a hundred years old, and after what happened to Chen and Miss Lu, she felt older, too.

As Yolanda was finally lifted into the palanquin, Ming held her head high and said in a whining voice, "I've been waiting for you for well over a lifetime."

Yolanda held her flabby chin up in the air and said, "Hmph."

Ming nodded. Good. You understood how to act the part.

Rika closed the thin curtains tightly before he and three other runners lifted the palanquin's four long poles. As they wound their way through narrow streets, Ming read the bold banners that hung from balconies above the shops: Four Happiness Tea; Long Life Fruits and Vegetables; Double Luck Mah Jong Parlor; Multiple Joy Funeral Cakes. Brass bells and gongs clanged. Crowds of people stepped back for the grand palanquin to pass, craning their necks to see who rode inside.

She smelled the tang of saltwater in the harbor market where merchants squatted beside makeshift stands, selling dried fish with dead eyes, wilted fruits and vegetables, cottons and silks, ceramic tea pots and bowls, wooden toys and tools. Customers swarmed the narrow passages between the stalls.

"Only a lord could buy rice today," one said.

"I've got to bring home something, or my family will eat straw tonight," said another.

"Just another hungry day."

"Another day to pray for the rains to come back."

"I'm praying for the prices to go down!"

The merchants were desperate, too. They ran after Rika's palanquin, shouting and begging them to stop, to taste their fine dumplings, to test the edge of their knives. When the runners had to slow down to let another palanquin pass, a dark-faced man jumped out of a stall with shiny brass plates and urns, ran to their palanquin and thrust a huge platter through the curtain.

"You've never seen such brass! Best in the East!" he said.

To Ming's surprise, Yolanda took it with both hands and looked into the shiny surface, as bright as a gold mirror.

"There's no time!" Ming put her hand on her shoulder. "We must get to the gate!"

Rika ran back and pulled aside the curtain, red-faced. "We'll send a runner to deliver it to your palace, Madame?"

Yolanda just stared into the brass platter as if hypnotized. What was wrong with her?

71

*Y*akos felt a tug on his spirit as if someone had tapped his shoulder. He spun around fast, but was alone in the battle tent. He'd experienced this feeling once before several days ago. It had been his sister Yolanda. He'd made contact with her then, but it drew so much concentration away. Too much.

"Not now!" he said aloud, irritated.

"Yes, my lord?" Yashi, his most trusted servant, bowed as he came into the tent. A cloud of red dust blew in, the same fine powder that ruined his food and found its way into all his clothes and even his wounds.

"It's nothing. You can go. But – wait. What is the news from the wall?" Yakos gritted his teeth to maintain the flow of power while he spoke.

"It's holding, my lord, but there's a breach. The Red line."

Yakos nodded, and Yashi backed outside to stand guard.

Again, Yakos felt the tug of Yolanda's presence, a reminder of an important lesson Nikolas and Narissa had taught him. "Use all that comes to you, in whatever form it may take."

This girl had more potential than anything he could imagine. He reached into his deep reserves of power and conjured a likeness that could speak with her again. It was excruciatingly difficult to keep the wall intact, and at the same time to create a smiling, pleasant face, so different than the fierce warlord he had become in this dry, hostile place.

"Yolanda, my sister. I'm so glad to see you! I have long suffered since we spoke last. Please, forgive what I said. I do need you here with me, now more than ever."

Though he could not see or hear her well, he sensed her reactions. Her lips had been pressed tightly together in an expression of hard resolve against him. She gulped, unsure what to feel or say now. He readied for a new task, to make her sure.

"Go west, into the mountains. I will lead you to a meeting place. I feel your strength, Yolanda. It pulls me to you. We can be so much more together than we are apart. When we meet – it will be very soon – nothing can stop us, my sister, my twin."

Yakos watched his sister's face slowly change, from a closed wall to an open, eager expression. She would come to him, soon. But he could not be sure what she would bring.

72

*M*ing's hand gripped her shoulder so tight that Yolanda couldn't ignore it any more.

"The guards!" she hissed.

"What?" Her twin's smiling face faded as Yolanda tore her eyes away from the brass platter. Through the curtain she saw a knot of guards rush toward the palanquin. For all her vision, she hadn't even noticed them coming.

"Who are your passengers, and what is their business?" The leader yelled to the runners.

Rika fell to a kowtow. "Two matrons of the Yung clan, sir, travel to the Fung Mountains to pay homage to the wind temple."

"The Fung gate is closed, by order of the Minister."

"Surely it is not closed to the honored aunts of Lord Yung!"

"All these relatives and their ridiculous whims," the leader said under his breath. "Was the trip officially recorded?"

"I see you are a captain of the Red level," Rika said. "Do these honored ladies need your permission to visit their family's temple? What rank will you have if Lord Yung hears of it?"

Finally the guard bowed toward the cab. "You may pass. I will send word to the Fung Gate. You'll not be delayed there."

"Please, please – do not trouble yourself. The ladies wish to be inconspicuous."

"Then get out of the market. It's clogged with gawkers." The leader ordered his men to clear the way.

As the runners hoisted the poles onto their shoulders, a small man kowtowed in front of the palanquin, blocking them.

"I humbly beg your pardon, but we are poor merchants. Your mistress has not yet paid us for the fine platter..."

Yolanda didn't realize she was still holding it. She passed the platter out through the curtain, but the man did not take it.

"Please, most honorable lady," he said, "just a few thousand taels, and it will be yours forever."

Ming jerked Yolanda's arm back inside, pointing to her hands. They looked way too young and smooth for old Aunt Kuo-fo.

"Rika Rika!" Ming wrapped the sleeve of her robe around the platter to hide her hand and arms, and thrust it out the window. "Return this to the merchant. We must go!"

The carriage rocked from side to side as the runners squeezed through the crowd of jeering onlookers. Ming turned to Yolanda, her eyes as fierce as a warrior again.

Yolanda wanted to tell her the truth – that she had seen Yakos – but something held her back. The closer they got to the gate, the thicker the silence grew between them.

73

$\mathcal{M}$ ing drew in a long breath and let it slowly escape through her nostrils. The palanquin moved slower than a thousand-year-old turtle, Yolanda was acting odd, and any hope of getting through the gate before dark was fading faster than the sun. She pulled the curtains aside and saw the street choked with guards in red tunics, their faces stern, unyielding. The Palace guard, in control of the city. Were they sent here to find us?

They wound through the streets to the Fung gate. It was supported by a pair of massive red-and-gold pillars, and arched with two gently curving beams. Rows upon rows of guards stood on either side. Beyond the gate, the Fung Mountains draped the horizon like veils of purple mist. She could see the dragon's breath curling in and out of the pines, hiding secret places only hermits know. We'll need luck to find the shelter in all that fog. If we get through this gate.

"Stop!"

The runners set the palanquin down. Ming peered through the curtain as the gatekeeper strode forward on stiff legs.

"This palanquin belongs to relatives of Lord Yung?"

"Yes, master." Rika's kowtow was perfect.

"Please inform your mistresses that the Fung gate is officially closed. We have sent for a pardon from Lord Yung himself. It should not be long before his messenger arrives."

Rika stammered a protest. "But –"

"Silence!" The gatekeeper shouted.

Ming gripped the carved arm of her chair. Too many guards to fight. But we must get through before their messenger returns.

"Ai-eeee-ah!" Ming added years of crustiness and bile to her voice. "It is getting COLD, and soon will be terribly DARK. We will never reach the temple by nightfall!"

The guard walked stiffly to the cab, bowing. "Ah hem, Madame. Good evening. We welcome such honorable visitors to the Western Gate –"

"If you honor us so, PLEASE let us pass NOW. I fear we shall not reach the temple before we see HEAVEN." Ming wailed, loud enough to be heard outside the gate even though the leader stood less than an arm's length from the palanquin. "Aii-eee!"

Yolanda looked dumbfounded. Her old woman's jaw dropped. "They should open the gate, if only because of your acting," she whispered. Ming prayed that the guard took no notice of her.

Thankfully, Rika threw himself down before the gatekeeper. "I beg you, open the gate! Madame Yung-So-Kuo will not let this matter rest!"

"She must wait. The esteemed Lord Yung will –"

"Lord Yung is far too IMPORTANT to be bothered with such trifles," she interrupted him in her haughtiest tone. "You'll be put to the LASH for this outrage."

"Madame, we are under the strictest orders –"

"WHOSE orders?"

"The Minister, Madame. His authority over the four gates is final! We will wait for the messenger."

Through the curtain Ming noticed a few Red guards on the left whispering behind the gatekeeper's back. He walked swiftly to their line and slapped each soldier on the cheek.

"Bad luck. Tough one in charge," she whispered to Yolanda, behind her fan.

"If only we could make a trance like Nikolas, to he would forget his orders." Yolanda tugged on her long sleeve, pointing to the gate. "Look! It's Chen!"

74

hat?" Ming looked confused, but Yolanda could see Chen's spirit standing tall on one of the pillars, unmistakable in the golden light of sunset. Luckily none of the guards seemed to notice as he stepped off the pillar and drifted down to the street, as graceful as a maple leaf on an autumn afternoon. He tugged the handle of the huge iron gate. It was way too heavy for one man, but it was just like Chen to try. The gate didn't budge.

"He's not strong enough," Yolanda murmured, and then Chen's spirit appeared in the palanquin next to her. "How the heck —"

"Shhh." Ming put her finger to her lips. "Who are you talking to?"

Chen looked at them both, eyes wide. "By the Four gods, if I was still alive I wouldn't recognize you old princesses!"

"It's Chen! He's right here with us!"

Ming shook her head. "I don't see him."

"It must be my vision, then."

"I'll keep an eye out. Rika is still begging, so you can talk – just be quiet!"

"I saw you, by the wall, with Miss Lu," Yolanda whispered to Chen. "It was so sad. Your spirit was there, too."

"Miss Lu's spirit went to her family in Chu province, but I didn't know where I belonged. My old body was no good. I am here to help you get past the gate, into the Fung Mountains." Chen bowed, and his spirit form intersected with Yolanda's knees.

"Back at the wall, your spirit didn't look real."

"Spirit is like wind. We can't be seen unless we affect something else. I wanted to help you, so I learned to make a material manifestation. It's a bit like putting on clothes. This ghost of my old body was not so hard, but that gate –"

"I can see you now," Ming said, excited. "You're faint, but I can see and hear you."

"I'm getting better at it." Chen lifted his chin higher.

Yolanda had an idea. "That gate is way too heavy... Can your spirit go into anything, like another person?"

"Yes, I can pass into any form of matter."

"Could you make them do something?"

Chen nodded. "I think so."

"How about him?" She pointed to the gatekeeper who stood near Rika at the front of the palanquin. "He's a tough guy."

"I can do it," Chen whispered, and then his spirit disappeared faster than the light of a blown candle. The gatekeeper jerked as if a cold wind passed through him, and stood up a little taller.

"Ming, it's Chen. He's inside the gatekeeper!"

He called out to the twenty guardsmen that blocked the gate. "Let them pass!"

The second-in-command stepped forward. "But, Sir! Lord Yung's runner has not yet arrived –"

"Do as I say! Open the gate!"

Ming smiled; the makeup didn't completely cover her dimples.

It took ten men to lift the huge latch and swing the massive gate open. Rika and the runners lifted the palanquin and ran through the pillars to the high road as fast as they could.

The keeper of the Fung Gate stood alone, rubbing his chin.

Yolanda lifted her curtain as the palanquin passed, and nodded in his direction. Well done, Chen!

75

*W*hen his messenger left, Narissa held Yakos' scroll in her hands, and noticed a chip in the pink lacquer on her fingernails. Thank the gods she received the letter first; Niko might have killed the poor man, the bearer of bad news. He'll turn colors when he learns that Yakos intends to change the plan. It will not be good for his heart.

Nikolas has never fully understood the ways of child rearing. And that's what we've been doing. We are much more than his mentors, making him strong enough to defeat entire armies by himself. We are his parents. And I want him to succeed.

Nikolas came in from his morning inspections and immediately saw the scroll. "That'll be Yakos' report. May I see it?"

"I'm not sure you'll want to," she said. "Before you read it, consider who Yakos is, and that he is for all purposes our child."

"Yes, yes, of course."

"Like any child coming into adulthood, there will come a time when Yakos must rebel against us."

"Naturally. Can I see the report?"

"That time has come." Narissa handed the scroll to Niko.

Nikolas read it aloud. "I hope this finds you well and the Yellow lands holding. Unfortunately the battle here has weakened me. I created a great wall to hold off their armies, fresh hoards of warriors on horseback. The tribes from the far northwest are skilled in practices unknown, and do not follow my seemings.

"I am also aware of Yolanda's escape from the Palace. She is now coming West, to me."

Nikolas nodded. "Makes sense, from the field reports."

"Call off the Palace guard," he read. "Let her travel unhindered."

Nikolas glared at Narissa and continued. "I believe her power, joined with mine, will defeat them. If only I were more sure of her abilities. If you had trained her properly, I would be."

Nikolas raged across the carpet. His neck muscles stood out like ropes, and Narissa could see the veins in his forehead pulsing. "How dare he question! He's not the master yet!"

"Niko, he only wants to find his own strength –"

"How dare you question me! This war is too important to leave in the hands of a rebellious teenager. I'm leaving now for the new world. I'll bring back weapons that we know can defeat the Red tribes."

"But, Niko –"

"Do not recall the guard while I am gone. We want her brought here."

76

The runners jostled the palanquin through the thick fog that clogged the steep mountain road. Yolanda still could not fully believe that Chen's spirit sat next to her in the palanquin, then jumped into the gatekeeper's body. "Do you think he'll come back?" she asked Ming. "I didn't get a chance to thank him."

Ming shook her head. "Doubtful. His duty has been fulfilled. I imagine he will soon join with Kua-ma's spirit."

"And be reborn?"

"If that is his destiny. Then he'll take a new form in this world."

"So, when he's born again, how will he find us?"

"It could be years. And he may not remember."

"I bet he'll remember," Yolanda said, "but how will we know it's him? I mean, he could even be a fly!"

Ming smiled, cracking the thick makeup around her mouth. "Only Kua-ma knows Chen's fate. But if he remembers, he can make himself known to us."

Yolanda closed her eyes. She tried to open her vision again, to find him. Although she couldn't see his spirit, a warm feeling wrapped around her, just like back at the wall. "Thanks," she murmured. Although she could not hear an answer, her heart knew that he had heard and wished her well.

Yolanda braced herself as the palanquin swerved and jerked like a carnival ride. Ming leaned out her window to direct the runners; how could she see anything in the dark fog that looked to threaten snow? At every fork in the road she ordered them to turn right, always steeper. Halfway up one slope a runner lost his footing in the dark. The palanquin rocked and buckled like an old horse falling to its knees. Rika and the other runners set the cab down and rushed to help Ming and Yolanda get down.

Rika came to her window. "Madame, we can barely see two paces ahead. We called the forest spirits to guide us through the dragon's breath, but they do not answer. We could slip off the mountain at any moment."

"Thank you. Please leave us here. You must return to the city with the palanquin." Ming must not have trusted the runners, because she still faked Madame Yung-So-Kuo's crusty voice.

"But Madame, it is still a long way to the Wind Temple. We can't leave you alone on the mountain at night!"

Yolanda agreed. How can Ming and I get anywhere by ourselves, with our feet all tied up in knots?

"But I, I –" Rika stammered.

"You are an honorable servant, Rika Rika, but the location of the Yung family shrine must remain a secret, even to you."

Rika's face fell but he bowed deeply. He took down a fancy gold lantern from the palanquin, and lit it, then reached under the seat for their two dusty road packs, over-packed with fresh supplies. He then ordered the runners to turn the palanquin around. He bowed to Ming one more time. "I am honored to have been chosen for your service."

"It has been our deepest pleasure," Ming returned his bow, her eyes shining through her disguise.

Yolanda didn't want to thank him like an old aunt. She waved her hand away to get him to come closer, that strange Eastern custom. Rika glanced over his shoulder and leaned in through the window. She smelled melons mixed with street smoke as she brought her lips close to his ear. "I wish I could pay you back for everything you gave us," she whispered. "Especially your smile! Thanks – and good-bye."

Rika's cheeks blushed red in the light of the lantern. "Hello, good-bye, all time same same – that's what I always say! Thank you, Madame. I will never forget you."

Rika bowed deep and long before he picked up his end of the palanquin and ran with the others down the steep trail back to the city.

Yolanda hobbled through the fog on her bound feet, trying to keep up with Ming. It looked as if she had just walked straight into the side of a hill, but then Yolanda found her crouching under a triangle of dried yellow-green moss that hid a tiny, hollowed-out cave, barely big enough for two. Inside they found dry sticks of firewood, a bowl and a bundle of skins.

"The hermits of the Fung mountains build these huts and leave them for travelers...who know where to look," Ming said.

Yolanda could barely wait to take off the makeup, headdress, robe and foot bindings and put on her baggy monk's clothes again. They ate some rice balls and dried fish Rika had slipped into their bags, then lay down on the soft furs to sleep.

In the morning they were happy not to see any signs of guards following them. The fog was so thick they had to inch along, taking tiny steps so as not to fall off a cliff or something. The next day's hike up the mountain was hard and slow.

"I know it's good for covering our trail, but I'm sick and tired of all this fog," Yolanda finally said.

"'Fung' means wind and water. My teachers told me stories of the Fung dragons that live in the clouds above these mountains. This fog is the dragons' breath. Without fung, our land – and the people – would wither and die."

"Real dragons!"

Yolanda wanted to ask her more about the dragons, but Ming only nodded and walked back into the wind and fog. Yolanda felt alone as she followed her on the rocky trails that never stopped going up. Along the way she searched for Yakos' face, but she couldn't see a lake or a stream or even a puddle through the pine forest, swirling with dragon fung.

He said he'd lead me to him. He said we'd meet very soon. He wouldn't ditch me again, would he? How will I know?

The closer she got, the more she craved finding him, the only one left in the world – or worlds – she could call kin. She dared to imagine what it was going to be like to have a brother for real. Maybe he'll look at me and just know things about me, things I never said to anybody. But will he like what he sees?

77

On the third morning, Ming rounded a sharp turn, and then stopped to wait for Yolanda, who grew more weary. "See, there? That fog is different. We're getting close to a tunnel."

"A tunnel? Through the mountain?" Yolanda leaned against a rock, puffing. "I can't even see the mountain in all this fog."

"The tunnels pass directly through the dragon's breath and lead to open ground. With luck, we'll find Ting and Tan nearby."

Ming hiked onward and upward, looking forward to seeing their kind, wrinkled faces. Surely they'll know about Ching's disappearance, and how to look for him.

I don't want to find Yolanda's brother, though. Yolanda acted so strangely in the market with the brass platter, as if she were under a spell. What was his power? She was always flushed with excitement after. Ming pressed on, not wanting to discuss the issue.

She found the tunnel hours later, a place where the fung swirled faster above and around them. As they moved through, the fog gradually drifted away and she could see the valley below; the grasses were dull and dry, not the brilliant jade green Ming remembered. Still, the sky was blue and the winds rolled the clouds into gentle waves worthy of the ancient scroll painters. Ming's heart soared when she spotted a pair of kites dancing in the wind. Two tiny figures, one white and one black, chased the kites across the meadow. The one in white ran in zigzags around the field, while the one in black remained still, rooted to one spot.

"Come on!" Ming took Yolanda's hand and ran down the side of the mountain until they tumbled into a tangle of arms and legs in the meadow at the bottom. While Yolanda caught her breath, Ming jumped up and ran to where Ting and Tan flew their kites.

These were the people she loved most in any world. She bowed deeply, but said nothing.

"Who's this? Another monk, looking for enlightenment?" Tan didn't stop weaving his kite strings. "We have nothing to teach, but you may fly a kite if you brought one on your pilgrimage."

"Uncle Tan! It's me, Ming." She jumped high in the air, flipped a circle of handsprings and landed in an arched backbend.

"Our Ming has long lovely hair, not a scrubbing-brush head."

"Only our Ming could do that so beautifully. It is her, husband." Ting smiled with knowing eyes.

Tan peered at her. "Eh? Ming has become a monk?"

"Aunt Ting, Uncle Tan – I am so happy to see you again."

"So very sorry, Minga, but you are wrong. It is us who are glad to see you." Tan loved to argue almost as much as kites.

Ting stood on tiptoe to kiss Ming's forehead. "Do I see sadness in your heart?" she whispered.

Ming looked down at her empty hands. She wanted to fold herself into Ting's robe and cry for the lost hope and suffering she had seen. She wanted Tan to hold her in his strong arms, but then Yolanda caught up, breathing hard.

"Who's this? Another monk?" Tan laughed.

"This is my friend, Miss Yolanda. She's not a monk, but she is very powerful."

"Yes, yes. I see those green eyes. Very auspicious!"

78

*Y*olanda bowed to Ting and Tan. They looked so much alike, they could be twins: the same wiry body type, deep-set eyes, nut-colored skin and chin-length hair, white with black mixed in.

"Where did you come from, my dear?" Ting asked.

"The Huskaloosa valley," Yolanda said, in almost a whisper.

"She came through a gateway," Ming said.

"Hus-ka-loo-sa," Tan said. "That gateway is not familiar. No matter. There is always more for us to know."

"I know that this dragon wind is dying down. No good for kite-flying, husband." Ting said.

"No, Mother. It's still good!" he said, but then his kite, shaped like a swallow and painted with flowers and bats, dove into the ground. "No matter. I want to hear your story, Miss Yo-lan-da, and I want to hear it with a good cup of cha in my hand. There's a hut that loves us, not too far up that grandfather mountain."

Tan pointed to the highest mountain in a range of peaks in the clouds. The steep-sided crags made Yolanda feel tired. At least now she could see where they were going, but the going was still tough. Ming leapt up the trail as fast as a mountain lion. Along the way Tan and Ting traded stories of the seven clans of the East, telling Yolanda about their foods, clothes, marriage customs, and what they believed in.

As they rounded the mountain most of the sunlight disappeared in shadow. Soon they came to the so-called hut: two rough stone walls tucked under an overhanging rock. Inside, the cave was cool and dark but for a circle of light from a hole above a fire pit. The dirt floor was smooth and hard, with big flat stones for tables. Bundles of stuff were tucked everywhere: knives, brushes, paper, string, sticks of bamboo, brightly painted kites.

"Why do you like kites so much?" Yolanda asked.

"Wind is a most powerful element," Tan said. "But like the spirits, it cannot be seen. A dancing kite gives shape to the wind."

He bent to the fire pit and blew on the dying coals while Ting filled a kettle from the water pouch. Soon Ming poured four bowls of tea that smelled of oranges and they settled on thick furs. Yolanda longed to look for Yakos in her cup of tea, but Ting and Tan's bright, black eyes never stopped watching her.

"From the beginning, then." Ting asked in a gentle tone of voice. "How did you come to be here with our Ming?"

Yolanda took a deep breath and told them about seeing her twin's face in a reflection.

Tan's shaggy eyebrows went up. "A reflection?"

"Yes, his face just kept popping up everywhere, in the TV and the toaster and –"

"What's a tee-vee?" he interrupted. "And a toas-tah?"

Yolanda smiled. "They're, um, machines that do things, so we can watch shows, like soap operas, and make toast – and –"

"Which was the gateway? Tee-vee or toast-ah?" Tan asked.

"Let her finish, Father!" Ting said.

Yolanda told them about meeting Miz Becca and Hanging Lake and how she lost sight of her twin at the glowing ball of light.

"Ah. The golden sphere. You were pulled into it, yes?"

"Yes! But I thought it was him, pulling me toward it."

"Many have had the same experience. If you go another way around the sphere, you'll choose another gateway, to the West, North or South."

"The West. That's where I –" Yolanda stopped. "Have you been there? Through the gateways?"

"The gateways are meant for only a few, to travel between worlds," Ting said. "Now, we watch."

"We have seen many like you stumble out in the fog. Some like Ming, listened to us, but some used their powers for –"

Ting put her finger to her lips. "There is a time to speak, and a time to listen, Husband," she said.

"No, please, tell me more!" Yolanda said.

Ting nodded. "Tan and I are very old. We've met many young people that fell into this land from the gateways to your world. Their stories are different, but all have the same questions: How did I get here? And why? The path we are on is not always clear, nor is what we are meant to discover on the way. We believe that all our experiences, good and bad, have something to teach us. So what did you find when you came through the gateway?"

"I wandered around in the fog until I met a little talking monkey in a banyan grove."

Tan nodded. "The Monkey King. Up to his old tricks."

"He's another of the old ones like us," Ting said.

"That little monkey? A king!" Yolanda told them about all the statues around the Palace, how she had met Ming and Jade at the door, how Narissa and Nikolas had trapped her, and how she saw their powers and got away, with Ming's help.

Tan was amazed. "How could you accomplish so much, with no training?"

"Well, a black bird flew in the window and kept cawing at me, pestering me to see, see, see, until I finally figured it out. How to use my – my vision."

"Hmmm. Birds of that kind are not native to this land. You say it 'pestered you'?"

"Not with words, but I could hear it telling me to see. That's how I finally saw the webs that Narissa makes. But it was Ming who cut them off, with a sword."

"Your power must be quite strong," Ting said. "Ming lived in the mountains with us for three years. She worked hard to find her individual power, and to align her strength with the Way. Yet still there is more to learn. There is always more."

"I, for one, would like to learn more about the face you saw in the tee-vee. Have you seen him since the gateway?" Tan asked.

"Yes." Yolanda's voice was a little shaky. "I sometimes see him in reflections."

"Can he speak? Does he say anything to you?"

"Yes. He says that I should go to him in the West, so we can be together." Yolanda looked up at Ming, who didn't look back. She didn't mention the battles or the danger. No sense in worrying them. Plus, they might not show her how to get to the West if they knew more about him.

"We have sensed trouble there," Ting said, nodding.

"An ancient seer predicted all of this," Tan said in a very serious tone. "A time of great change will come to Tessar, when the green-eyed twins appear."

79

*M*ing dreaded the mention of her twin, but Yolanda was excited to hear any news of him. "Green-eyed twins! What else did they say? Anything about my brother?"

And now she wants to go to him again. It felt wrong.

"The prophecy is wrong," Ming said as she stared into the fire. "How can there be change if the cycles do not turn? How can there be change if Ching is gone?"

Ming told Ting and Tan about the many sad things she had seen along the way, about the spring that never bloomed.

They only nodded politely.

"Have you been so long in these mountains that you no longer feel? Nothing grows! The spirits have vanished! Where is Ching?"

"Tsk, tsk, Daughter." Tan clicked his tongue. "We feel it."

"No change. That is a kind of change, isn't it?" Tan said.

"Forgive me," Ming hung her head. "Of all the wise ones, I thought you'd know what happened to Ching. I thought you'd be angry. I thought you'd help." She made herself stop before she said another unkind thing.

"Things are not always as they seem," Ting said in a gentle voice. "The cycles of life have not stopped. Not even a god can do that. Everything still changes, only very, very slowly."

"Think of a stone. Perhaps it takes its own kind of breath. Perhaps it takes a thousand years for one inhale," Tan added.

Ming herself took a slow, deep breath to quiet her heart. She'd already waited so long to meet her father; to wait one minute longer seemed to take all of her strength.

"Time to consult the oracle." Tan leapt to his feet, while Ting pulled a familiar red silk pouch from the folds of her robe. She took out the three old coins with square holes in the center.

"A square hole in a circle. I've seen it before," Yolanda said.

"The gate at the Palace of the Ten Thousand Things," Ming said. "It's the same shape."

"The circle represents Heaven, or Yang, and the square is Earth, Yin." Ting smiled.

"What?" Yolanda said.

"See the design on that kite?" Tan pointed to the yin-yang symbol. "Yin-yang is a whole circle made of two halves, one black and one white."

"Swirling around like two fish in a pond." Ting said.

"They signify the elemental male and female principles we call yin and yang. Each has a spot of the other inside, to show the opposites are always moving toward each other."

Tan sat taller on his haunches and told the old story that Ming had heard many times.

>*"Long ago, in the time before time,*
>*before there were any worlds, or any living things,*
>*all was chaos. And out of the chaos arose a sphere.*
>*The inside of the sphere was an egg, made of two parts,*
>*the dark and the light.*
>*The egg broke, and the dark force separated from the light.*
>*The heavy elements became the Earth and Moon*
>*and the light elements became the Sun and Sky.*
>*Yin and yang.*
>*Yang is the male force of light and creation..."*

Tan paused and nodded at Ting, who took up the story:

>*"..and yin is the receptive, the female force of darkness.*
>*Wherever there is yang, there is also yin.*
>*Wherever there is light, there must be dark.*
>*Wherever there is action, there must be rest.*
>*There cannot be one without the other.*
>*Together, yin and yang balance the opposing forces of Nature.*
>*That is the Way."*

Ting and Tan each put their hands together, like a prayer.

"I like that story," Yolanda said. "Except the part about the female being dark. Isn't that bad?"

"No bad, no good. Only different." Tan's eye's twinkled.

"Hmmm, that sounds familiar," Yolanda said. "Oh! It's like our friend Rika said, 'good, bad, all time same same.'"

Tan smiled. "Your friend is a master."

"He's a thief!"

"All time same same, eh? Yin and yang are very useful for understanding this very old knowledge we call Tao, or the Way,"

"'The Way!' Ha! That's what the monkey kept jabbering about! The Monkey King, as you call him."

Ting and Tan nodded. "The Way is a great pattern of change that is always moving, manifested in everything all around us." Tan moved his arm in a slow arc above his head.

"Long ago, our ancestors discovered a key to the pattern, using these coins." Ting let the three coins dance out of her palm and across the dirt floor.

"But isn't a coin toss just random?" Yolanda asked.

"Nothing under heaven is truly 'random,' as you say." Tan smiled. "Everything in nature, no matter how small, reveals the larger pattern. Ming, will you read the coins?"

Ming noted the symbols on the coins' faces, and drew two lines in the dust, with a space between: — —. Ting threw the coins five times and Ming added five lines above the first, two sets of broken lines with straight lines in the middle. "It's the double trigram Kan."

— —
——-—
— —
— —
——-—
— —

Tan smiled. "These six lines, a hexagram, represent the condition of the world at the moment the coins fell, a pattern that tells us the changes of the Way. This hexagram, 'Abysmal Water,' means there is great danger ahead."

80

*D*anger. We've had enough of that already!" Yolanda rubbed out the lines in the dirt with her foot, as if that could make the danger go away.

Ming touched her hand. "Don't worry. Though the hexagram shows danger, there is also success. We will overcome it."

"Water shows the way to move forward, *through* the danger," Ting said. "So. The way to overcome danger is not to avoid it, but to keep moving and to hold on to your goodness. 'If you are sincere, you have success in your heart, and whatever you do succeeds.' That is also in the hexagram."

"Enough sitting, with oracles and teachings. I'm hungry!" Tan jumped to his feet.

"We need water for our supper, Husband." Ting said.

"I'll fill our pouch at the spring," Ming picked up the bag.

Yolanda had been dying to find some water, anything that reflected, ever since they left the city. All the talk of danger made her want to find Yakos. Now. She practically grabbed the water bag out of Ming's hands. "I'll get the water. Where's the spring?"

Ming frowned. "Behind the hut. Marked by a pair of pines."

Yolanda hiked over crumbling rocks to the spring, which was barely a trickle. She filled the bag then found some water trapped between some rocks, just big enough to see a reflection. A shadowy rug of short red hair had grown on her scalp.

The surface of the water twirled before Yakos appeared.

"Hey," she said. "It's been a long time."

"Yes, and a challenging time." His voice sounded colder than the spring water running down her arm. "Where are you?"

"I did what you said: came west. We're up in the Fung Mountains."

"Yes. You are close now. I can feel your presence. I've been waiting a long time, Yolanda."

"Long enough, I'd say!"

"The time is nearly come. But first, you must go higher. Climb the highest mountain you can see, the mountain they call Grandfather, and wait for me there."

"How will I know where to go?"

"Trust me, Yolanda. I will send a sign. But you must go alone."

"But I don't know the way!" The blasted way. Again.

Yakos smiled. "You are strong. And powerful. You'll find it."

"But I don't want to go all the way up there without Ming!"

"You must. And don't tell her where you are going."

"But she'll worry about me."

"Do you want to see me?" He stiffened, and sounded colder than before.

"Y-yes, but —"

"Yolanda, think of it. The first time we meet, after being apart for so long, we will only want each other."

81

ecca's spirit rose with the fierce updrafts of fung that swirled among the peaks. The spirits high above these mountains were more free and wild, less confused than the ones below in the domestic plains and valleys. She tumbled with them, dancing where the fung took them, and found energy in their strength.

As she grew stronger, more and more she felt the anguish of her people coming from the West. It was as if a hundred thousand souls were tortured all at once.

Want to go to them, help them. End the suffering.

Must stay here, near the girl Yolanda.

She sensed the girl was held in safety now, for the first time in her long journey.

But she was drawn to the West, too.

Coincidence? Not likely. There is no such thing.

82

olanda woke up and saw Ming's fuzzy dark head sleeping soundly on the woven mats. She wanted to tell her so badly, but Yakos made such a point of it, not to tell.

I've come too far to risk him leaving me again.

She tiptoed past her and ducked under the door, out into the moonless fung. She thought surely that Ming would hear her leave, but no one followed.

Yolanda could barely see her own feet on the skinny, steep trail that seemed to lead straight up into the clouds. In some places it was barely wide enough, and with no edge to the drop-off below. Could be a million miles down.

A loose patch gave way under her foot. She fell against the mountain and clawed the dirt and rock with her bare hands to keep from sliding into that awful nothingness.

He'd better not be pulling one of his tricks on me again.

She struggled back up as the wind whistled around her, wondering what Ming would think of her, sneaking off like that.

Wish I could have told her.

Her bones ached and her muscles felt like rubber, but she kept on going. After hours of climbing straight up, going no faster than a crawl, the faintest light of dawn began to peek through the fog. She rounded a tight stretch that ended in a wall of smooth gray rock. The trail was only six inches wide and the wall was too steep and slippery to climb. As she stood wondering what to do the wall started to melt and swirl, like a storm on a TV weatherman's map. Slowly his face came up through the whirlpool, a moving, breathing picture on the rock.

He blinked, and his green eyes danced. "Yolanda..."

"How can you do that? In a wall?"

"I'm getting stronger, as you get closer. Can you feel it?"

"Yeah, I guess so. You look real, even in that rock."

"This is the sign I promised. I want you to know you can always trust me."

Hmm. "How much farther to the top of this dang mountain? Are you up there now?"

"Climb to the highest peak you can see. You will find me there." He smiled as his face sunk back into the rock.

Yolanda set out again. She did feel a little stronger, just like he said. She spotted a nicely notched handhold in the same spot where his face had been. She pulled herself over the rocks and kept on going – up, always up.

82

From the moment Ming opened her eyes she knew something was wrong. Yolanda's bundle of skins was disturbed. "She's gone," she said. "Yolanda is gone."

Ting stoked the morning fire. "The Northern girl is not a trained warrior. Perhaps she's not ready to face the dragon."

"She is very strong. Maybe the dragon is not her journey," Tan said. "Where might she have gone? Back down the mountain?"

"I'm not sure which way, up or down, but I am certain why she left: for her twin brother."

"Hmmm. She said that she could see him," Tan said.

"I saw him, too, in the flesh, at the Palace of the Ten Thousand Things before I fell into the Northerners' trance. He stood with them. He is part of all that is wrong."

"Did you tell your friend?"

Ming looked down. "She wants to find him as badly as I need to find Ching. She has no other family."

"Minga. Sometimes we must speak what we dread most," Tan said. "If she knew how you felt, it might confirm her fears."

"What do you mean?"

Tan stood up. "Did you see her face, when she came with the water? Full of worry. He is very important to her, yet there is something else, something hidden, not spoken."

"Yes! But it's so hard to speak of things that I know so little about!"

"Do you know how you feel?"

"Yes. I am worried. Afraid for her. Afraid he will not be good to her, that he will hurt her. But –"

"Then you know what to say." Tan smiled.

Ming took a short, deep breath. "Yes. Next time, I will speak my feelings, even if I am afraid."

Ting nodded a half bow. "Very good, Minga. Now, do you know where he is?"

"She said only that he was in the West."

"There is a gateway at the peak of this grandfather mountain. He could be using that gateway to move between the lands."

"The peak! That's where we were going - to find the pathway to the mountains of clouds. This may be a happy accident."

"No accident, Daughter," Tan said. "Your destiny is entwined with the green-eyed twins."

83

Yolanda trudged on higher. The dawn sky was the same grayish green as the rocks under her feet, so even though there was lighter, it was still hard to see her way. Her lungs felt tight as if there wasn't enough room for air. With every step a burning ache shot up her shins and ankles. She kept climbing until she didn't feel it anymore.

She came to a rock face so steep and smooth she thought she'd fall off for sure. Somehow she found another handhold and then another toehold. She clung to the wall panting, like a cat on a tree. She prayed to her Sunday school God and to the Four gods of Tessar, just in case. "Please, don't let me slip and fall."

One last push and she was over the worst of it. She raised her head and saw the last trail where the grandfather mountain jutted up into a craggy point. The wind blew so fiercely that it took every inch of her willpower to hang on, and then to keep moving forward. An old county song came into her head, "Against the Wind," and she sang it out loud into the howling fung. She could hardly get enough air to breathe, much less to sing, but it kept her mind off the distance she still had to go.

84

*A*s Yakos strode past the row of rounded cliff dwellings a cold wind blew over the cave openings, which played an eerie music like a human wail. It reminded him of the voices of the Red people as they ran off the cliffs high above his head. He had avoided this place because the stench of the bodies rising from the ravine below was overpowering. He did not like to be reminded of all the suffering. Painful, but necessary.

His mind and body felt equally empty as he made his way to the gateway at the back of the third cave. Hard to concentrate. Hard to gather the energy needed for his encounter with Yolanda. He'd planned to use the geography at the peak; his knowledge of the place was an advantage, but still, it would be taxing.

It would be so much easier not to test her. To simply meet her as my cherished sister, and then watch her grow, slowly, over time. But there is no time. And I must know what she is made of. Damn! If only Nikolas and Narissa had done their part, everything would now be in alignment. I wouldn't have to leave here.

If only I could be sure that the wall will hold. If only I could be sure that Yashi is capable of maintaining the order I've worked so hard to build.

Now I am truly alone. Can't trust them. Can't trust her.

Not yet.

85

*Y*olanda's arms shook like crazy as she gripped the wet rock ledge, the last cliff. She couldn't hold on for another second. She hurled one leg up and over. With a huge push that she didn't know she had in her, she dragged her chest and legs over the edge.

She lay on the cliff top, a small piece of flat ground at the foot of the peak, sweating, breathing hard, looking around.

Is he here? Can't see squat in all this fog.

A giant circle shape suddenly loomed above her head, like a big sign, or? She hadn't seen it at all. It was a large ring with something dark in the middle. She stood up and reached out to touch the ring. Cold, metal. The fung swirled away for a bit and she could see an iron statue of a man standing in the middle of the big wheel, as if his arms and legs were the spokes. He was a man of the East, with strong cheekbones and fierce, wide-set eyes. He wore an awful look of shock, as if he wanted to roll his wheel right over the edge, to get away from something. Or someone.

"How did you get up here? And where is Yakos?" she said aloud, not expecting the iron man to answer.

As she stared up at him, the statue's face began to melt into another person's, his almond-shaped eyes becoming round and green. She stared, not breathing, as a warm pink skin color spread down the whole statue, starting from his forehead, moving down through his chest, and then out to his arms and legs, fingers and toes. While at first the statue had been as black as iron, from his proud head to his outstretched feet, this figure wore a shock of red hair.

Yakos!

Her brother smiled and leapt away from the metal man like the peel of an orange. Before she could speak he landed on the ground and ran out onto a skinny outcropping of rock that jutted out from the cliff-top plateau. Yolanda hadn't noticed it before. The tiny ledge didn't look strong enough to hold even a squirrel, yet he stood solid, hands on hips.

"Yakos!" she shouted. "Aren't you even going to say hello?"

His green eyes shone bright as emeralds. It was the first time Yolanda could see all of him. He wore a red uniform that crossed in front and was cinched up with belts and decorated with rows of buttons. A tough soldier. "Come. Follow me."

She sized up the narrow ledge of rock he stood on. It stretched out farther than she saw at first; still, it looked a lot more precarious than the worst of the cliffs she'd just climbed. She was dying to see him up close, maybe even touch him, but not out there.

"Why'd you go over there? Why can't you just stay by me?"

"You can do it, Yolanda. Show me your strength."

She made herself take a few steps. The trail was so skinny and steep, and there was nothing on either side to catch her if she fell. "But it's so narrow. And take a look at that drop-off."

"The path of the great is always difficult. Don't be afraid, Come to me."

you can't make it

Yes, I can. Just watch me.

Yolanda took a tiny step further, and glanced up at the iron man, still in his iron wheel, safe, not moving.

Yakos laughed. "I knew you'd be strong, like me. I know it's in you. I can feel it."

you're not strong enough to survive that fall. no one is.

Shush, Mama. I can do this.

Yolanda inched forward, feeling the ground ahead, and then took another step with her left foot.

"That's it. Come to me, Yolanda."

Her left foot fell down a lot farther than it should have, like stepping down a too-tall step on a staircase. A tumble of rocks

251

slid out from under her. She waved her arms to catch her balance.

"Yikes! That scared the holy living daylights out of me!" Sweat dripped down her forehead into her eyes.

Yakos didn't say anything, but Yolanda felt him pushing her to a place she'd never been. It was scary, but she wanted it so much. Wanted to prove she was like him. Strong and sure.

She could almost touch him. Just a few steps more. She lifted her foot and reached it out way in front, like a trapeze artist or a ballerina. She was just about to let it down on the small space Yakos had left for her, when she heard a horrible scream coming from down below.

86

*A*drift high above the borderlands, Becca's spirit heard a terrible scream echo through the mountains.

Was it from her people? What could be so wrong, that she could hear them cry from the next realm?

No. The people in the West were suffering, but the shout did not come from there. It came from below, from the world of dust. Yolanda's world. But it wasn't Yolanda, and it wasn't a call for help. It was a warning. Perhaps from the other god-child, Ming?

Becca let the physical plane take shape in her mind. She sensed where Yolanda stood on the peak of the tallest mountain. With one foot on the steep, rocky slope and the other groping the air in front, she prepared to take one more step. If she did, it would be her last.

I must stop her.

How? Spirit cannot make sound. I can't become the bird I was, to tell her. That body does not exist any more. Yet she would listen to a black bird; she would trust it.

Becca drew up her strength and tapped into the deep well of power. She created a little vortex of wind to sweep up bits of dust, dragon debris and other loose matter that swirled in the soup called fung. She gathered them together and shaped it all into a loose body, a small form that she could inhabit, if only for a short while.

It was a rickety, wobbly sort of a thing. The trick was to get it to move. She didn't have time to make it self-propelling. Instead, she caught the next sweep of wind that came along and rode it down to where Yolanda stood precarious.

One more challenge. Becca drew on all her powers to make it happen.

Talk, you scrap of life-stuff! Tell her!

87

olanda blinked twice when she heard that shout.
Was it Ming? She's up here! On the mountain! I
should call back to her... but then Yakos will think I
didn't come alone.

As she decided, a raggedy black bird appeared
out of nowhere. It didn't look quite right, not like the bird back
at the palace. It had no feathers and a loose, lumpy body that she
could see through in a couple places.

It wheezed and croaked, then finally made a sound that
Yolanda could understand. "Caw – Caw – Look. See."

"So it is you!" she said.

"Of course it's me," Yakos said from where he stood down
the precipice. "I'm leaving now. Follow me to the West, or you
may never see me again."

"Wait! I –"

Yakos turned his back on her and took a step further on the
narrow trail. The bird zigzagged in his direction, and then flew
right through him.

"What the heck?!"

The bird fluttered like crazy right in the middle of Yakos'
chest, in the place where his heart ought to be. The bird hovered
there, screeching: "Caw! Caw! Look! See! See!"

Open the vision. That's what the bird is telling me!

Yolanda tried to relax so she could feel it inside her. It wasn't
easy standing on the edge of a tiny bit of rock, with her only
brother about to walk away, leaving her alone again, maybe
forever. She squinted and stared at him, but the vision just
wouldn't come. She nearly lost her balance.

maybe it's not real, maybe you don't have it

I do. I do! She felt the truth inside her. It just needed to find
a way out. She closed her eyes and waited until the sight rose up

through the knot of fear in her belly, until it flowed through her like air, like her own blood.

Yolanda opened her eyes. Her vision reached out to Yakos as he walked down the narrow crag of rock, and then he disappeared. He didn't just walk into the fog; he wasn't there at all. The skinny trail to the West was gone, too. She looked down at her feet, at the place where she had almost stepped. Below her she saw only clouds, and a long, long fall.

He tried to kill me. My own brother.

Yolanda's heart sunk like a lead weight. She took a couple of steps back to more solid ground. She heard a weak 'caw' and looked around for the bird.

A streak of red flashed around the side of a boulder.

"Congratulations! You passed my little test." Yakos stood three feet behind her.

She spun around. "Get away from me!"

"Bravo. You have proven yourself to be more than worthy to be my sister."

He was gone, again, faster than a flame on a birthday candle.

"Damn you, Yakos!" Yolanda's chest choked with fury.

"I'm down here!" Yakos yelled from somewhere down the trail. "No tricks this time. I promise you. I'm really here..."

Yolanda half-stomped, half-slid down the steep mountain in the direction of his voice. She couldn't see very far in the fog, but she was gonna find the real Yakos, no matter if he was in the East or the West or the next galaxy.

I'm going to give that boy a piece of my mind. Once and for all.

88

*M*ing scaled the grandfather peak like a mountain lion, looking and listening for any sign of Yolanda. When she saw that tiny figure on the very edge of a precipice, about to jump, she knew it was her friend. She'd shouted her loudest warning: "TAK! Stop!"

Yolanda did stop, thank the Four gods. But then a wave of fung wrapped around the peak like a blanket, so thick that Ming couldn't see the top or even the trail ahead.

She groped for a solid place to hold before she could take each step. Treacherous and slow. The air thinned nearer the peak. Each breath was harder than the last, and provided less strength. The muscles in her legs, back and arms begged her to rest.

Remember: it is the will that perseveres. To the top!

She finally came to the slick, sheer cliff that Ting had told her to watch for. Like a camel draws water from its hump, Ming drew on her deep reserves of strength to pull her body up and over the final edge, and onto the plateau.

She lay on the rock and took a few breaths to calm her wildly beating heart. The peak was shrouded in thick fung.

"Yolanda? Are you here?" she called.

No answer. Did she fall? Was she hurt, in need of help?

Ming crawled over the sharp rock with arms outstretched, feeling her way through the fog until she touched cold metal.

She followed its shape with her hands. It curved up and around, like a giant ring. When a stiff gust of dragonwind blew the fog away, Ming saw a figure of a man balanced inside an iron ring at least six stones tall. His body formed the spokes of a giant wheel. The sculptor was a master, the features were so lifelike. She stood on tiptoe to examine his face, his high cheekbones and firm, square lips.

"By the Four gods!" Could it be? The wheel was unmistakable. Was this iron statue her father, the god Ching, the one she had searched for, for so long?

He did not look grand and powerful as she had expected. He was small. Skinny. She sank to her knees and kowtowed, giving thanks for the many kindnesses that finally brought her to him.

"Father, if you can hear me, I am Ming, your daughter."

He didn't answer.

"I will not rest until your wheel turns once more. I'll go anywhere, do anything, to restore your powers. Even to the Imperial Dragon himself."

The wind only whistled around him. Ming looked up at the pillar of fung, the mountains of clouds that reached to the sky. She was ready. But what if Yolanda needed her? Or was in pain?

Ming took a breath to let the answer come, to listen to the inner voice that knows what is right, and what to do.

Yolanda will be all right. I must do what I came here for.

The clouds piled in huge drifts around the peak, like snow. So moveable, so fluid. How can they hold me?

Ming filled her lungs with fung, and recalled what Ting and Tan said: 'Remember the hexagram: danger, sincerity, success.'

She lifted one knee high into the fog. Her foot sank down, then finally caught on something firm, like a sponge or a bed of springy moss. She let her weight fall onto the raised leg. It sunk a bit more, but it held. She took another, higher step. Though her leg sank past her knee into the fog, she now stood on the clouds, a full arm's length above the grandfather mountain.

Danger, sincerity, success.

One breath for every step: in, out. The rhythm helped her go on without fear. She did not let herself think of how high she was or how far she could fall, but of only the next step. Soon she climbed as if it were an ordinary mountain of rock and earth.

Ming pressed on higher, until she caught a glimpse of green-gold scales and a slender tail snaking through the fog. A dragon!

He was forty feet long, with sharp claws that wheeled through the fog like throwing stars. He looked as fierce as a temple dog, with long whiskers and huge, popping eyes. He reared his head back, snorted and opened his mouth. A puff of cloud shot out from between his sharp teeth.

He's terribly, horribly angry. At me.

89

*Y*olanda half-slid, half-crawled down the rocky face of the mountain. She couldn't see much in the fog, but she went toward the spot where Yakos' voice had come. Soon she saw a small opening under a ledge where a strange greenish-gold glow seeped out. It reminded her of the shining ball under Hanging Lake.

It's a gateway! That's how he got here.

She stooped to go into the mouth of the cave. As her eyes adjusted to the bright light toward the back of the cave, she saw a dark silhouette of a young man walking toward her.

"Yolanda, my sister! Finally, we meet." Yakos reached out to her with arms wide, grinning.

Yolanda shoved his chest with both hands. He staggered back.

"So I finally get to meet the real Yakos. Flesh and blood," she said. "I should kick your butt to Kingdom Come."

"I'm sorry. I didn't mean to upset you." He pouted.

"I could have died up there!"

"If you had not used your power, you would have revealed a weakness. I had to be sure you are strong."

"Is that all you want me for? To be strong?"

"Yolanda, there are many reasons, many things that only twins can share: secrets, knowledge. Please. Sit with me." Yakos sat down cross-legged in the dirt.

Yolanda didn't trust him farther than she could throw him, but she had to know more. "Just tell me the truth. What in God's holy creation are you up to? Why did you call me here?"

"You were supposed to know all of that from the beginning," he said. "Once you found your power, and learned to use it at will. But Nikolas and Narissa failed us, tried to control you."

"They're totally evil! Why are you with them?"

"I'm not sure I am with them. Now that you're here –"

Yakos looked into Yolanda's eyes. She felt a shiver of excitement, like when he first called her from the mirror.

"Nikolas and Narissa are my – teachers," he continued. "They were very good to me. They taught me the ways of power. And I've learned so much! Now I can tell you, now that you're here. My power is illusion. But my illusions look, feel, sound, and even taste, completely real."

"Like the path back there? The one I almost walked off?"

He nodded. "That wasn't much of a demonstration. I can do so much more. I've learned to combine the very essences of matter and spirit in a completely new way. It's all energy! It's never been done before! You wouldn't believe all that is possible."

"I did believe it. I thought it was real," she said. "You could do a lot with that."

"Yes. I can and I will. And I want you to be part of it. Here, I'll show you!" Yakos closed his eyes and took a breath.

The walls of the cave melted away, and the two of them sat cross-legged on a tiny plateau in the middle of an enormous cavern, surrounded by a lush green jungle. A huge waterfall splashed beside them, sending sprays of mist on Yolanda's face and arms. Bright orange and red flowers nodded in the warm breeze. Yolanda could almost taste the scent of honey. Purple and blue birds chattered in the trees.

"Oh, my lord!" she said. "It's beautiful!"

Yakos folded his arms across his chest and smiled. His jaw muscles looked tight, as if he were holding something very heavy but didn't want to show the strain.

90

*Y*akos forced himself to keep from trembling as he spun the illusion of paradise for Yolanda, adding more and more living details to make her feel the breadth of his power. To make her want it for herself.

At the same time, he felt the breach in the wall at the Red lands cracking wider. Opening to the Red warriors. Failing.

So this is too much. Good to know one's limits.

Nikolas would never admit to any limits. And that will be his downfall.

He took another breath to feed the turbines of power that turned inside him. He loved the feeling of controlling the particles of matter in that cave, making them dance into new shapes and to refract the energy of light in new ways.

"Is it hard?" Yolanda said.

"Yes. But with you here, it's easier. I feel stronger."

It was true. The energy she added, with just her presence next to him, made the illusion so much deeper. Yakos was surprised by how the droplets of water freshened his skin, and all the saturated colors made him feel more alive. He gave more attention to the wall in the West, building up the gaps, filling the holes.

I must keep her.

91

*Y*olanda was a little sad when the ferns and birds and flowers melted back into slimy cold rock. "That power of yours, it's incredible," she said. "So, what'll you do with it?"

Yakos let out a big breath. "Nikolas and Narissa said that I would become a god one day. The one true god of Tessar."

"What?!"

"Yes, it's true. I am as strong as a god, even now."

"Oh, come on! That's crazy."

"That iron man, up on the peak. Do you know who he is?"

Yolanda did know, but only just realized it. "Is it Ching?"

"Yes. He's the god of Change, the most powerful being in the East. Do you know how he got there?" Yakos winked. "He resisted change. Ironic, isn't it? Ching didn't want to make way for the new. He tried to use his wheel against me, to destroy me. I was forced to put a stop to it."

Yolanda frowned. "But his cycles, the rain and the crops, are messed up. There's no food. Everybody in the East is starving!"

"Of all Tessarians, I thought the Easterners would understand. Change is a fact of life. When Ching and his people accept the change that's coming – a new god, a new way – then they will get their rice and fish."

"But it's awful, what you did to him, to all of them!"

"Yolanda, we are different. As leaders, we have to look beyond the discomfort of a few. Of even a god."

"But Yakos, it's just not right!"

"I know the pain you feel. But it's only temporary. Everything will be better soon. You and I, together, we can make the Four into one. We can put aside all the differences of the Black, White, the Yellow and the Red. We can create a whole new balance. Imagine it. Tessar, as one land!"

The cave walls disappeared again. Yolanda looked onto a wide yellow plain with gently rolling hills in the distance. Streams of people came from four different directions wearing colorful costumes. One group of people had white skin and wore mainly blue and purple. Others were brown, with deep red and tan clothing, and one group were dark-skinned, wearing bright gold and green.

"Look!" she pointed to the Easterners in yellow tunics and loose pants. They all looked happy, doing acrobatics or juggling.

Yolanda watched as all four groups met in the center, bowed to each other and held hands. Then they began to dance, in an amazing pattern that wove all of their colors and costumes together. "It's so – so – beautiful."

Yakos stood and reached for her hand, pulling her into the light. His eyes burned with excitement. "Together, we'll make this happen. Come with me. Through the gateway, to the West."

She wanted so much to be part of this incredible, joyful experience. But as she stood up, a picture came to her mind: a lone fisherman on the half-moon bridge in the Chua's village, waiting for fish that would never come, unless he bowed down to Yakos. Then she saw the guard's empty eyes as they chopped down the two young acolytes in Kua-Ma's temple. Finally, she saw Chen's body as he lay beside Miss Lu, his arm draped over her.

Yolanda looked up into Yakos' face. His eyes flashed with brilliance. He was so knowing, so strong and sure.

Her vision leapt up from deep inside, more powerful than ever before.

It's stronger now, because he's holding my hand!

She looked directly into the very center of his being. She found a diamond in his core, brilliant and beautiful and hard. But this diamond had a flaw. A crack. It was just like all the empty places she had seen in herself and Ming, the ones Nikolas filled with dream clouds. But the opening inside Yakos was so much bigger. She saw the huge appetite it gave him. She saw how he tried to fill that awful emptiness, with power and control.

How desperate he is to win, to be in charge. How fiercely he believes in what he's doing. He won't ever stop, not until he makes his ideas real. He'll do anything, kill anybody, if they get in his way. Even me.

Yolanda then saw all the pain he could bring trying to make his dreams come true: mothers screaming for babies, torn from their arms; sons killing fathers; brothers hurting sisters. She saw a multitude of disasters, small and large, in and out of war.

She wanted to run, get away from him, go back home, anything to get away from all that pain. Still, she would never get away from the truth, that he was the cause of it all.

He's my brother. He wants me to help him do this.

"Come with me, Yolanda." Yakos pulled her toward the light.

"No!" She screamed. Her vision shot out of her eyes and burned into his, ten times more powerful than before.

Yakos jumped back as if he'd been scorched. He covered his face with both arms and dropped to the floor, rolling in torture.

"Stop! What are you doing?!" His voice was thick, muffled.

"I don't know! I was just —"

Maybe all the pain she saw him bring to the world was reflected back to him. Whatever it was, she didn't mean it to happen. She closed her eyes fast to turn off the vision, slowly letting it trickle back down to nothing.

Yakos crawled away from her and sat back up. He gripped his head, closed his eyes and kept still, as if he was trying to concentrate very hard.

Yolanda felt the ground shake under her feet. She jumped up and backed away toward the mouth of the cave. The mountain groaned as if it were about to break into a thousand pieces. Big rocks fell from the roof, crashing down all around them. A huge chunk hit Yolanda's head and broke into a pile of rubble.

"Oww!" Her skull screamed with pain.

She staggered into the cave opening, and reached up to touch her head. There was no blood, and no bump, either.

That rock felt hard. So how come I'm not hurt? Am I in shock?

Slabs of rock fell from the sides and roof of the cave, as though the mountain itself was breaking into a million pieces. Yolanda staggered outside, and looked back at Yakos. Rocks fell on his head and back as he crawled on all fours to the ball of light at the back of the cave. Suddenly, dust and shards of rock flew up everywhere, as if a stick of dynamite had gone off. Then the whole cave collapsed in a pile of rubble.

"Yakos!" she shouted. "Get out of there!"

92

*W*hen she felt the dragon's hot breath on her face, Ming tried to run, but she could only trudge through the clouds. Dragon fung hissed around her legs as her feet fell through the insubstantial mass.

Her heart beat faster as the dragon lifted a giant wing and brought it down again, making a great whoosh as it shot straight up into the clouds above her.

She felt dozens of pinpricks fall onto her robe. The force wasn't too heavy at first, but built more and more intensity.

The dragon writhed like a snake and let loose a flurry of silver streaks that fell fast against her, cold and wet.

Rain! Dragons make rain. That's what it is. Oh, thank the Four, the dragon makes rain still. But it feels so *hard*!

Slices of rain fell into her shoulder. Another whizzed past her ear, and bit into her back.

Is it because I'm too close? Maybe by the time the rain reaches the land, the drops lose their force.

One huge drop drove itself into her thigh. She groaned as more and more silver came raining down from the dragon. It was like dodging the wooden knives that Ting and Tan used in fighting practice.

Breathe, and avoid them. Just like any other weapon.

The air was thin so high on the mountain of clouds. Still, each breath raised her chi to a higher state of alert.

Danger. Sincerity. Success.

Move like the water. Move through the danger. Don't get stuck in it. Ming bore down into the onslaught, fending off the rain with her elbows from the right, left, ahead, and behind.

The dragon loomed overhead, so close that his trailing whiskers could whip her. His golden skin was burnished with purple. She counted five claws. Of course! Only the Imperial dragon could make a dragonwind that strong.

As he lazily opened his mouth, she saw four rows of teeth inside, as long as swords. A gust of fung poured out, full of silver rain. She spun and rolled to avoid the blows.

He's not attacking me. It is only the dragon's way to make rain. I just happen to be here, in the rain's path.

Ming put her hands to her mouth and called up in her loudest warrior voice, "OH GREAT AND POWERFUL IMPERIAL DRAGON OF THE EAST!"

The dragon raised one giant eyebrow.

"I HAVE COME TO BEG a small bit of your infinite MERCY, just one of a thousand gifts you bestow among the four lands."

She kowtowed very low, keeping watch as the dragon lowered his head until his huge beady eye came within a few arm's length of her. A slow hiss of fung came through his nostrils, ruffling her short hair and scattering swirls of fog in all directions.

"OH GREAT ONE," she shouted. "Though I am not worthy to stand before you, I humbly beg you to listen." She kowtowed again. "The East is dying. Your rains no longer fall to the ground! Nothing grows or blooms, because the cycles of Ching can not turn."

The dragon raised his eyebrow again. His expression said that he knew everything since before the beginning of time, and nothing could surprise him.

Ming politely kowtowed one more time and went on. "Ching is my father. He is trapped in an iron gate at the peak of the grandfather mountain. I pray that you can free him."

The dragon's dark eye was deep and unknowable. Was he angry? Would he pelt her with rain for her impertinence?

With a grunt, the dragon bent his massive arms and raised his belly from the cloud. His whiskers whipped and snapped above her head as a powerful burst of fung blasted from his teeth.

The cloud of fung came fast. Ming readied herself for the blow. She stood in warrior stance and took a deep breath. The fung smelled oily and ancient. Instead of knocking her off the small cloud that she stood on, the dragon's breath slipped below and gently lifted it.

Ming wanted to shout a thousand million thanks. Before she could speak, the Imperial Dragon arched back and blew another narrow stream of fung at the cloud beneath her feet. The cloud bounced a bit, and then drifted downward, as if on a cushion of air.

She was flying, on a cloud! Ming nearly lost her balance. She sank to her knees and took a breath for courage.

Above her, the Imperial Dragon unfolded his wings. The span was so enormous that it darkened the sky. With a burst of chi that she felt in her bones, he lifted his torso into the air.

He drifted behind her, shielding her like a giant umbrella. He blew another gentle puff and her cloud picked up speed, flying down and around the mountains of clouds she had just climbed.

He's taking me back down to the Grandfather Mountain!

Ming leaned downwind with a smile and wished that Yolanda could see her now, flying – really flying!

Except for a few updrafts and dizzying plunges, the ride was gentle. All too soon, the dragonwind slowed to a gentle drift down to the top of the grandfather mountain. From her perch on the cloud Ming could just make out her father's wheel on the highest of the rocky peaks.

"There he is!" she pointed, as if the Imperial Dragon needed her help.

93

*Y*olanda peered into the deepest part of the cave, but couldn't see Yakos among all the broken rocks and boulders. She let her vision open, to find out if he was okay.

The cave looked exactly as it did when she first got there — dark, musty, and cold, with the faintest glow of light hiding at the back. Not one rock had fallen!

But it was so real. Especially the rock that hit my head!

Yolanda went back to the trail and dragged herself up the grandfather mountain, alone. Yakos was gone. And she knew better than to follow him.

When she first saw him, he gave her hope that she wouldn't be alone forever. It was like something new got born, and then was taken away fast. Now, she had an ache in her chest. She missed him and hated him at the same time. Now, just feeling lonesome, the way she'd always been, felt worse than before.

Why did you have to call me here!

Yolanda made it to the top and flung her body on the ledge. She looked up at Ching's iron wheel and let her vision flow. She saw residue of terror and pain like veins of rust inside his metal body. She saw the golden veins of power within him, too, but it could not move through him. Because he was solid. Stuck. Frozen in metal.

"I can't believe my brother did this to you," she said. "Damn him!"

Way up over her head, something made a wild howl that sounded like a cross between a turkey vulture and a hyena. A huge gold and purple snake flew down through the clouds, so big that it cast a shadow on the peak. Yolanda crouched behind Ching's wheel and stared up as it writhed and glittered between puffs of gray and white fung.

It's the dragon, the one Ting and Tan told us about!

This dragon was a lot skinnier and longer than the drawings in the fairy tales, the ones that were slain by a handsome prince. His wings were small, and he had five claws and a big tail that coiled and curled. Instead of fire, he blew steam at a little cloud right in front of him, making it fly ahead of him. Ming sat on that puff of cloud.

"Hey, Ming!" Yolanda jumped up and waved both arms.

Ming rode on the dragon's breath, only a lick away from its mouth full of sharp teeth, but she didn't look scared. She waved back at Yolanda as the cloud floated gently down toward the peak. When it got close enough, Ming tucked herself into a neat ball and rolled off the cloud onto a small patch of mossy ground.

"Thank the Four gods. You're alive!" Ming said.

Yolanda was so glad to see her she couldn't help but give her a big hug. "Ming! You were flying! Actually flying!"

"Yes!" Ming smiled, showing both her dimples. She looked up at the dragon, still twisting in the sky, and then clambered up close to Ching. "He's my father. This is Ching."

Yolanda only nodded. Her throat felt too tight to say anything. She wanted to shout, 'Yakos did this to him!' loud enough so the whole world would hear. She looked up at the dragon and hoped it would do something to help, like Ting and Tan said.

The dragon loomed over Ching, and with a warm moist hiss, he shot out a little puff of cloud that clung to the iron ring a minute or two before it dissolved into the rest of the fog. Then the dragon coiled up his tail and sprang back up to the sky.

Ching stood inside his wheel, just as cold and hard as before. It seemed as if the dragon fung hadn't helped him. At all.

Ming stared up at him and blinked. She tried not to show her worry, but her warrior face wasn't so proud anymore.

"Oh, Ming!" Yolanda wished she could do something. Maybe there was still some of Ching's life force – his chi – buried under all that iron. It was hard to let her vision come again, after all that pain she'd seen back in the cave with Yakos, but she had to try.

She took a big breath, closed her eyes, and felt – nothing. She was like a squeezed-out tube of toothpaste, without even a drop of vision left. Her shoulders drooped. She felt like giving up. Instead, she stopped trying so hard to do something. It felt like *being* a door instead of forcing one to open.

Her vision came through the opening like a wide river of knowing. That dragon's breath – the fung – must have made a difference, because now she could see Ching's heart pulse like a wavering light bulb, on-off, on-off, deep inside the metal.

"Ming!" she cried. "He's alive in there!"

"What?" Ming's eyes opened wide, shining with hope.

"His heart! I can see it! It's beating now. There's life in him."

Yolanda took a deep inhale and felt the whoosh of power rise up again, even stronger. Suddenly she was aware of so many things – almost too many. She heard the scratching and clawing of thousands of small animals, on the mountain and down in the valley. She felt minerals crystallizing, deep inside the rocks. Tiny microscopic beings like curls of energy danced in the fog. She felt oxygen move through her lungs and into her bloodstream. She even tasted the coppery scent of her own cells dying, and felt the pop! of new ones being born.

Yolanda turned back to Ching, to let all that vision flow into him. Although she could see the same pulses of life going on under the iron, he didn't move. She'd have to do more.

isn't it too much? can you go any further?

I can, and will. Yolanda closed her eyes. A dizzying surge of power flooded her. She could see way past the grandfather mountain, and even beyond Tessar. Her view got bigger and wider until she felt like a grain of sand in a universe of black velvet. Her mind swam like a dolphin through the wide reaches of space. She felt her own shape expand, until she felt as big as a planet, as if she could reach out and touch the stars. She was the darkness itself, and life itself, all of it, all at once. Nothing had ever prepared her for this hugeness of this vision, yet she knew the truth of it. She knew she was both the creator and the one being created. That sense of knowing was a real power, but it didn't belong to her. It simply blew through her like dragon wind. Time to direct it, channel it into something.

She brought her vision back from space and turned it on Ching's body.

The metal seemed thick and hard on the outside, but when she looked at each tiny particle that made him, Yolanda was surprised to find the greatness of space there, too. The man looked like iron, yet he was more space than anything else. Her vision danced through the open spaces to where his heart beat.

What an amazing fist-size bundle of muscle his heart was, with zillions of blood cells rushing through little tunnels: in, out, in, out! As her vision wandered through his heart, the flow of energy spread out wider and warmer. It looked like pure yellow light, a glowing spark breaking free from the iron.

Then his wheel moved. Just a small turn, but Yolanda felt it.

Did I do that?

Yolanda opened her eyes just in time to see a quarter of Ching's outer ring break off. The curved piece of iron didn't clink against the stone like regular metal; it faded into nothing as soon as it hit the fog. The rest of his metal sheath cracked off in big hunks, leaving only a man, standing on a rock. His skin slowly warmed from cold black iron to a tawny gold shade. He stretched all four limbs in every direction, just like her kitten Jimson after waking from a long nap. He rolled his head a bit, to stretch his neck, and then finally opened his eyelids.

How wonderful to see Ming, his daughter, there! But he didn't notice her at all.

Instead, his eyes pierced Yolanda like a sword.

94

*M*ing was so astonished that she stood frozen in place. Ching spoke to Yolanda in a rusty voice that didn't try to hide his anger. "So, you've come back to play with me again! You should know, the penalty is high for such reckless use of power."

"W-what?" Yolanda shivered.

Ching leapt to the ground, faster than a tree frog. Very fast for a man who only a moment ago was made of iron. He stood close to Yolanda and spat his words into her face. "How long has it been since you did this to me? Have all my people died of starvation yet? I'll never bow down to you, even if there is not one soul left in the East, or anywhere else in Tessar."

"Oh! You think I'm Yakos!" Yolanda tugged on her hair, as if surprised to find it so short.

Ming stepped forward. "Father, I beg forgiveness for what I am about to say, but this girl just freed you from the gate. She is not your enemy."

The long black braid at the base of Ching's neck whipped around as he spun toward Ming. "Who is this young woman who looks like a nun and calls me 'Father?'"

It felt like a slap. Ming stood her ground, took a deep breath, and made an even deeper bow.

"I am Ming. I come from Taipei," she said in as strong a voice as she could. "Ting and Tan found me at the gateway. They taught me to follow the Way. They said I must find you to continue my training. I have searched for you for a long, long time."

Ching's stance seemed to soften. He reached out his hand and lifted her chin to get a better look at her face. His eyes were like pools of midnight, as deep as forever, as if he knew the mysteries of the universe.

"I want to believe you," he said quietly. "But how can I be sure you are not another illusion?"

"See me, Father. I am your own flesh and blood." Ming gently pulled herself away from him, bent backwards in a high arch, then flipped herself up into a ball and performed the double happiness roll she had practiced over a thousand times for this very moment, the moment of meeting her father, the great god Ching. She landed precisely on both feet, although the terrain was rocky and far from level. She bowed again, unable to look up to see if it had pleased him. What if it had not pleased him?

"If you are an illusion, then you are as worthy as any of my children!" Ching bowed down to Ming so low that his forehead touched the ground. When he stood up again, he wrapped a long arm around her waist and brought her close to his side.

Tears ran down Ming's face into her dimples.

From the corner of her eye she saw Yolanda turn away and mutter, "Damn him! Damn, damn, damn!"

"What did you say?" Ming asked.

"My brother did it," Yolanda said. "He did this to Ching."

"Your brother. Is he your twin?" Ching asked.

Yolanda nodded, her face a mask of frowns.

Ching looked up and down at her. "Ah. I understand. The young man that challenged me was a child of the North, with fair skin and round eyes and hair as red as fire, like yours."

"I was afraid of this," Ming looked at Yolanda. "I'm sorry. Please. Tell us what happened."

"The young man found me at the Palace, during my annual visit to the Ten Thousand Things. He said it was his destiny to become the one true god of Tessar, that if I did not bow down to him he would destroy me and my people. I did not take him seriously. Others have tried to change the balance of Tessar, but his powers were greater than all of them put together. Now I see why. He is one of the green-eyed twins."

"The prophecy," Ming murmured.

"Yes," Ching nodded. "The fight was long and bitter. First an army of warriors swept the Palace, then a firestorm, a flood and finally an earthquake. I suspected they were illusions, cobbled together from bits of matter. I thought I could see the edges unraveling, but to the people at the Palace, his illusions were as devastating as if they were real. I had to protect them."

Yolanda nodded, as if she knew something about illusions.

"I brought him here, to the grandfather mountain, where I could drive the wheel of time forward without disturbing the cycles of nature so much. I planned to age him back to the dust that he came from, but the devil got to me first. Although his illusion of iron was not real, I felt as stiff and cold as any metal from a forge. I could not move, and gradually lost all awareness of my own body. I forgot who I was. I became the iron."

Ching looked at Yolanda again, with an expression both fierce and kind. "So the young man called Yakos is your twin?"

"Yes." Yolanda looked down.

"And did you, as my daughter said, free me?"

"Well, the dragon got your heart going, with his fung."

"Dragon?"

"The Imperial Dragon," Ming said.

"The Imperial Dragon?!"

"Yes. Ting and Tan said I should go to him, in the mountains of clouds, so I begged him to help. Praise the Four gods, he came down from heaven and blew a gust of fung on you. Still, you did not move until Yolanda used her vision. She is very powerful."

Ching looked to the sky and put his hands together. He turned to Ming and bowed deeply. "My debt to you, and to the Imperial Dragon is very great." Then he bowed to Yolanda. "My debt to you is eternal."

Yolanda only hung her head and looked very sad.

"I see that your twin Yakos is a great disappointment to you," Ching said. "Despite your sorrow, this is a time of great change, as the prophecy foretold. We must return to the Palace."

"Father, you should know. Two other Northerners took control of the Palace." Ming glanced in Yolanda's direction.

"We shall see about that," Ching said. "But first I must restore the cycles. So many are suffering. Please, come stand close. The wheel of change can be very dangerous."

95

*Y*olanda inched over to Ming, hoping she wasn't mad at her for sneaking out in the middle of the night to meet Yakos. She resolved to tell her everything, as soon as she had a chance.

Ching raised his arms to shoulder height and stretched his legs out into the same position he'd been in the iron. Then he flipped onto his hands and did cartwheels in a small circle around them. As he spun faster and faster, Yolanda could see another ring of colored light forming around him. Once the ring connected the tips of his fingers with the bottoms of his toes, everything changed.

First, all the colors of the rainbow appeared inside the ring. Ching's body seemed to disappear in the whirring blur of colors. Then the center of the ring became an opening, a tunnel that gyrated around him, twisting into space. Though she hadn't moved an inch, Yolanda found herself inside the tunnel with Ming.

Colored rings of light shot past them, lightning fast. Between the rings Yolanda saw glimpses of yellow fields and misty plains. Ching's arms and legs appeared every so often, like the spokes of a bicycle wheel as it slows. Finally the colors stopped changing, the ring faded away, and Ching sprang out and flipped a few cartwheels around them. When he finally stopped, Yolanda saw the walls of the Palace just ahead, shining gold.

96

*N*arissa felt seasick. Her chair rocked and shook, as if an earthquake shook the palace.

Where is Nikolas when I actually need him? Still in the modern world, finding his weapons. Toys.

When the violence stopped, she rushed to the window and pushed aside the screen to look outside. A circle of rainbow light spun over the wall and through the gardens, flooding the trees with light, and burning off the fog in an instant.

What the hell?

A man with a long braid popped out of the circle and did handsprings all over the grass. Ching!

What happened? Where is Yakos?

Narissa gathered her essentials, the small bag of cosmetics she always kept close by, and slid out the side passage that led through the servants' quarters. With the excitement in the gardens drawing all the attention, she slipped past the guard and out the rear without attracting any notice.

The trees were in full foliage, so it was easy to move from one to the next without being seen. If only the blasted gateway were more conveniently located.

Yakos will be so happy to see me!

97

*M*ing heard the welcoming song of hundreds of birds, a sound that had been missing before. Beauty bloomed everywhere. Instead of fog, morning light filtered through the willow vines, leafy and full. A thousand flowers scented the air with delicious nectars. The orchards buzzed with bees and butterflies.

Ming hurried down the wide lane to the Palace, stopping with the others to admire the ripening pears. She chose a perfectly round yellow one, tasted its sweetness and felt the juice run into her sleeve. Everything was as it should be.

"Thank you, Father," she bowed with deep appreciation. "Thank you for this fruit, for the birds and the butterflies."

"Yeah!" Yolanda bit into a pear, too. "It wasn't so good here while you were gone. How did you do it, bring it all back?"

"I didn't do anything," he said. "It was the wheel. I am only the wheel's guardian. It turned the cycles of time forward as it brought us through space, here to the Palace." Ching's smile turned dark. "How many suffered, while I sat rusting on the grandfather mountain?"

"It was a hard time," Ming bowed her head. "But Ting and Tan say, all things come to an end before a new beginning can arise."

"You have learned much, my daughter." Ching laid his strong hands on her shoulders.

Ming's heart wanted to soar with the birds.

Still, not everything was as perfect as her happiness. As they walked to the Palace they came upon a tiny figure of a beautiful spirit lady among the willows. Her long, flowing gowns trailed behind, but instead of waves of sea foam, she was the color and texture of granite, cool and still.

"A water spirit cannot abide such a form." Ching frowned.

"It was Nikolas' trance," Ming said. "His power tricks the mind, numbs the body and paralyzes the spirit. He did it to me, though my trance was not so deep as these spirits."

"There are more?"

Ming nodded. "The garden is full of spirits, elements, animals. There are many. It is terrible."

Ching spun to face Yolanda. "Could you use your power again – the vision, as you called it?"

"I don't know if it'll work or not."

"Please, try. These spirits need to be freed, too. As I did."

Ming beamed with pride. Only a very great man was not afraid to say that he'd been weak and needed help.

Yolanda nodded. Her eyes crossed slightly as she looked deeply into the water spirit's face. Did she see through her, as it appeared?

Ming watched, amazed, as the spirit's body gradually became a lovely shade of turquoise. She bowed with a shy smile and rushed to join the bubbling stream that rippled through the center of the garden.

Yolanda stared as if she had never seen a water spirit change form. Probably she never had, not in Hus-ka-loo-sa.

They walked on toward the Palace, pausing to admire the fragrant wisteria that hung over the garden walls, the golden carp that swam through the reflecting pools, and the delicate grasses between the iris and tiger lilies. When they came to the garden where dozens of spirit statues stood silent, Ching walked from one to the next, touching the stone. His expression grew darker with each one.

"Please, Miss Yolanda. Free all the spirits, if you can. They have suffered enough."

98

*Y*olanda leapt onto a short wall, so she could look out over the whole garden. She took a breath to let the vision flow and run loose over the garden of wild animals, people, people with animal's heads and vice versa. As soon as her vision touched one of the frozen shapes, she saw the true form hidden inside each. It wasn't too long before the chi that pulsed inside them flowed to the outside.

That was the end of the peace and quiet in the garden.

The elephant-head spirits were the loudest, shooting off their trunks like horns. Lions roared, tigers growled, monkeys chattered and black-and-white panda bears didn't make a sound. The Buddhas laughed, shaking their big bellies, while wise men with long white beards stared up at the sky. Dancers spun into dizzy twirls and slow gyrations, a hundred arms and legs wiggling at the same time. Ching flipped handsprings all around the garden, greeting each of them one at a time. It was like a fantastic circus, a zoo and a carnival show, rolled into one.

Ching bounded back to the wall where Yolanda watched. "A thousand thank yous," he said, bowing almost as many times.

"I'm just sorry I didn't try it sooner."

"Your powers may not have been as effective until now. This is a very auspicious time. Never before have all the spirits of the East been gathered in one place. My heart warms to see them all here at the Palace, despite their suffering and the wickedness that brought them."

"What do you mean?"

"These spirits came from all over the East, lured by Yakos' illusions. Now they are wild and free again. They'll soon return to a form they choose, and most will go back to their homes. But not before we celebrate. This banquet will be beyond anything ever imagined in the East!"

As Ching rolled off again, Yolanda felt a bit like her old self: alone, apart from everybody else, kind of empty inside. Though she was glad that Ching was saved and Ming was happy and everything was alive again, she didn't feel like celebrating.

She spotted Ming walking on a path of river rocks, arm in arm with an older woman. Jade! The other lady she'd first met at the Palace. Yolanda jumped down from the wall to catch up.

"Miss Jade, I'm glad to see you again."

"Miss Yolanda." Jade bowed deeply. "Who could have guessed that the scared little round-eye girl we found at the door would turn out to be so important?"

Yolanda blushed. "Yeah, but if you hadn't of helped us get away, we'd probably still be here. Right, Ming?"

"Pooh! I only kept the guards busy," Jade said.

"So what happened? After we left?"

"The Master and Mistress eventually came back to their senses. They sent guards after you, but they all came back empty-handed. I was so happy, even with the pain –" Jade covered her mouth with her hand, as if she'd said too much.

"Your pain? What did they do to you?" Ming asked.

"They thought I would tell them where you went," Jade stood taller. "They were wrong. Not to worry. Soon they tired of – ah – testing my will, asking me questions. Then I was sent to the garden with the other statues."

Ming frowned darkly. "I will find those two demons and punish them for what they have done."

"Yes, and you should. But Minga, I did not suffer long. When I was out here in the garden, I felt nothing. We did not even notice the sun or moon. But all that is ancient history now. Come, I have to make those good-for-nothing servants get busy. The Palace must look its best, for the banquet."

Jade hurried them through the East gate, the one shaped like Ting's throwing coins – round, with a square hole in the middle. The guards who had stood in the halls day and night were all gone. Yolanda found the hall that led to her old room and went in. She half expected to see the black bird again, pecking at the window, but the room was empty except for the miniature pine tree and the big bed with the flimsy draperies. She fell back into the feather mattress, soft and deep.

"Just don't let your mind fall asleep this time," Ming teased as she went to the dressing room. She was different now, not so serious, since Ching came to life.

"Uh huhm." Yolanda didn't realize she drifted into a nap and almost screamed when Jade touched her cheek with a cool hand. To wake up in the same bed, in the same yellow room, was like her worst nightmare all over again.

"Don't worry! It's only me, Jade. No Master or Mistress to bother you now. Time to get ready."

Yolanda dragged her feet over the side of the bed, still sluggish. Jade led her into the big bathing room where Ming sat on the chair, tended by two young girls.

"I'm not going to undress you for your bath," she said, smiling. "Not like before."

"I didn't want your help!" Yolanda grinned. "Especially with my underwear."

"I remember that fierce look you gave us, like a green-eyed tiger. But we were under Master's orders."

"And now I'm under orders from Ching," Jade said. "He wants you to look like 10,000 pieces of gold. That's impossible, since you cut off all your hair. But we'll do what we can."

Yolanda peeled off the baggy blue trousers and tunic that Chen's family gave her. She still missed him. It seemed like years, not days, since they left him at the Fung gate, and it had been even longer since she'd bathed. She sank into the marble tub. The steamy scent reminded her of that very first day she came to the East. She felt so different now. Older. A little less stupid, and a whole lot more tired. Tired of running. Tired of all the hiding and hoping, and the hard work of opening her vision. Tired from all the steep slopes and sleepless nights, the guards and the ghosts. Tired of looking everywhere for someone who wasn't worth looking for.

Jade came to offer a hand up and a silky robe, but Yolanda wanted to sink down under the water and never come back up. "Just ten more minutes..." she said.

"You can rest here all day," Ming said as she left, "but you'll miss quite a feast. Dim sum! My favorite."

Ming looked like the daughter of a god, in her wig hung with silver charms and jewels, and her robe embroidered with a fan-tailed phoenix and fat peaches.

Yolanda's eyelids drooped and she drifted off again. When she woke the water was freezing and she was alone. She put her hands on either side of the deep tub to lift herself out, when the reflection in the bath water started to swirl.

99

olanda expected to see Yakos' face. Instead of green eyes and a smiling mouth, a hand reached out from under the water and gripped her arm. This was no reflection.

"No!" She jerked back against the marble tub. "Get away!"

He wouldn't let go. He pulled her down so hard that her arm went under, up to her shoulder. Her chin slapped the icy water.

She fought back, but he was stronger. Her vision tried to rise up, to see what was real. But she had to stop trying.

Take a breath. Look. See.

The hand faded, leaving the dirty bath water rocking gently. Yolanda jumped out of the tub and flung on her robe.

I'll never take a bath again. Just showers.

"Ming! Jade! Where are you?"

The two young servant girls hurried in. "So sorry. Miss Jade said to let you rest. You must be very tired, to sleep in a tub."

"Where is everybody?" Yolanda heard strains of music and the din of voices down the hall. The party had already started.

"Come, we'll get you ready," the younger girl said.

Yolanda avoided looking in the mirror as the maids dusted her skin with white powder, painted her lips, cheeks and eyelids from little pots of color, and set a towering hairpiece on top. They draped her in a bright green robe painted with dragonflies and irises and guided her out the door. She felt as foreign as the first time she'd gone down the halls of marble.

The little alcoves were empty. She pictured the fat Buddhas rolling off their tiny couches, and lizards and tigers leaping up from the small boulders where they'd crouched for so long.

The maids slid open the doors to the same room where she'd first met Narissa and Nikolas. Musicians sat under the mural of the East, playing a lively song on box-shaped guitars, small drums and wooden flutes. The spirits sat or sprawled at long, low tables, waving arms and tentacles and any number of heads. With so many colors, feathers and scales, stripes and spots, it could have been a party of aliens from another planet.

Ching saw her standing in the doorway and motioned with his hand. The music stopped. Ming slid across the room to stand by her side. "Three hours in a bath? You look beautiful."

Yolanda blushed. "You're the one who's beautiful."

Ming's headdress, a glittering tower of silver leaves, tinkled as she bowed her head. She seemed more like a real goddess every minute. "My father will introduce us now."

"No, really, I – don't," Yolanda protested the whole way as Ming dragged her to the table where Ching sat between Ting and Tan. Ting smiled sweetly and Tan winked. Both nodded a quick bow.

Yolanda grinned and bowed, glad to see them. "How did you come here so fast, all the way from the grandfather mountain?"

Before they could answer Ching leapt into the air, tucked his body into a ball, rolled down a strip of cloth on the center of the table, and then jumped up into perfect bow, to Yolanda. "Welcome to the banquet! I'll introduce you."

"Sire, I, ah, don't –"

"I'm only a peasant who knows how to do a few good turns. You must mean our friend, the Monkey King!" Ching nodded to a little monkey sitting on a purple pillow with his chin held high. with three bird spirits gently fanning him with their wings.

It was the exact same monkey Yolanda met back in the banyan grove, and the same little stone monkey that sat on the chest in the yellow room.

"Aaaaiieee-ah!" The Monkey King laughed very loud and long at some joke that nobody else had heard, and then bowed his chin slightly at Yolanda.

She bowed back in return. Bowing seemed very natural. She did it without thinking, to say "Hello, I know you," or "Thank you," without saying a word.

Ching rang a small bell. The guests all quieted down, even the Monkey King.

"Spirits and people of the East, my guests," he began. "We have in our midst two most unusual young ladies."

Ching took Yolanda's hand and pulled until she was forced to stand up. Here it comes. Nothing worse than a long, drawn out speech.

"Not long ago, this child of the North, Yolanda Mae Crick, came into our land, lost and alone. Yet she has already changed the course of our history."

The crowd clapped politely.

"And this young lady," he took Ming's hand and pulled her to stand beside Yolanda, "is my own offspring from the world of dreams, who came here according to the tradition of the ancients to play an honored role in our present and future."

The clapping got louder.

"These young women were destined to meet here, at this Palace, home to all that is sacred to the East. Just before they came, a conspiracy of great powers from the North took the Palace, stopped the wheel of change, and made all of you their prisoners."

Angry shouts, snorts and roars filled the room.

"Yes, the balance of the Four has been changing, as the great prophets of old foretold. I have felt it coming for some time, as have the seers," he nodded to Ting and Tan. "However, we were not well enough prepared to face the powers that seek to undo the harmony we all hold dear.

"Among all the brave warriors, kind hearts and wise spirits of the East, these two young women overcame their bindings and sought to free us all. They alone believed I had not abandoned you. With no army to protect them and no leaders to guide their way, they came by foot and humble ox cart. They endured bitter fights and long days of hiding. Finally they reached the gate of heaven at the top of the grandfather mountain, where I was imprisoned in an illusion."

The crowd hooted and hollered loud enough to raise the roof. Ching waved his hand to calm them down.

"They did not stop there. Ming, my daughter, went farther, beyond where any have dared go before. She climbed the mountains of clouds and braved the dragonwinds to ask the Imperial Dragon himself for help. She did not rest until the dragon flew down from heaven to blow his mighty fung on the wheel of Change. It was a great deed! I am so proud of her courage and strength."

Ching's eyes gleamed at Ming. Yolanda wished somebody would look at her like that.

The crowd yelped and shouted and stomped their feet and hooves. Ching waited until they calmed down.

"And this young woman, Yolanda –" He turned to face her. "Her extraordinary powers of vision destroyed the illusion that bound me to the iron gate. I owe an eternal debt to this girl of the North, the one who set me free to turn the Wheel of Change, and restore the cycles of life to the East!"

Ching lifted Yolanda's sweaty hand high over her head, then took Ming's and joined their hands together.

The whole room full of spirits exploded in a frenzy of snorts, coos, and roars. They beat chopsticks on rice bowls, tables, silver platters, anything to make noise.

Yolanda would have run if Ching wasn't holding up their arms. She didn't have to use her vision to see that Ming was just as embarrassed as she was. Though her face was painted with white makeup, a red blush peeked through at the edges. Ming squeezed her hand and smiled, a little smile that didn't show her teeth.

Ching lowered their arms, thank goodness. "Even as we lift our glasses and drink to the courage and vision of these two young women, danger has not forgotten us. Nikolas and Narissa

– the cruel ones that ruled this Palace – are gone, but we do not know where, or for how long."

The spirits growled and hissed. Yolanda felt like hissing, too. She didn't want to tangle with those two, ever again.

"And Yakos, master of illusion. He may return any moment."

Yolanda's spirits fell. Would Ching say that Yakos was her twin brother?

"We must be ever vigilant! But tonight, let us honor the chi that flows in us, and enjoy the riches of this bountiful land. Celebrate! For that which was cold is now warm, that which was stone is now flesh, and that which was blind can now see!"

As the roar of the crowd rose up like a cyclone around them, Ching looked into Yolanda's eyes with the same shiny look he'd given to Ming.

Funny how even a good feeling can press down awfully hard, so you feel like you can't breathe.

Finally the servers came in balancing dozens of platters of steaming food. Everybody waited with chopsticks raised until Yolanda, Ming and Ching had tasted their first bite. Then the guests dove into the steamed and fried dumplings, long rice noodles covered with savory sauces and vegetables, and tasty bao – buns – filled with delicious meats and sweet red bean paste. The banquet lasted hours. Yolanda ate so many shrimp dumplings, pork bao and tangy broccoli in oyster sauce that she thought the silk rope around her waist would bust. Finally she sat back and watched the elephants lift small bits of dim sum with their trunks, while the tiger spirits attacked their food like wild beasts and water spirits splashed their soup joyfully.

The musicians started playing again. Seven golden ladies made a chorus line of a hundred hands and feet. The Monkey King jumped over the tables, yanked off their headdresses and juggled them with some fruit he'd stolen from their plates. Then the nature spirits came in colors of spring, summer, winter and fall to sing of wind rustling through lonely pines, sea foam splashing, and of fire at the center of the world. Their songs brought tears to many eyes in the room.

Soon after, the guests began drifting outside in pairs and threes to view the full moon rising from the jade pavilion. Ching did handsprings around the room, keeping things lively, while Ming entertained Ting and Tan with more tales of their journey.

"Tell them how you convinced me to shave our heads," Ming said.

"No, you're much better at stories," Yolanda teased.

"That is not true! Anyway, Yolanda saw Chen shaving, and she –" Ming began.

Yolanda slipped outside through one of the sliding screens. She wandered through the garden, avoiding the others until she found a quiet brook with a mossy rock to sit on. Cool breezes grazed her cheeks, and fireflies danced among the trees. She took off the heavy headdress, bells a-tinkling, and set it down.

It's nice here now. And the people are good to me...

Yakos' face came into her mind, but she didn't want to think about him. A whoosh of wind ruffled her robe, and then Ching stood up beside her.

"Ah, so here you are. I've been looking for you," he said.

"Oh. I just –" Yolanda still felt shy around him.

"All things must change. Even celebrations come to an end. May I join you?"

She nodded, and he settled on the moss beside her. "Did you enjoy the party?"

"Oh, yeah! The dumplings were great! And the dancers, and the spirit songs...that was my favorite."

"Did you like my speech?"

"Well, thanks for not saying Yakos was my twin. The rest was nice, but, embarrassing!"

"Every word was true. Soon the spirits will sing songs of your deeds. Not only of what you did for me, but also for my daughter, Ming. She is more precious to me than the moon and the sun; you delivered her from slavery and brought her to my side."

"No, she's the warrior! She's the brave one!" Yolanda said.

Ching laughed. "Are you certain you were not born here? Your humility is more than admirable! Have you learned to trust your vision? You could not have come to the East without it. And I would still be on the grandfather mountain, standing in a piece of iron."

Yolanda bit her lip and felt the rush of vision flow through her again, opening her to the truth.

She heard him speak into her mind without talking out loud. He said, "You are worthy. You are unique. You are powerful, and you are loved."

it's true just don't get all stuck up about it

Mama! A warm buttery feeling came up from Yolanda's insides. She hadn't felt it many times, but knew the name of the feeling: pride. She felt proud of what she had done, of how she helped to save Ching, and all the spirits and the people of the East.

She looked up at him with a wet shine to her own eyes. Ching smiled, showing his dimples.

I did something good. It *was* good!

That buttery feeling swelled up inside again, until it filled her up, even into her fingers and toes.

you're right to feel proud

Ching's eyes glowed like stars in the moonlight. "The change has come," he said.

100

hing was right about the change, but he would know all about that! Yolanda smiled. She didn't feel so nervous around him.

"What do you wish for now?" he asked.

"I'm not sure. For so long I wanted just one thing." Yolanda covered her face to hide the tears rising up. She felt one of Ching's long arms wrap around her shoulder.

"I wanted to find him so bad. Since Mama died, he's all I've got. My only family. But he's no good, I know that now. Anybody who would do that to you –"

"Yakos simply defeated me in a challenge. Perhaps he would make a better god. It is the natural way of things, to ebb and flow. Even gods are born, grow strong, and then pass away into obscurity. My time may be drawing to a close."

"Don't say that! You can't die now."

Ching smiled. "I'll still be here for a while, at least until a new god who can be entrusted with the balance comes forward. Then I can pass on the wheel of change to them."

"Where do they come from, the new gods?"

"From the other world. Your world."

"I don't get it." Yolanda frowned.

"Ming is my daughter, from Taipei. I come from there, too, only it was so long ago I can barely remember the first time."

"The first time?"

"Yes, I have returned many times. In Tessar, the cycle of re-creation lasts about a hundred years. When the right moment comes, all the gods and goddesses of Tessar return to the world you call Earth, to seed the next generation."

"That sounds like something animals would do."

"It is instinctual. I feel it deep in my belly, the urge to begin again. Then I go through a gateway to your world, to find the one who will be my mate."

"How do you know who it is?"

"I always see her clearly, in something like a dream. She was chosen by fate to make a child with me. Since I am only allowed to stay one night, sadly, I don't get to know her."

"What about the babies? What happens to them?"

"It depends. Only nature knows how much is human, how much is god. Some of them find their way here to Tessar, though very few fulfill the promise of their destiny."

Yolanda got quiet. Ching's eyes burned into hers, hinting at something. *Am I one of them? Like Ming, the daughter of a god?*

She felt the old longing again. Her whole life, something had always been missing. She thought finding Yakos would make it go away, but maybe it was something else, something she'd made herself forget. She'd asked Mama so many times, and got turned down so many times that she shut that door a long time ago. But now Ching made her wonder again about him.

Who is my father? Maybe he came from Tessar.

"So, anybody who goes through a gateway, does that mean their mom or dad is a god or goddess?" she asked.

Ching nodded. "You can't enter a gateway unless part of you came from Tessar, one of your parents."

"So that means I'm –"

"Yes. You wouldn't be here if your father wasn't one of the four gods of Tessar."

"No way!"

"Yes, it is the Way."

Yolanda smiled. "You sound like the Monkey King. He kept talking about the Way."

"He's one of the old ones, a spirit of a former god. He's a good one to have on your side."

"Do you know the other gods, then? Do you know my – my father?"

"No, I'm sorry. The Balance keeps us apart, each in our own domain, so the weight doesn't tip too far in any one direction. That's why it was a shock to find your brother here in the East, claiming to be a god. Clearly he was trained in the use of power, but not in the Way or the Balance."

"So if you're part god, you don't just grow up to be one?"

"Not at all. That's why I must wait for the right god. Many of the new ones, the children we create in your world, do not come to Tessar. They use their powers for other ends. It is a great sadness to the old ones when this happens, because they try very hard to make sure the young ones come through, and are trained. Thank the Four that you came, and learned so much – even without a teacher!"

"I did have someone. Miz Becca. She told me to come here, and to use my vision," Yolanda said. "And the bird, too! A black bird. It's been with me, telling me to use it, too."

"Sometimes the teacher will appear, where there is a need."

Yolanda was quiet. She knew she still had a lot more to learn. "I still need a teacher. I think it's Miz Becca."

"And she's in your world?"

"Yes, she's back in Huskaloosa."

Home. Mama wasn't there, but it still felt like a place she belonged to, where she had things to take care of: feed the chickens, water the garden – it's probably overrun by weeds now –and fix that screen door. And Jimson! He needs looking after, if he's still alive.

"Ming will be very sad to see you go," Ching said.

"So will I! I mean, she's my best friend. My only friend. I'll hate to leave her, and I'll miss her more than anything. But I think that home's the best place for me now."

"The heart knows best what should be done. I will take you to the gateway at dawn, so you can see the sun rise in your homeland. But go now, and speak to Ming."

"I will." Yolanda picked up the clumsy headdress, and then bowed to him. "Thank you, Ching."

"It is I who thanks you." The god of the East bowed deeply to the red-headed girl from Huskaloosa.

"What I mean is, thanks for showing me that I –"

"It's just another trick of the Way, that those with the most powerful vision can be blind to the truth inside themselves," he chuckled. "Good night."

101

When Yolanda burst into the yellow room, frowning, Ming didn't know what to expect.

"I'm going home in the morning," she said, matter-of-factly. "I'm sad, though, because I don't really want to leave you. It's just that I'm going to find my teacher. So I can learn, like you did with Ting and Tan."

Ming turned away to watch the drapes drift before the open window. It was so hard to say what she was thinking. Yolanda always talked so freely, so openly. It was one of the qualities Ming didn't understand, yet admired most in her.

"Ming, are you ok?"

She swallowed hard, and tried to speak the way Yolanda would. "I've never had a friend," she finally said. "Even in Taipei, with all my brothers and sisters, and crowds of strangers on the streets, I always kept to myself. Always the strong one. Silent."

"You *are* strong," Yolanda nodded. "And mostly silent."

"When I learned to be a fighter, many people approached me, followed me, and called themselves my friends. But not one of them wanted to really know me, the way you did. I've never met anyone like you."

"By the Four gods! I'd feel sorry for you if you did," Yolanda teased. Then her face got red. "Back home in the valley, with other kids, I was always so different. Maybe I didn't try to be friendly, either, but I never had a real friend before. Not like you. I've never been – just ok, being with somebody –"

"Or trusted them." Ming added.

"Or had more fun." Yolanda smiled.

"Or got through so much danger."

"That's the truth. Remember when we hid in those trees? I thought I was going to fall right on top of that guard. And back at the gate, with Chen. I'll always remember that."

"Chen was so good to us."

"Yeah. I miss him. Rika, too. Even Uncle K'an!"

"I will miss you one thousand times as much!" Ming covered her mouth with her hand, shocked at herself for saying something so revealing. Yolanda made it easier to say what was in her heart.

"But you've got Ching, and Ting and Tan, too. I've got nobody except my kitten, Jimson, Miz Becca if she'll have me, and my neighbors, the MacGroders. They're pretty nice to me. But I'll be thinking about you all the while I'm doing my chores."

"Chores?" Ming asked.

"Oh, mostly working the garden and feeding the chickens. If they're still alive."

"I have an idea! If you stay here at the Palace, Ting and Tan will teach you. We'll get chickens for you to feed, and a kitten, and we'll eat dim sum every day!"

Yolanda smiled. "That does sound good. We could go exploring the East, you could teach me tai chi, and –" she stopped. "I'm not sure why, but the feeling is strong, that I should go back home. Maybe it's part of my vision. Seems like I should start to trust it. But you could come with me! Help me feed the chickens?"

Ming looked down. "I must stay with Ching, now that I've found him. But what about your brother?"

Right away Ming sensed that she shouldn't have asked the one question that could hurt her friend. Maybe her old habit of not talking was a good habit to keep after all.

"Oh, he's not what I thought he'd be." Yolanda's face lost the glow it had when she was taking about her vision. She lay back down on the bed and closed her eyes.

Ming lay down next to her, and watched her friend's chest rise and fall with each breath. She wished that she could ask more about him, but worried that it could hurt her even more. She wished that Yolanda would laugh again, and make her laugh, too, the way she had so many times.

How will I ever laugh like that, without her?

dull glow lit the eastern sky outside Yolanda's window. Her eyes flew open. "Pssssst...Ming..."

"Is it morning?"

"Yes. I have to go, but I really don't want to ... Thanks, Ming, for everything." Yolanda's eyes burned with tears as she gave Ming a big hug. When she let go she realized she wasn't the only one that was crying.

"Jade's going to be upset about this robe," Ming said, rubbing the tears off the silk.

"Don't worry. You're a goddess, remember?"

"Good-bye, Yolanda." Ming bowed lower than Yolanda had ever seen her. She bowed back, as long and low as she could.

"'Bye. Oh! I thought of something. I can come back someday! Or you could come to Huskaloosa sometime, through the gateway."

Ming nodded, very slow.

It was hard to go, but Ching was waiting just outside the eastern door, rolling around in the moss. "I'm ready," she said, though she didn't feel nearly so sure.

Ching opened his arms and legs in the same pose as when he carried them from the grandfather mountain. "Come stand close to me. That way I'll take only you, instead of the whole Palace."

The ring of light appeared around him, as bright and electric as before. Yolanda hesitated, and then stepped into the blur of colors.

Ching's wheel flew faster than the wind past fields of golden millet. In a moment the wheel slowed to a stop in a green valley surrounded by trees. The branches swayed, waving good-bye. Yolanda noticed an odd shimmer in the trees. If she stepped out of the ring, she would walk right into it.

"Is that the gateway?" she said.

"Yes. Each one is different, but once you get inside the passage it's always the same. The globe of light – do you remember it?"

She nodded.

"Always keep it to your right. And also, this is very important. Keep the image of your home in your mind. Don't let anything distract you, or you may end up somewhere else. The gateways connect all four lands of Tessar with your own world, so you could end up in danger."

"I'll remember," she said, but Ching had already begun rolling his wheel back and away from the trees.

He put his hands together into a praying position and bowed to her with his whole wheel, tipping nearly to the ground. Then he flipped back upright in an explosion of color that sent him reeling back into space.

Yolanda stood on the threshold of the gateway and bowed to him, long and low, then took a step into the trees.

Swirls of gold and green light surrounded her, flowing and pulsing toward a burning globe of light. Everything was the same as before, except that Yako's face was not there to lead her. Still, the same magnetic force drew her on toward the center. She made sure the glowing ball always stayed to her right, like Ching said, and kept the picture of Hanging Lake sharp in her mind. Drifting, reeling, spinning, swimming, she rose up, then down, over and through the swirling mists. Finally she saw clear water sparkling above. She swam to the surface and broke through the cold waters of Hanging Lake.

Dawn had begun to streak across the morning sky, feathers of pink and gold that reminded her of Ching's wheel. Yolanda swam to where she could touch bottom, then stood knee-deep in the chilly water.

She looked down at her reflection, and this time saw only herself: short red hair, pale skin, green eyes, and wiry body inside the baggy yellow silk pajamas that Ming had loaned her. Not ugly. Just wet.

Yolanda took in a long breath of blue spruce and Huskaloosa pine, while a lone black bird circled the sky above.

Upcoming books in the "Tessar" series:

Book II: Gift of the Gods, 2014
Book III: North Quest (title TBD)
Book IV: South Quest (Title TBD)

Book III:
Yolanda's
father in the far North
holds the keys to her past and
Tessar's future, but first she must
complete three impossible
tasks with the help of
her Tessarian
friends.

Book II:
Yolanda
falls for Orion, a
young runaway, but
leaves him to return to
Tessar where she must learn
to follow the red path to
fight the battle that
still rages in the
West.

Book I:
Yolanda
follows her twin
through a gateway
to the East – first of four
spirit realms of Tessar –
where she befriends
Ming, a young
warrior held
captive.

Book IV:
The South
faces total
annihilation unless Yolanda
and the other young gods of Tessar
can descend into the black volcano and face
their future King, once and for all.

To receive e-mail notices about *The Twins of Tessar* and future books in
the series, please subscribe to our email list by sending an email to
fans@twinsoftessar.com, or visit www.twinsoftessar.com.

ABOUT THE AUTHOR

Christine Castigliano worked as a magazine art director, multimedia producer, film set artist, video director, website designer, gospel singer, T-shirt designer, travel writer, newspaper artist, computer instructor, bra factory seamstress, waitress and gas station attendant. She lives in Washington State with her husband and daughter in a renovated barn overlooking Hood Canal and the Olympic mountains. *The Twins of Tessar* is her first novel.

Made in the USA
Charleston, SC
11 February 2014